CURSED TO DREAM

CURSED TO LOVE
BOOK TWO

KJ WARAWA

MYSTIC
CITY
PRESS

Tuesday, December 31

Mae hadn't meant to fall asleep on the couch. Every time sleep claimed her, it felt like Russian roulette—dreams instead of bullets, but the same effect in the end.

She pushed herself upright, remnants of her dream lingering. Pieces flitted through her mind and she exhaled in relief. They were fuzzy, disjointed fragments—like her dreams used to be. Nothing unusual.

A heavy head landed in her lap. "It's okay, Solo," she crooned as she scratched his ears with both hands. "A normal dream this time."

She scooted into the corner of the couch with her legs stretched out and patted her thigh. Solo jumped up, shaking the couch with his weight before he lay lengthwise, sprawling his mass across her. At 230 pounds, her mastiff shouldn't have been a lapdog, especially since he outweighed her five-foot-one frame by over 110 pounds, but she loved to cuddle with him. He beat a weighted blanket.

She smoothed her hands down his back as far as she could reach and let her head fall back on the cushions, eyes closed. Thirty years old and it was just her and Solo on New Year's Eve. "Not truly alone, am I, Solo? I have you."

She opened her eyes and reached for her phone on the coffee table, Solo anchoring her as she stretched the short distance. She'd stopped keeping it on the couch a long time ago because Solo chewed anything in reach.

"Ten o'clock, Solo. A new year begins in two hours." Mae leaned over and buried her face in his short fur. "I don't want the new year to come," she whispered. The horrific dreams began a couple of weeks after her thirtieth birthday. Only four of them so far, but they announced the beginning of the end. She knew it.

Her mom was thirty when her first episode hit. Mae remembered how they progressed and worsened. Her mom would be fine one minute, spaced out the next, and then she'd snap out of it and babble nonsense. Never knowing when her mom would change was a nightmare.

"Ha." Mae chortled at her own joke. "Nightmares. Get it, Solo? That's what my dreams are." She'd woken up from the first dream—nightmare—at the end of November and tried to brush it off. But all day it had clung to her, not like a regular dream. No matter how bizarre her dreams were, they usually faded from her memory within a few minutes, along with whatever feelings they elicited. Sometimes snippets stuck with her for a few hours, but unless she replayed them on purpose to make them stick, they vanished.

Last month's nightmare had been different—vivid, precise, and detailed in full color. Each replay etched it deeper in her mind until the day itself felt wrong: coffee tasted tinny on her tongue, overhead lights took on a hospital glare, and every sound turned too sharp. The sadness didn't dim with the daylight. Instead, it rode her shoulders into the night.

The images refused to blur. Even now she could call up every detail. For ten days she told herself it was a one-off, a vivid dream she'd overthought. Then came the second one. Eight days later, the third.

Each time she had one, it felt real—terrifying. Four days ago, the fourth one woke her in tears. She'd felt a deep sorrow, unlike anything she'd experienced since childhood, when her life first fell apart. Tears streamed down her cheeks then too, but for a different reason. A social worker—a stranger—had dragged her away from her mom.

"No, not tonight. Right, Solo? No sad thoughts on New Year's. Want to go for a last walk of the year? Should I wear that purple dress I bought? It's still hanging in my closet." Mae shook her head at the crazy thought as she lifted her legs, giving Solo a nudge. He slid off the couch and sat, waiting.

"I've got to go pee, and then we'll walk," she told him as she headed to the bathroom. A few minutes later, bundled against the cold and with Solo on his leash, they stepped into the night.

Jake Young checked the text from the PI. Now he had a call to make.

Laughter and music spilled out as someone opened the sliding glass door at the back of his house. Clenching his phone, he turned to greet the intruder. "Hey." He smiled at his sister before crouching down to scratch his St. Bernard's ears.

"Chewie was looking for you." Chelsea shut the sliding door behind her, dampening the party noise. "You okay?"

"Break," he told Chewie, letting him know he could run free, before standing and propping himself against the railing. "Yeah, fine. I was talking to Blake out here when I got a phone call."

Chelsea grinned like a Cheshire cat. She'd always smiled big, except for the years she hadn't smiled at all.

"I saw Paige's ring." She mock-fanned herself. "My, oh my. Blake did good with that one. I had to get my sunglasses."

He scoffed. "You say that as if your own husband didn't do the same."

"Yes, Cam did good too."

They turned in sync, leaning on the railing to watch Chewie sniffing around the yard.

Chelsea leaned into him. "It's cold out here, but a nice break from the heat of the house."

He wrapped his arm around her, tucking her into his side. "I kept the house cool all day, hoping it would help. When we go in, I'll turn on the air conditioning."

"Good. A few people complained about the heat."

He groaned. "No one is ever happy, not even family, it seems. Funny, Blake and I were just talking about family before my phone rang."

"As much as I love our family, I'd rather talk about your phone call instead. Are you ready to tell me what's been going on? Is it about the curse?"

Catching Chelsea up on recent events would give him a few minutes before he made the phone call. He usually wasn't nervous about talking to someone. "Actually, it is."

She rubbed her hands together in excitement. "Oh good. When you first told me about it, I thought you were joking since it was near Halloween. I mean… a curse, really? When you never mentioned it again, I was going to ask you about it, thinking I'd missed the punchline, but I forgot. It wasn't until Christmas at Blake's place that I realized that it wasn't a joke. Blake and his brothers were talking about it. They were all serious and I've been around them enough to know when they're joking. They weren't. I was curious but didn't want to pry." She looked up at him and frowned. "I get that you all think it's real, but it's still hard to wrap my head around."

"I get that. It's not every day you hear about a curse, but it's real." He let out a breath, visible in the glow from the little lights he'd suspended. "I've talked about it so much with Blake and his brothers that I'm not sure what I told you. Short version: Hundreds of years ago, a spirit cursed an ancestor on Blake's mother's side. Now each member of the family must fall in love and have their love reciprocated by their thirtieth birthday, or the curse will take effect. Blake's mom said the curse affects each person differently."

"You told me Blake went into trances, and they lasted longer and longer. I think that's what made me question whether it was a joke. You've teased me before, but you don't lie."

"I saw him go into a trance, so I know it's real. I guess I assumed you would believe me, as far-fetched as it sounded." Jake remembered watching his best friend go stiff as a board as a trance locked his body and took his mind back in time. The first time Jake witnessed it, he'd been frantic as the minutes ticked by, wondering how long it would last. "If he and Paige hadn't broken the curse, he might have been stuck in one trance after another."

"Was he aware of what was happening?"

"Not where he was, no. His mind traveled back in time. His body didn't move. Each time, Blake witnessed a couple experiencing failed love."

She glanced back toward the house. "I want to hear more about them, but I told Cam I wouldn't be gone long. And since the curse broke and Blake and Paige are madly in love, I know that's not what's been bothering you. You've been distracted for the last few days."

She pulled out of his arms and looked up at him. "Who was on the phone? And don't tell me it was someone wishing you a Happy New Year, because I swear everyone we know is inside your house right now."

"A private investigator. Blake's brother, Cade, hired her to find their aunt."

"Her? Hmmm… Did she call because you're seeing her?" The corner of Chelsea's lips turned up in a hopeful smile.

"No, I've never met her in person. I hired her."

Chelsea's eyebrows pinched together. "You said Cade hired her."

"He did. To look into his Aunt Chrys. Blake's mom told him that their aunt died when he was really young, but they found photos that made them believe their mom lied."

"I'd be suspicious too, since she never told them about the curse. I can't imagine learning about something like that in a letter, especially since they were grieving."

"Exactly." Jake watched Chewie give himself a shake and head toward the stairs. "The PI found their aunt, and Blake and I went to see her the day after Christmas. She kept a picture of a teenager in her room." He unlocked his phone and showed his sister the photo he'd taken of the picture in the frame.

Chelsea studied the photo for several seconds before meeting his gaze. "She's striking, even as a teenager. What is she? Fifteen? Sixteen?"

"About that. The photo is old, the last one her mom had. She's only two months younger than Blake. She turned thirty in November, so the curse has—"

"Wait." Chelsea gripped his forearm. "You hired the PI to find her, didn't you?"

"Yes. She doesn't know about the curse, and it will have started. She needs—"

"No." Chelsea threw up her hands. "She's Blake's cousin, let him find her. Or one of his brothers. He has enough of them."

"Blake is busy, so he's letting me take the lead on this." It was the truth, so he didn't have to tell his sister that he hadn't given Blake a choice. As soon as Jake saw Mae's picture he knew he would be the one to find her. The thought of someone going through what Blake had didn't sit right with him. If it turned out she had a huge support system, he'd back off, but it didn't sound like she did.

He'd never given much thought to destiny before. He wasn't even sure he believed in it, but seeing her picture and knowing she might be alone spoke to him. It could have been seeing her as a teenager and knowing what Chelsea went through at that age. He wouldn't be able to explain the compulsion to find her, even if he tried.

"Letting you? Or did you not give him a choice?"

Shit. His sister knew him too well. If he didn't confirm, she wouldn't know for sure.

"I know it was her picture that got to you. Not the fact that she's now thirty and cursed." Chelsea sighed. "This is you trying to make amends again. You told me you forgave yourself for what happened to me, but obviously you haven't."

He would never forgive himself. If he hadn't been so caught up in his own shit, he could have saved Chelsea years of suffering. "I want to make sure she's okay. Then I'll introduce her to Blake and his brothers or just give her their contact info and let her decide what to do."

"You won't go über protective on her?"

He frowned at his sister. "I'm not *über* protective. I look out for people I care about."

"Really? What about Marissa? Or Shannon? And Des… Destiny… No, Desiree, the woman you dated last year. They all broke up with you because they felt like you were suffocating them."

"I care about the women I date and want them to be safe. There's nothing wrong with that. Marissa walked by herself on the campus in the dark and wouldn't let me meet her. It was dangerous."

"You showed up everywhere to escort her. She was an adult. So was Shannon and you wanted her to quit her job."

He remembered his request to Shannon that turned into a yelling match and internally cringed. Not because he regretted asking her to find another job, but because she told him he was crazed and delusional. "She continued to take the late shift at the sports bar. The place was crawling with drunk assholes, and she wouldn't even let the manager walk her to her car. Anyone could have hurt her."

Chelsea crossed her arms. "She said she knew self-defense."

"A big, drunk guy could have overpowered her anyway." He hated that people weren't more careful about their own safety, physical or mental. "And before you mention Desiree, at first all I did was suggest she talk to someone because she was acting depressed." Looking back later he realized that he had gone too far. Making her an appointment with a counsellor had been overstepping. She told him she'd look into it herself, but all he could picture was Chelsea's lifeless-looking body. "I get it. I went a bit overboard. I've learned my lesson. I won't drive anyone away again."

The look Chelsea gave him said she didn't believe him, but she let it drop. "What did the PI say?"

"Lyra—the PI—said Blake's cousin legally changed her name from Maeve Montgomery to Mae McFadden. She hadn't tried to hide it, so there was a clear paper trail."

"So, now what?"

Good question. Jake still held his phone in his fist and itched to call her, but how exactly did you tell a stranger they're cursed? "I'm going to call her."

"Tonight?" Chelsea waved him off. "Forget I asked that. You have a possible damsel in distress, which means it doesn't matter that it's New Year's Eve and you have a house full of people."

He glanced at his phone. "It's not late. No one's going to miss me for a few minutes."

"Okay." Chelsea gave him a quick hug. "Don't be long, it's too cold. Come on, Chewie, let's get you dry."

Jake waited until Chelsea ushered his dog inside. She drew the curtain to keep people from peeking at him outside in the cold. She might not agree with what he was about to do, but he knew she understood his driving force.

Unlocking his phone, he stared down at the number Lyra had texted him. Had Chelsea been right? Should he let Blake make the call? Jake knew what would happen if he came to care about Mae, but one phone call couldn't hurt.

Before he forgot, he texted Lyra back to check about the other person he asked her to look for. She responded immediately, saying she was still working on it.

Jake hesitated for a moment, his finger hovering over the number. He could either help her or drive her away, but deep down he was already committed, and he had truly learned his lesson. He wouldn't drive Mae away.

He hit call and brought the phone to his ear.

On the third ring, a breathless voice answered. "Hello?"

2

"*R*emember our first walk? It was cold and late like this." Solo had only been three months old then, but already fifty pounds. Mae had been terrified he would bolt and she wouldn't be able to hold him back. His owners had barely trained him.

Living on her own again after the divorce, she toyed with getting a cat. Her neighbors' shouts had changed all that. The young couple next door argued loud enough to carry through the wall.

"You're the one who wanted the dog, so you can get rid of him," the woman shouted.

"You wanted him too. And it's your job that's making us move," a male voice responded.

"I know, I..."

The woman's voice dropped too low for Mae to catch the rest, but she'd heard enough. She knew what it felt like when someone gave you away because you weren't wanted. Even as she crossed the hall and knocked, she didn't care if she was wrong. She would give that dog a loving home and he would know he was wanted.

Mae huffed a laugh, her breath haloing in the glow from the streetlamps. "We have no regrets. Right, Solo? And once I'd researched how big you were going to get and the shock wore off, we were fine, right? And Solo is a way better name than Bob." She scoffed. Who names their dog Bob?

In less than an hour, she had the right name for her new companion. Briefly, she'd considered Luke, since he was the young, immature one, but it hadn't felt right. Solo was the misfit and untrustworthy in appearance, the way a huge mastiff might look. The original Solo was a loner too, like her, but eventually committed to the cause and loved. Mae knew her Solo would be like that too.

At the dog park, Solo led the way, tracking the winding path by memory. She never let him off leash, always afraid he'd get lost, but lengthened the lead to give him more freedom to roam. The same as not being wanted, she refused to let him learn what being lost felt like. Mae mothered him, hoping she helped him feel safe and loved, like she expected a good mother would. Not that she'd had much experience with that, but she remembered some of what her mom had done before her illness had taken over.

For years she'd pushed thoughts of her mom from her mind, trying to forget, but they always came back. It could be she was melancholy because it was the last day of the year, or that no matter how much she told herself she wouldn't go crazy like her mom, she now knew it was inevitable. She wanted to lie to herself and say they were just dreams, but she knew better.

One thing she would do differently than her mom… she'd get help. She couldn't go to a doctor yet because four nightmares didn't equal a diagnosis. But when they got worse, and before they were too bad for her to know her own mind, she'd get medication. As a teenager, she'd been old enough to understand mental illness, and spent years angry. Her mom could have gotten help and didn't. Instead, she'd abandoned Mae to the system.

She and Solo walked for a long time, enjoying the crisp air and quiet. When her eyes wouldn't stop watering and her lashes were frozen, Solo turned back toward home, as if he knew what she needed.

They passed a family out on their front lawn with sparklers. It wasn't midnight yet; the kids were little, so they were likely ringing in the new year early. It was something she'd wanted once.

Now all Mae needed was Solo. They were a family of two —not the large family she'd hoped for as a kid, but enough. Solo was loyal and would never abandon her. She'd had enough of that to last a lifetime.

A block from home, her phone rang. She stopped and fished it from her coat pocket. She didn't know who could be calling her on New Year's Eve. The area code was Colorado. Hopefully not a telemarketer.

Yanking off her glove, she answered on the third ring. "Hello?"

"I'm looking for a woman who was born Maeve Montgomery."

She frowned, wondering what the caller wanted. "Why?"

"I just want to make sure I have the right person. My name is Jake Young. I met your mom, Chrys, and I know your cousins."

Figures. The year would end with a crank call. "The last I heard, my mom was in an institution and I don't have any cousins." She lifted the phone to end the call, but Jake spoke.

"No. Don't hang up. Please. I visited your mom in the psychiatric hospital."

She stared at the phone with her ungloved finger freezing as it hovered over the end button.

"Mae? Please. Will you let me explain?"

It was his please she couldn't ignore. It was such a simple word, but one she'd seldom heard while growing up. She was told where to go and what to do. Rarely was she asked, and no one ever said please. *Set the table. Do your homework. Fold the laundry. I'm taking you to see your mother.* Even in work emails people didn't say please. They stated what they needed, and Mae responded. She'd never thought much about it until she heard Jake say the word.

Lifting the phone to her ear, she started walking again. It was too cold to stand still. "I'm here."

"Thank you. I know it's late, but I just got your number. I'm best friends with—"

"How did you get my number?"

"I hired the same private investigator one of your cousins used to find your mom. Your cousin—Blake Akerman—is my best friend. When he found some pictures of your mom and you—or a little girl they think was you—that proved what they knew about their aunt was a lie, Cade hired a PI."

"Who's Cade?"

"Blake's brother. You have five cousins."

She'd always wondered what it would be like to have a big family. Cousins wouldn't be the same as brothers and sisters, at least she didn't think so. Not that she had any experience with either.

At her building, she rode the elevator to her apartment on the third floor, still holding the phone to her ear.

Jake had to be wondering what she was doing since she was breathing hard from her walk. Before she could speak, he filled the silence.

"As soon as the PI found your mom, Blake and I went to see her. That's when we learned about you."

"It's nice that my cous—" Saying cousins seemed weird;

she didn't know if this Jake guy was telling the truth. Jake and Blake? If he'd made up those names, he wasn't very creative. Could she really have a family? A tiny spark of hope came to life deep inside her.

"Look, Jake. It's nice that Blake wanted to find my mom, but she hasn't been in her right mind in decades. At one time I had hope she would seek medical attention and get the right medication, but she didn't. Or maybe her disease had progressed too far by that time, and it was too late."

"She doesn't need medication. Your mom is cursed. Your entire family is. Blake is your oldest cousin and his curse was triggered but he broke it. No one can help your mom until she breaks her own curse. That's why I wanted to help your cousins find—"

When Jake's words finally sank in, she went back to her first thought—her last call of the year was a crank call. And perhaps she'd gotten it wrong, and Jake was original. A curse?

As Mae disconnected the call and turned her phone off, the little spark of hope winked out. She should have known better. Family wasn't in the cards for her; it never had been.

Thursday, January 16

JAKE GLARED at the calendar on his computer and second-guessed himself for the hundredth time. If "hundredth-guessed" was a thing, he'd coined it. For two weeks he'd ping-ponged between calling Mae and waiting her out. And every time he decided to wait, it felt like a mistake.

After she'd hung up on New Year's Eve, he called back but got her voice mail. He left a message with his phone number and asked her to call, saying he wasn't a crackpot and would only take a few minutes to explain things to her.

Her call still hadn't come.

Knowing how the curse affected Mae wouldn't change anything, but he couldn't help but worry about what she was going through. He'd already seen firsthand what it had done to Blake and his aunt. The curse could already be affecting Mae's life and he was worried, like he'd be with anyone.

In the letter she'd left with her will, Blake's mom said the curse affected each person differently, and so far that rang true. Blake had been haunted by ghosts of failed love, and his aunt Chrys said she experiences delusions. Jake hadn't been back to see her, but maybe that was his next step. Showing up at Mae's house without an invitation screamed too much like stalker.

On New Year's Day, Blake visited his aunt and introduced his new fiancé, Paige. He'd invited Jake to tag along and as much as he would have loved to talk to Chrys about Mae, he declined. Chrys was the only relative Blake and his brothers had left—except for Mae—and Jake hadn't wanted to intrude on their brief time together. Chrys was only lucid for a minute or two each time she surfaced from a delusion.

Jake's worry over Mae was becoming an obsession. Or perhaps it was past *becoming*. He thought about her all the time and wondered if she had anyone to talk to. He didn't know why, but he wanted to be that person for her. It wasn't the first time he'd become obsessed with something or someone, as he'd do whatever it took to keep someone safe. What he didn't know was whether he was obsessed with protecting Mae or with wanting to get to know her.

Blake and Chelsea were worried about him, but they didn't need to be. This wasn't like what happened with Chelsea, and he wasn't trying to control anyone. It was alright to care about someone, and after seeing what Blake went through with the curse, he wanted to help.

That's what he told himself every day. Mae would reach out.

He unlocked his phone. After he'd left a voice message for Mae, his phone had pinged. He'd hoped it was her, but it was a text from Lyra, the PI. She said she was still investigating the witch they'd heard of when at the house where Blake's curse broke, but she'd found pictures of Mae. She sent three graduation photos. One was from Mae's senior year in high school. She didn't look much older than she had in the photo her mom had. In her college grad picture he could see some slight differences, her cheeks were narrower, her hair shorter. The last photo was taken two years earlier. Mae was smiling in the photo, but something was off, like she forced the smile through a cloud of sadness because it didn't quite reach her eyes. He could be completely wrong since he didn't know Mae, only the superficial data Lyra had provided, but he didn't think he was.

Chewie nudged the chair; Jake hadn't noticed him come up. Swiveling around, Jake bracketed Chewie between his knees and rubbed his head. "I'm okay, boy. Got a lot on my mind, that's all."

He grabbed a towel from a stack in his large, bottom desk drawer and wiped the rope of slobber from Chewie's jowls before wiping his own hands. Blake was his human best friend, but he didn't know what he'd do without Chewie. His dog was an empathic genius, always knowing when someone needed attention.

"You done for the day?" Blake asked as he walked in and sat across from the desk. Chewie ambled over to Blake to say hello and Jake tossed him the towel.

"Yeah, nothing urgent that can't wait until tomorrow. You?"

"I'm taking Paige to see Aunt Chrys again tonight. Paige's idea. She hates that Aunt Chrys is alone. Last time we had to wait an hour before she was able to talk to us and didn't stay longer because Cade and Jessica had Emmie. Cade is flexible, but we hate imposing on Jessica as kids don't seem to be her thing. We've hired a babysitter for tonight, so we won't be rushed. Want to come with us?"

He did. For a brief moment, he considered canceling on his sister, but he wanted to see her too. "Can't. I'm going to Chelsea's for dinner." He glanced at the time on his computer. "Speaking of my sister, I need to leave soon."

"Before you go," Blake said, catching Jake halfway out of his chair.

He sat back down. "You don't need to say anything."

"Sure I do. The same way you walked me through things during my curse."

"This is different."

"I know. You're not the one cursed. Mae is. My offer still stands," Blake said. "Let me reach out."

Jake let out a long sigh that had Chewie padding over again. Jake met Blake's gaze as he ran his fingers through the dog's fur. "I can't explain it, but when I saw Mae's picture, she… hit me." He snorted. "Not in a creepy, thirty-year-old-ogling-a-teen way."

"I get it."

"Knowing that she doesn't have her mom or any siblings and might be facing the curse all alone is eating at me."

Blake leaned his forearms on his knees, his stare tense. "She's not Chelsea and you can't protect everyone."

"For fuck's sake. I know that. You and Chelsea keep reminding me of that." Jake held up his hand. "And before you say it, I know what happened to Chelsea isn't my fault." He didn't believe it, but the lie came easy to him because he'd said it many times over the years to reassure those he loved.

Blake's expression said he didn't believe the words either, but neither of them pointed that out. Jake would always regret not doing something sooner for his sister. He could have prevented Chelsea from suffering, and now he could prevent Mae from suffering more than was absolutely necessary. It's not like he could make himself fall in love with her and end the curse, but he could explain what's happening and help her navigate it. Be there for her if she needed someone.

"Today is two months since Mae's thirtieth birthday. How many curse episodes had you had by this point?" Jake already knew the answer, but he needed Blake to understand why he was worried.

"Seven. The eighth came two days later." Blake stood to leave. "Since it's Thursday, and Mae might be busy on the weekend, I'll give you until Sunday night. If she hasn't called you by then, Cade or I will reach out."

Jake nodded. Waiting for a call that might never come and letting Mae suffer when Blake or Cade could call her was selfish. Jake had never been a selfish guy, but something in Mae's voice—hope maybe—made him want to be the one she called. His reasoning wasn't logical—even he knew that—and could be wishful thinking on his part since she'd only spoken a few words, but he couldn't brush it off.

By the time he and Chewie walked into his sister's house, he'd shoved thoughts of Mae to the back of his mind.

His St. Bernard didn't waste any time and settled in his favorite spot in the living room. Delicious smells pulled Jake into the kitchen after he took off his work boots and hung his coat on a hook.

"Hey there, munchkin," he said, picking up his niece out of a playpen sitting in the middle of the kitchen. She smiled at him, showing four front teeth, as drool rolled down her chin. Jake used the sleeve of his flannel shirt to wipe away the drool. "Where's mommy and daddy?" he asked her as he nuzzled her neck, eliciting toddler laughter.

"I didn't hear you come in," Chelsea said from behind him.

Jake spun to face his sister, and the smile dropped from his face. "What's wrong?"

"Nothing, I'm fine." Chelsea didn't look him in the eyes as she crossed to the stove and stirred something in a large pan.

He put Chloe back in her playpen and got in his sister's space. "You're not fine. You're pale. Tell me what's wrong."

Chelsea slapped one hand over her mouth and used the other to push the pan off the element before she spun and left the room. Jake turned off the stove and followed her until she slammed the bathroom door in his face. A moment later he heard the unmistakable sounds of retching.

Hearing his sister retch wrecked him. He'd had his fair share of injuries over the years—that was life in the construction business—and none of them had ever bothered him. Seeing Blake and his brothers bleeding didn't affect him like seeing Chelsea suffering.

A couple of minutes later he heard water running and then Chelsea stepped out. "I'm fine."

"Puking is fine?"

She ignored him and walked back to the kitchen.

"Do you have the flu?"

"No."

"Did you take too much medication?"

Chelsea spun around and faced him. "No," she hissed. "I would never do that again."

He gripped her shoulders. "You're right and I'm sorry. It's been years and that was insensitive of me. I don't know why that just popped into my head. I hate seeing you sick. You're scaring me, Chels. What's up?"

She glanced toward the front door, as if checking to see if anyone was there. "I haven't told Cameron yet."

"Told him what?" He nearly shook the answer out of his sister.

She grinned. "I'm pregnant."

Jake hauled her against his chest. "I'm so happy for you." He knew how much she and Cam wanted to have several children close together in age. At one time Jake thought he'd have a couple of kids of his own by now. He'd only turned thirty the August before, but, like Chelsea, he'd always wanted a big family. There had been just the two of them but maybe growing up with a horde of aunts and uncles and too many cousins to count had rubbed off on them.

Chelsea finally pulled away and she paled again. With her hand covering her mouth, she took a step back and pointed at the stove. "Can you take that outside?"

"The pan? Is it ruined? It smells delicious."

"It's making me sick."

"Got it." Jake grabbed two tea towels and lifted the pan off the stove, before lifting his chin toward her back door. "Open it for me?" He stayed back with the pan until Chelsea opened the door and backed away.

A cold wind hit him, and dampness soaked into his socks at his first step outside. Not caring about himself, he took the three steps off the deck and walked through the snow to deposit the pan in the middle of the yard.

When he walked back into the kitchen and lifted a foot to remove his sock, Chelsea laughed. "You didn't have to go that far. Out on the deck would have been good enough."

Jake took off his other sock and shook the snow off the bottom of his jeans. "I wanted to get it far away from you."

"Well, I appreciate it," she said as she handed him a towel. "Now, I have to figure out what to have for dinner."

"I can order from the Thai place around the corner."

"Maybe something milder?"

"But you love—"

She tilted her head as if to say, *Think about that for a minute.*

"Oh, right, spices. How about some simple pasta from the Italian place down the street?"

"Perfect. I should be able to handle that."

"Handle what?" Cam said as he walked into the kitchen and pulled his wife to him for a quick kiss.

Chelsea's eyes widened and she looked between him and her husband.

Jake couldn't imagine what it would be like learning the woman you loved carried your child, and at the rate he was going, he never would, but he expected he would want privacy to enjoy the moment. "Come on, munchkin. Let's order some food," he said to his niece as he scooped her up and took her into the living room.

As soon as he sat on the floor with Chloe, she let out a loud squeal. "Chew chew." Jake put out his hand to steady her as she hoisted herself up and toddled over to his dog, flopping down half on and half off him. Chewie lifted his head enough to give her a lick and lay back down. While Chloe chatted away to his dog, Jake called in an order for food.

A couple of hours later, Cam bathed Chloe as Chelsea walked him to the door. "Thanks for ordering dinner."

"My pleasure, and thanks for having me." He pulled her into a hug and repeated his words from earlier. "I'm so happy for you and Cam."

When she stepped back, her eyes were watery, but her smile was big. "I know you're not seeing anyone, but I want you to have this too."

He swallowed and plastered a small smile on his face. "Me too. But first I need to find a woman who can put up with me."

"You will. As long as you cut out the caveman act."

That might not be possible. Chelsea's near-death experience almost wrecked him, and that was enough for one lifetime. Having anyone he loved put themselves at risk wasn't something he would be able to easily ignore.

"You saved me," she said softly, something she'd repeated more than once over the years.

His response was always the same. "Not quick enough."

"If it wasn't quick enough, I wouldn't be here, and I am. All because of you."

"Thank you for proving my point. I need to be vigilant with the people I love." Chewie rubbed up against his leg and Jake reached a hand down.

"There's a difference between vigilant and overprotective to the point you drive people away."

Only sometimes. "Chels, let it drop. Okay?"

"Okay. For now."

He gave her arm a slight squeeze, shoved his bare feet into his boots and grabbed his coat, shrugging into it.

"Oh, your socks."

"I'll get them next week." Laughter reached them from upstairs and Jake swallowed, pretending the sounds of family didn't affect him like they always did. He tilted his head toward the stairs. "Go join in the fun. I'll see you next week."

It didn't take him long to get home. He and Chewie entered the dark, silent kitchen from the garage. There were moments, like right then, that he regretted buying the modern, spacious, four-bedroom house. He had an empty house that he only filled on occasion, like on New Year's, and his dream of filling it with a family felt out of reach.

Chewie had already laid down on his dog bed by the unlit fireplace, but Jake wasn't ready to call it a night yet. "Want to play with a ball?" he asked, forcing some excitement into his tone.

By the time the large St. Bernard flopped down in the snow, Jake's arm burned from throwing the ball. He got them both inside and had just wiped off Chewie's feet and under-belly when his phone rang.

Mae's number lit up on his screen because he'd programmed it in after the PI had texted it to him. He wiped his suddenly sweaty palm on his jeans and answered the call. "Hello?"

3

All day Mae fought to forget last night's dream. The harder she shoved it away, the sharper it got.

One of her retainer clients emailed at dawn with an emergency change—revising a massive section. All day while she worked, her thoughts drifted to the dream—more of a nightmare—like it dragged her toward a pool of despair. Each time she forced her focus back and, barely, met the deadline.

The dream was her sixth and there'd only been six days between it and the last one. Something was definitely wrong with her, and since she refused to be like her mom, she knew she needed help. A slot was canceled, and the doctor fit her in that afternoon.

As soon as Mae tried to explain her problem to the doctor, heat climbed her neck and into her cheeks. The doctor met her gaze with empathy. "You're under too much stress. Do you have a support system?" That was a big fat no, but Mae brushed it off—sure, she had friends. The doctor handed her a prescription for a mild sleep aid and referred her to a psychologist.

She'd left feeling foolish. She couldn't explain the sudden nightmares, or the despair that lingered after. She saw nothing while awake, only at night, and as much as she wanted to blame stress, Jake's words wouldn't shake loose: *"She doesn't need medication. Your mom is cursed. Your entire family is."*

Mae didn't believe in anything outside of the physical world. Not God, nor Santa Claus, and certainly not witches and curses.

Jake's talk of family curses had sounded crazy, but each time she woke from another nightmare, she wondered if what he said had some merit. If a curse had her in its clutches, she might not slowly lose her mind. Or maybe she would. Her mom had.

Jake said her eldest cousin had broken his curse. If he had, could she? If a curse actually existed—she still wasn't sure—it could mean she might not end up in a facility like her mom. Weather her mom was cursed or had a mental illness, the result had been the same. But if Mae was cursed, maybe she could break it before it was too late.

The tree from her recent nightmare flashed in her mind. "The tree was huge, Solo. I mean, gigantic. You would have loved it. I stood under it and had the sense that it would protect me forever."

Mae ran one hand through Solo's dense fur as she remembered looking up at the tree feeling a sense of safety she'd never felt before. Her life had been a series of moves, disruptions, and new families. Not once had she felt safe.

Now, living alone, she often felt like she was biding time, waiting for something bad to happen. But, standing under that tree, with its strong branches creating an umbrella overhead, she'd felt safe. She couldn't see the tree's roots, but somehow she knew they were unshakable.

Knowing that steadied her.

Then the leaves began to fall one by one.

As the leaves fell, unease rippled through her.

The ground beneath her shook, causing her to stutter-step to stay upright. Mae looked up as a massive crack opened in the trunk above her head. The crack snaked down the bark like a viper ready to strike.

She jumped away from the trunk. In her haste, she tripped, falling to her hands and knees. Beneath her palms, the roots heaved from the ground, pushing up dirt all around her. Scrambling to her feet, Mae rushed forward to the edge of the tree's canopy and watched in horror as the tree collapsed and turned to dust, leaving her exposed under a stormy sky.

She sensed the dream was warning her about something she already knew: no matter how stable a bond felt, eventually it would fail, leaving her vulnerable, alone, and exposed.

"Good thing I have you," she told Solo as she stroked his head. When she first got Solo, she looked up Mastiffs and knew their lifespan was six to twelve years, and that eventually he would leave her too. It hadn't mattered because she already loved him. As soon as he walked over to her and pressed against her side, she'd been a goner.

From the moment she heard his former owners fighting, she promised herself that he would never know what it felt like to be abandoned, and she never wavered. When Solo eventually left her, the only difference between him and everyone else who'd abandoned her would be that Solo wouldn't do it voluntarily.

But what if she had to abandon him? If she couldn't stop the dreams and became like her mom, what would happen to Solo? Abandoning him was more terrifying than anything that could happen to her.

She thumbed the phone in her lap. Instead of blocking

Jake's number after he left his voicemail, she'd saved it. Just in case. Tonight might be that case.

He could still be a crackpot, but she didn't think so. She searched and found two photos of him on the Akerman Contracting website, one the official picture of the executive and the other in the company's brochure. He was good-looking in a mountain-man sort of way. He had a full beard, neatly trimmed, and his hair ran long on top, but swept back. Both his hair and his beard were a deep auburn color, near dark red. In the formal picture he wore a suit, which was such a contrast to his rugged backwoods look. In the other photo he wore a flannel shirt and jeans on a job site and came off as more approachable.

The site also featured four Akerman men. In a sleep-deprived fog one morning last week, she called Akerman Contracting and asked them to verify Jake's number. The woman on the phone told her that Jake was out of the office, but she could speak to Blake Akerman, the CEO. Mae nearly said yes, but something at the last minute stopped her. It could have been remembering how Jake pleaded with her to listen to him. How he'd said "please" twice. Or the possibility of talking to Blake and being rejected by a family member—even one she didn't know—was scarier than talking to Jake.

If she asked for his help, it wasn't like he could abandon her. He was a stranger. She'd ask him what to do and then they'd go their separate ways. Would she even get to know her cousins? They likely had families and close friends and might not even have time for her. Whether they did or not, it was always best to keep her distance. Get the help she needed and sever all ties. She couldn't be disappointed or hurt that way.

At one point in her teen years she'd become so accustomed to being abandoned, tossed from one person to the next, that she no longer cried. It wasn't until her husband left her that she finally shed another tear. For an entire day she wallowed in the loss and another abandonment. After that she resolved never to let anyone else in because she would never put herself through that again. Solo was different, and if she left him, he wouldn't understand.

"I won't abandon you, Solo." With courage she hadn't felt in a long time, she unlocked her phone and clicked on Jake's name.

The phone rang twice before she heard his deep voice. "Hello?"

MAE DIDN'T SAY anything when he answered the call, but he could hear her breathing. "Mae?"

"Uh, hi."

"Hi." Jake waited for her to say something more, but after a couple more seconds of silence, he worried she might regret the call and hang up.

She let out a nervous-sounding laugh. "This is weird for me."

"In what way? Besides calling to ask me about a family curse."

Mae scoffed. "Yes, besides that. I don't normally call strangers out of the blue."

"The PI mentioned you own a business, so your clients start out as strangers."

"That's different because they're calling about work and usually start off with a question."

"I can ask you a question. What type of dog do you have?"

"A Mastiff. How did you know— oh. The PI told you I have a dog. What else did he tell you?"

"She. The PI is a woman. She told me you have a business, a dog, changed your name when you got married, and that you're now divorced. You live in Green Springs, Colorado, and you went to college." Lyra also gave him notes about several of the foster homes Mae had lived in. Repeating those facts now felt too impersonal to tell Mae because those families would have been more than names and dates to her. The facts felt intrusive, as he shouldn't know any of that unless she told him.

"That's a lot. Now you have me at a disadvantage because I know nothing about you."

When Jake first got the file, it hadn't felt like a lot. All he needed was a phone number, but he had wanted to know so much more. Mae's likes and dislikes, how she'd felt in all those foster homes, and what made her get married so young and then divorced.

From Mae's side, he could see how intrusive it sounded. "I didn't mean to pry, I wanted to find you. So… a Mastiff. What's his or her name?"

"Him. Solo."

Jake laughed. "Well, I see we already have a couple of things in common. I have a large dog too, a St. Bernard. His name's Chewie."

"Hmmm… A St. Bernard. Not really a large dog, then?"

He heard the teasing in her voice. "Only the owner of a Mastiff would say that. How much does Solo weigh?"

"The last time we were at the vet he was 230 pounds."

"He's definitely got Chewie beat as he's a measly 180 pounds."

Mae laughed and it warmed something inside Jake. "Besides Star Wars and large dogs in common, let me even the playing field. I work at Akerman Contracting, the company owned by your cousins. I have a business degree, my name has been Jake Young since birth, I've never been married, don't have a girlfriend, and I live in Blue Mountain. Did I miss anything?"

"I think that was it. I…"

Mae hesitated and he wished he could see her face. Video when they barely knew each other might freak her out, but maybe one day. "You can tell me or ask me anything," he said gently.

"Really? Anything?"

He smiled to himself. "Did I walk into something?"

"Maybe," she said drawing out the word. "So you wouldn't care if I asked if you sleep naked?" Mae sucked in a breath loud enough for him to hear. "Oh my god! I can't believe I asked you that. I don't even know where that came from. Don't answer."

Now he was grinning. "Okay, I won't answer that. Not right now, anyway. Seriously, though, I know you wanted to say something earlier. Say or ask away."

"I called you because of Solo. Idon'twanttoleavehim." She blurted it as one word, as if she wasn't quite sure she should tell him.

"How do you mean?" Jake figured she was worried she'd end up in an institution like her mom, but he didn't want to put words in her mouth. He knew from Blake's experience with the curse that first he had to accept that the curse was real and then open himself up to love. One problem with that was that he didn't know if Mae had anyone she could love. It would be arrogant of him to even think that Mae might want to be friends with him—a complete stranger—let alone that she could one day love him so they could break the curse. He didn't know if either of them was right for the other, but he liked what they had in common so far.

"If I'm cursed or sick I might not be able to care for Solo, but a part of me doesn't want to know about either. You know… the whole head in the sand thing. If I don't know about it, it doesn't exist."

"I think a lot of people would feel the same way in your position. That if you ignore it, it will go away."

"Yes. But what if it doesn't?"

"I haven't told you about the curse yet, so maybe I should explain—"

"Wild that we're talking about a curse at all."

"I know, but since I've seen it, I know it's real. The curse—"

"What do you mean you've seen it?"

"Mae?"

"Hmmm?"

"If you stop interrupting, I'll be able to explain everything," he said without rancor.

"Oops, sorry. It's a bad habit I developed when I was younger and was either ignored or talked over."

Jake could imagine Mae as a young girl thrown into strange situations and unfamiliar families trying to be heard. His family went through some hard times when Chelsea was a teenager, but his parents had always been there for him. Never once did he worry about not being heard. He felt for Mae and decided to do what he could to alleviate her worries. "I'm going to make you two promises right now. Okay?"

"Maybe," she said drawing out the word like she had earlier, teasing once more in her tone. "It depends on what the promises are. If you promise to give me chocolate, I'm all in, but if you promise to toilet paper my house every Halloween, I'll pass."

The way she switched from worry to teasing surprised him. Since he didn't know her, he should have expected anything, but perhaps knowing how she'd grown up and that she was facing a curse had made him jump to conclusions.

He liked this unexpected Mae and that she had an inquisitive mind.

"No toilet papering, I promise. The first promise is—"

"Wait. Does that mean no chocolate either?"

"You'll have to see about that one," Jake said and paused, waiting for Mae to say something so she didn't have to interrupt him again.

"Okay, I can live with that. You can continue."

He chuckled. "Thank you." He paused again and she didn't disappoint him with a murmured, *You're welcome*. "My first promise is that if something ever happens to you, I'll make sure Solo is well cared for. As a dog owner, I completely understand so either I would take him in, or one of your cousins, but you'll never have to worry about him. You should add my phone number or Blake's to Solo's dog tag as backup." He tossed out the offer before he thought. To downplay his pushiness, he added, "Blake's number is on Chewie's tag."

"Thank you, I'll think about it. And the second promise?"

"For however long we talk, I'll always listen to you, and I'll never speak over you." Jake expected Mae to say "thank you" again, but all he heard was silence. After a few seconds, she sniffled. He kept quiet, not quite sure what to say. "I'm sorry that no one's ever promised you that before," could be taken as patronizing, but he *was* sorry. No one deserved to be ignored or treated as Mae obviously had been.

He wanted to promise he'd always be there for her. Since he was trying to tone down the caveman act, that wouldn't be good. He also couldn't guarantee that he'd even be able to keep it. She might consider him insincere, as who promises that when they barely know someone? For now, he'd have to settle for listening while they sorted out her curse, which he still needed to explain.

"Are you ready to hear about the curse?"

"Sure."

She didn't sound sure, but he'd take it. "In August, your mom's sister, your Aunt Alex, Blake's mom—"

"Aunt Alex? Like my mom is Chrys but her full name is Chrysanthi Desdemona Montgomery. Chrysanthi means golden flower. Is Alex short for something?"

"Yes, Alex was short for Alexandria and her middle name was Evangelina. The only reason I know her full name is because it's on a plaque at the office."

"You said *was*."

"She died in August."

"How?"

"A car accident." Jake let Mae process the information. She'd learned she had an aunt at the same time she discovered she would never meet the woman. On top of that, Jake was going to throw the information about the curse at her.

A full minute passed before Mae spoke. "I don't think I want to hear any more tonight. Does that sound crazy? I mean, I could be cursed, but it's all a bit too overwhelming right now."

"It's a lot to take in. Hearing about it today or in another day or two won't make a difference." He hoped it wouldn't, but he still didn't know how the curse was affecting her.

"You can tell me about it some day."

Her words gave Jake hope that she would talk to him again. It was getting late. Time to let her go, but he didn't want to. He'd been enjoying talking to her. "Any other questions I can answer for you?"

He was getting used to her pauses, knowing now she wouldn't hang up.

"How and when did you and Blake meet?"

"Our *how* is the same as our *when*. In kindergarten."

"The whole Jake-Blake rhyming thing is weird."

"In kindergarten we thought it was cool. Now, I don't even think about it."

"You've been close friends the entire time?"

"Yes, even through high school and college. His dad died while we were in our freshman year of college. Blake took over Akerman Contracting with help from the existing executive team. We'd both been working for the company for several years by that time, only part time. The following year we took all the same classes so I could take notes for him if he couldn't make a class."

"I can't imagine what it's like to know someone your entire life." Her last word was garbled as she yawned. "Sorry, it's been a long day."

"I'll let you go." He didn't want to. What had started as an obsession over a picture and wanting to keep her safe, suddenly felt like a friendship. "Can I call you tomorrow?"

"Yes, I'd like that. But I can't guarantee I'll be ready to talk about the curse. It just doesn't seem real."

"No problem. Whenever you're ready." As long as she didn't wait too long, he wanted to tack on but didn't.

"Good night."

"Pleasant dreams, Mae."

Mae scoffed, but before he could ask why, she'd hung up on him.

After he let Chewie outside one more time, he was in bed with him lying at his feet when his phone pinged with a text.

A laugh rumbled up from deep within him when he opened the text to find a photo from Mae where only the top of her head and chin were visible. Solo lay stretched out lengthwise of top of her. She must have held the camera above her to even take the picture.

Jake clicked on the camera icon and took a similar

picture, capturing his torso and legs underneath the blanket with Chewie laying at his feet. He sent the photo and set his phone on the nightstand. Tomorrow night couldn't come fast enough.

4

Wednesday, January 22

*H*anging up her coat after wiping the snow and wet off Solo, Mae realized she'd slipped into a new normal. Jake had called her every night during the last week, and she looked forward to talking to him. Instead of settling in with a book after dinner like she used to, she would take Solo for an early walk, get him settled, make some tea, and be ready for Jake's call.

She set the kettle to boil and glanced at Solo, waiting for a treat. "A new routine isn't so bad, is it?"

She loved it. Too bad it could be dangerous for her. Dangerous because of how much she looked forward to each call. Her day felt incomplete if she didn't talk to Jake. She couldn't remember the last time she enjoyed talking to someone as much as she did with him. Topics ranged across everything, as if they were friends getting to know each other, which she supposed they were. They only avoided one item—the curse. He'd brought it up the first couple of nights they talked and both times she'd brushed him off. Finally, she told him she'd ask about it when she was ready.

Mae still wasn't ready to talk about it, wanting to keep her head in the sand for a while longer. That reprieve was ending; the newest dream came five days after the last one, not ten. Shaking off the daytime despair kept getting harder.

Each morning Mae woke resolved. That night would be the night she would ask Jake all about the curse. All throughout the day she'd remind herself, tonight she would ask Jake, tonight she would ask about the curse. Then she'd get on the phone with him, he'd ask her something about her day or a random question, and off they'd go.

Their conversations never lagged, and she found herself laughing more than she had in years. By the time they hung up, she'd realize another night had slipped by and she hadn't asked about the curse. She kept shoving it to the backseat for the joy of talking to Jake. She'd never had anyone to rely on, but she'd been content. Lonely at times and lacking family, except for Solo, but still content. Then Jake popped into her life and she'd started to rely on him to brighten her day. A dangerous position to be in because she knew all too well that people leave.

Two nights ago, she let it ring. Not because she didn't want to talk to him, but because she freaked out knowing how much she wanted to. Right now, she was relying on him to brighten her day, but then what? Would he end up in charge of her mood—of whether she felt okay at all? Thinking of that possibility had terrified her too much to answer.

Jake left a voicemail asking her to let him know she was safe. No one had ever done that for her before, not even her ex-husband. She sat on the couch with a book and reread the same page twenty times, her eyes flickering to her phone.

She lasted two hours before texting him back that she was fine.

Settled on the couch with Solo, she looked at the sticky-note reminder she'd placed on the coffee table earlier.

Her phone rang; she exhaled slowly, trying to calm her excitement. "Hello?"

"Hello there."

"Is that a coincidence or are you quoting Star Wars?"

"Wondering how much of a fan you are."

"Ha! You want to go there?" Mae couldn't stop her grin.

"I do. What is Luke Skywalker's home planet?"

Mae snorted a laugh. "Is that the best you've got? Too easy. Tatooine. My turn. What is Yoda's home planet?"

"You're going to be like that, are you? That's a trick question. Yoda's home planet was never revealed."

"I mean, after your first super-easy question, I needed to know if you were a *real* fan. Okay, give me another."

"Not only do I have more questions, one day I'll show you all my Star Wars LEGO sets—even the Tatooine Homestead."

"You are a geek, aren't you?"

"And proud of it."

"Some of the foster homes I was in had boxes of old LEGO. I never had a kit."

"You could buy a kit."

"Maybe." She didn't want to talk about all the things she'd never had. Buying a kit as an adult and putting it together on her own hadn't felt the same. She steered the conversation back to their earlier teasing. "Your turn. Let me have it."

They shot questions back and forth for over half an hour, trying to trip each other up, but neither did. Mae laughed so hard she felt a stitch in her side. "Okay... Let me... catch my... breath."

"Trivia aside, how was your day?"

Long and boring as I waited all day to talk to you. "Fine."

"Did you have any difficulty with the project for that new client?"

Part of her addiction to Jake's phone calls could be the way he always seemed to care about what she did and thought. Not like the people who asked how you were and couldn't care less. He remembered everything she told him.

"No, it turned out easier to do than I first thought." Mae gave a quick rundown about what she'd done and the new client she'd gotten through a referral. "What about you? How was your day?"

Mae listened as Jake told her about a new project. The entire time, the sticky note on the table taunted her. She couldn't put it off any longer. When Jake finished, Mae took a deep breath and exhaled slowly. "I'm ready now."

"Ready?"

"To hear about the curse. Well... Maybe not everything yet."

"I'll tell you as much as you want to hear," Jake said without judgment in his tone. "When your aunt Alex died in August, your cousins read the letter she left with her will. Cade—the second-oldest—is a lawyer and handled Alex's will. He had always figured that the letter was a goodbye letter, so after the funeral they gathered to read it."

"I'm guessing it wasn't a goodbye letter?" Mae couldn't imagine what it would have been like for them to get that kind of shock, except maybe to get some closure. She'd never had that herself. A social worker had taken her away from her mom, and that was the end of it.

"Depending on how you look at it, you could call it a goodbye letter. I had Cade email me a copy of the letter. Would you like me to email it to you? Or read it now?"

"No, not yet." Maybe one day she'd like to read it, but right now, reading or hearing a letter from a dead aunt she'd never met felt strange. "For now, can you sum it up for me?"

"Sure. Hundreds of years ago, one of your ancestors was cursed by a spirit because she heard rumors that he didn't have enough love in his heart. The curse was to affect his children and all the generations that followed. If a person in his family did not fall in love and have that love reciprocated by the time of their thirtieth birthday, the curse would take effect."

"By their thirtieth birthday? It didn't start until a couple of weeks after I turned thirty." Mae pulled her phone from her ear, put it on speaker, and opened her calendar app.

"Mae? Are you still there?"

"Yeah, I was looking at a calendar. My curse didn't hit me… well, what I think is the curse… until ten days after my birthday."

"That was the same with Blake as well. I think his hit eleven days after his birthday, but it's pretty close. Your aunt said the curse affects each person differently, so we interpreted that to mean both when it starts and how it manifests itself. She also said that if a person isn't in love and loved in return, by the time they turn thirty, the curse takes effect after that, but not necessarily on the day of their birthday."

The feelings of despair she felt after a nightmare settled around Mae like a scratchy, too-tight sweater. "I'm going to be sick, like my mom."

"Your mom isn't sick, she's cursed. She could have broken it. Blake did. If your mom's curse was like Blake's, it would have likely been only a few months from the time it first came on until she was spiraling multiple times a day, but she could have fallen in love."

Mae tsked. "You say that like falling in love is easy." Even if it was, it wouldn't last. It never did. The other person eventually left.

"No, I don't think it's easy." Jake paused, thinking it through. "But it's possible. My parents have been married for thirty-three years, and Blake's parents were married for decades before your uncle died. My sister is happily married, and Blake and Paige love each other."

Mae had seen happy couples too. That didn't mean it would happen to her. "Why aren't you married or have a girlfriend?" she asked. As soon as the words were out of her mouth, she realized that while she was enjoying her conversations with Jake, he could be looking at them differently. "Or boyfriend?"

"I prefer women." She could hear the smile in his voice, but he sounded sad when he said, "The right one hasn't come along yet."

"Are you picky?" Mae felt the mood shift when Jake didn't answer right away.

JAKE DIDN'T KNOW how to answer Mae's question. Picky? About safety and love, yes. Weren't most people? No one wanted to settle for someone who didn't love them. As for the rest—a woman's career, looks, background, whatever— he didn't think he was too choosy. When he looked back at past girlfriends, none had been *the one*. He may have stayed with them for the company or because he became obsessed with keeping them safe.

"Jake? I didn't mean to offend you."

"You didn't. I'm trying to figure out how to answer your question. I'm picky about people's safety."

Mae hummed, puzzled. "You'll have to explain that one."

It had been years since he'd talked about the incidents that changed his life. He cleared his throat and swallowed away his discomfort. "When I was seventeen, I walked in on our neighbor sexually assaulting my sister. Chelsea was fifteen."

He heard Mae suck in a breath, but pushed through. "The guy was in his forties and lived across the street with his wife and kids. My parents were friends with him and his wife. Chelsea babysat for them. That day I got home later than usual because Blake and I stayed after football practice to work on some drills. Chelsea usually hung out on the bleachers and watched my practice, but that day she didn't want to wait while I did extra drills, so she walked home."

Thirteen years later, he still saw that afternoon: the frantic search, the wrongness, Chelsea's panic-stricken face.

"On my way home from practice, I texted Chelsea to see if she wanted me to grab her a blue-raspberry slushy—her favorite. When she didn't respond, I got her a slushy anyway." At the end of the day, that slushy still sat on the kitchen table, melted, a puddle of condensation around the cup. To this day, the sight of anything blue-raspberry nauseated him.

"When I didn't find her at home, I worried. Chelsea and I always chatted after school. Usually she wanted to share some gossip she heard, or chat about the players on my team, especially the quarterback she was crushing on. I called her phone, and I heard it ringing, faintly. It went to voicemail, and I kept calling."

Thinking about the number of times he paced the house, listening for the ring to get louder, got his heart racing almost as fast as it had that day. "I found her phone on the front lawn. That was when I knew something was wrong. Chelsea always had her phone on her and was never careless with it. She wouldn't have let it fall out of a pocket."

"What did you do?" Mae asked, her tone anxious, as if anticipating his answer.

"I started calling Chelsea's name." Standing where the grass met the sidewalk, he yelled her name as loud as he could. By the time the next-door neighbor came out to see what he was shouting about, he sounded like a two-pack-a-day smoker. "I didn't want to go too far and miss Chelsea if she came home. At the same time, I wanted to search inside every house. The woman who lived next door came out to ask what I was doing. She worried I'd wake her grandson from his nap. When I said I was looking for my sister, she told me not to worry because she'd seen Chelsea go across the street with Mr. Howell.

"I'd known Mr. Howell almost my entire life, so I relaxed. Then Chelsea's phone vibrated in my hand. She'd set an alarm to start making dinner. It was her turn. Over breakfast, she'd bragged about how good dinner was going to be. I knew then that something had happened to her."

In that moment, his world had narrowed to the house across the street—the drapes all drawn—spiking his earlier feeling of unease to a twenty on a scale of one to ten. So many details from that day stuck in his mind, but he didn't remember the sprint. One moment he was on the sidewalk, the next he was at the Howells' front stoop, lungs burning.

"Funny," he said quietly and huffed a humorless laugh, "I didn't knock at the Howell's door, even though I expected it to be locked. It wasn't. An oversight or cockiness—I don't know—but I barged right in and called Chelsea's name. She didn't answer and there was a moment when I second-guessed myself. But only a moment. I called Chelsea's name again and ran up the stairs. She was in the master bedroom. Howell had backed her up against a wall. He was towering over her with one hand between her legs and the other holding a knife to her throat."

Jake felt his fingernails bite into his palms and loosened his fists. The terrified look on his sister's face still haunted his dreams now and then.

"Please tell me you beat the shit out of the guy," Mae said, and he blinked, focusing him back in the present.

"No, but I wanted to. I yanked him back so hard he crashed to the ground. Chelsea didn't say a word, and the fucker jumped up and immediately spewed lies. He said that he asked Chelsea over to help him with a recipe to surprise his wife, and he claimed Chelsea lured him into the bedroom."

Mae scoffed. "Really? A fifteen-year-old girl enticed a grown man into a bedroom? How did he explain the knife?"

"He said he had it in his hand from cutting vegetables for the recipe when Chelsea told him she wanted to show him something."

"No one believed him, though. Right?"

"At first the police weren't sure who to believe. I took Chelsea home and called my parents and the police. Chelsea had no marks on her and the fuckwad had staged his kitchen to look like they had been in the middle of cooking. He said he mentioned his anniversary and the gift he got his wife and Chelsea asked to see it. When he said it was in his bedroom, Chelsea led the way. The demented pervert could have won an acting award for his performance, looking all embarrassed, saying he hadn't wanted to go to his bedroom with a teenager, but followed Chelsea to get her to go back to the kitchen, so he could go get the gift for her to see."

Mae scoffed again, but let him continue. "He even said I barged into his house and threatened him. The situation turned into a he-said-she-said mess. A fifteen-year-old girl against a successful businessman and upstanding member of the community with a perfect-looking family."

"What about Chelsea's phone? She wouldn't have dropped it if she was going over there to help, right? And since she had to cook dinner, she wouldn't have gone over there anyway, right? Of course, she wouldn't have. The police would have been crazy to take his word over hers, especially since you barged in. Now please tell me they believed her."

If the memories weren't so painful, Jake would have chuckled at Mae's rapid-fire questions and comments, not letting him respond before she shot the next one out. He liked her fierce protective streak.

"At first they didn't, and Chelsea…" Jake wasn't ready to say what finally made him obsessive about protecting people. "Eventually, another girl the bastard assaulted came forward, and then the wife. He abused her too, but her worry about what he might do to their twelve-year-old daughter was what finally got her to talk. Still… Chelsea fell into a dark time."

"Why hadn't the other girl come forward before?"

"She felt scared. He threatened to do the same to her little sister if she said anything. After word got out in school about what happened to Chelsea, the girl finally went to her parents."

"Sick bastard."

Mae summed him up nicely. "Yes, he was."

"I'm so sorry that happened to your sister, and it makes sense why you're protective of people you care about. That's not a bad thing."

As bad as the assault was, the harrowing time later was worse. It forged Jake into the man he became. "No, it's not a bad th—"

"Wait. Did you first call me because of what happened to Chelsea? I'm like a pet project you need to save."

It wasn't a question. He said he'd always listen to her and not talk over her, and to him those went hand in hand with being honest. Because if he was going to lie to her, there wasn't much point in listening to what she truly wanted or needed. "Not a project, but when your mom said you'd turned thirty, I worried you didn't know about the curse and would wonder what was going on."

"Why didn't Blake call me?"

He heard the accusation in her tone. "Because when I saw your picture in your mom's room… something about you spoke to me. If you hadn't called me back when you did, Blake would have reached out that weekend."

"My picture? Oh. I know which one. I think I was fourteen or fifteen."

"I think so." Jake tensed as he waited for Mae to put the pieces together.

"Oh, my god. The picture shows me at the same age Chelsea was when attacked. I *am* a project to you."

"Not a project." Jake could feel Mae slipping away from him. "I already said I wanted to make sure you knew about the curse, but you're more than that to me now. We're friends. I look forward to talking to you every night. Don't you?" He held his breath as he waited for her answer.

"I do… Jake?"

"Yeah?"

"Since we're friends, you…. uh… you won't walk away, right?" she said, lowering her voice. He noticed she did it when she was worried about something, as if saying it too loudly would jinx it.

"No, Mae, I won't walk away." But he had no way of knowing if the curse would take her away from him.

They talked for a couple more minutes about their plans for the next day before they hung up.

Jake walked into his kitchen and checked the contents of his fridge to see if he needed to go shopping soon. After adding a few items to a grocery list, he put in a load of laundry, then went into his living room and straightened items that didn't need it. Chewie lifted his head and watched him sit down and pick up his book. When Jake settled into the chair, the dog put his head down but picked it back up five minutes later when Jake stood, not even one page further into the story.

"Chewie, outside. Let's play with your ball." Jake grabbed his coat, shoved his feet into his boots at the back door, and stepped onto the deck. He'd been throwing the ball for about ten minutes when his phone rang.

He checked the caller ID. "Hey, Lyra. You got something for me?"

"Hi, Jake. Following up on your other request. I found the witch you were looking for, but she won't be any help."

"Why not?"

"She's old, and her family doesn't want her talking to anyone."

"Then you're not denying she is a witch?"

"Why would I?" Lyra said with a half laugh.

"Not everyone believes in witches. When I first asked you to look for her, I think I may have been testing you. Waiting to see if you were only humoring me."

"Again, why would I, considering what our company does? That would be like a wolf denying it has sharp teeth."

Jake frowned. "I think I'm missing something. You're investigators."

"Yes. Didn't you look us up?"

"No, Cade Akerman gave me your card. It said Lyra Statera, Lumen Security and something about magical investigation. That wasn't simply a catchy tagline?"

"Nope," she said, popping the p. "Our company name is Magical Protection and Investigation Service. Sure, a chunk of our bread and butter comes from catching cheating spouses and dealing with insurance fraud claims, but most of what we deal with is about magic and the paranormal."

"Do you know the witch I'm looking for?"

"Yes, but that's a dead end, Jake. We're very protective of

her, so please drop it. If you can tell me something specific you need help with, maybe I can find some answers for you."

"Do you know someone who can break a curse?" Since that's why he wanted to find the witch anyway, he didn't see any point in pushing Lyra to tell him about someone she didn't want to talk about.

"It depends on the curse. Who cast it and when?"

"A spirit about five hundred years ago."

Lyra let out a low whistle. "I'll ask around, but don't hold your breath. Since you said spirit and not witch, I don't think I'll have much luck. I don't know much about spirit curses, but I've heard they're almost impossible to undo. Spells can also change through the generations."

"I'd appreciate it if you looked anyway."

"I don't want to waste your money, so all I'll promise is to ask around."

"Thanks." Jake hung up and called Chewie, taking him into the house.

In bed a while later, Jake couldn't stop thinking about his conversation with Mae. She was a contradiction—asking him why he wasn't married when she'd lost faith in the institution herself. Having had a more stable environment than her and the perfect example of marriage, he always expected to get married someday. He didn't know if Mae could be *the one*. It was too early to tell, but he wanted to help her. He still didn't know how the curse was affecting her. Or how much time she had left. The more he cared, the more he wanted to be there for her. But it was up to her. She was going to have to let him in.

Thursday, January 30

The cold stung Mae's cheeks, making her eyes water. Freezing temperatures weren't her favorite, but for once, she was thankful for the cold. The wind whipped around her, forcing her to walk faster, invigorating her. All day she'd fought off tiredness and a sense of despair. For the past week, she'd considered what Jake had told her about Chelsea. Mae couldn't imagine what it would be like to have a brother who loved you so much. Or anyone who loved you that fiercely.

"Solo, home." The brisk walk through the park had eased some of her exhaustion, but they'd been outside for twice as long as usual and she was always conscious of the cold and snow affecting Solo's paws.

Pulling her phone out of her pocket with her mittened hand, she checked the time. Jake wouldn't phone for a while yet. She'd have time to get Solo settled and make her nightly cup of tea. As Solo led them home, Mae thought of her last dream. It had come early in the morning, not long before her alarm was set to go off, and hadn't been far from her mind all day.

Mae wandered down a dim hallway in an old house, skimming her fingers along the paneled walls. With each step, the hall stretched, a never-ending tunnel. Framed portraits of long-gone ancestors, hung on the walls on either side, lined up one after the other like soldiers standing at attention for inspection. Their expressions were dour, as if the painter forced them to stand still for a long time, sucking the happiness out of them.

From out of nowhere, Mae heard voices, as if close by, distracting her from the portraits. The people's chatter grew louder, making her quicken her steps. A doorway appeared on her left, leading to a formal sitting room. A fire crackled, swallowing the voices and drawing her attention to an enormous stone hearth. A vase of fresh roses sat on the mantel, along with photos of ancestors in freshly polished frames.

Two wing-backed chairs stood in front of the fire. A small table between them held a novel and a cup and saucer of tea, the steam still rising. Mae wondered if the tea's owner would be back soon.

As she debated whether to stay, laughter reached her. Following the voices to a doorway off the far end of the room, she found a long dining table that would seat twenty people. A china plate and silverware for many courses sat in front of each chair. Full platters lined it end to end. Her mouth watered from the delicious aromas wafting off multiple dishes.

"Hello?" The people couldn't be far since the food was still hot. More voices murmured, and another doorway appeared. She walked into the room and found it empty too. Each time she walked into a room, she could hear voices, but they soon faded.

Mae walked back into the dining room with the long table of food. She covered her nose and mouth with both hands from the horrible stench. The serving dishes were still full, but the food rotted.

Fleeing the horrible smells, she traced her way back to the room with the fireplace. Only ashes lay where the fire burned moments ago, the once warm room cold and dark.

The message was obvious—no therapist required for this one. Her fear of abandonment came through loud and clear, but it was the portraits that Mae had been seeing in her mind all day. Funny thing, as she'd never really thought of portraits before. She couldn't ever remember seeing one up close.

Sitting for hours for a portrait must be gruelling, but knowing your family would look at it for generations would be cool. Or creepy. She couldn't decide. Not that it mattered, since she didn't have any family who would want a portrait of her.

She huffed a dry laugh. Thinking about portraits felt ridiculous when she could take a photo. Not that she ever did. Besides the photos she had of Solo and the selfies she'd taken of the two of them, she only owned six other photos. Three were from graduations—high school, college, and her master's program. The other three were of her with her mom. She didn't even have a picture of her wedding. The entire affair had been a quickie at the courthouse. A week after she and her ex had left the foster care system, they were living in a cheap one-bedroom apartment and felt like as long as they had each other anything was possible. The next morning, they'd gotten married. She'd worn the only skirt she owned and her groom had worn jeans and a button-up shirt. The clerk had offered to take a picture for them, but neither of them had a phone. Mae had smiled at the older woman and told her they'd take a photo every year on their anniversary instead.

"Ha. What a joke that was, Solo. We didn't even make it six months and we still couldn't afford phones." She scruffed his head as they reached her building and walked into the warmth of the lobby.

She didn't even have a copy of the picture Jake had seen in her mom's room. A social worker had taken it, gone to the trouble of printing it and getting a frame for Mae to give her mom the last time she'd seen her.

When she and Solo settled into their usual spot on the couch—him as her blanket, covering her legs, her phone in her lap, and a mug of tea in her hands—she waited for Jake's call. Same as the past two weeks, except for the one day she didn't answer.

In the week since Jake told her about his sister and Mae accused him of treating her like a project, their chats flowed, easy. She hadn't seen the over-protective streak he talked about. He'd said he had it around people he cared about, so maybe he didn't care about Mae that way, but she got the sense he did. And she wanted someone to care. But not just anyone—Jake.

Yearning for that, she finally told him about the dreams. Two nights ago, during a pause in a friendly debate about which is the best Star Wars movie, she blurted out that she was having dreams she thought came from the curse.

Jake asked if she was ready to tell him about a couple of them or if she wanted him to explain more about what happened to Blake first. Opting to hear about Blake's curse because it had a happy ending, she'd listened as Jake told her how Blake witnessed a woman confessing her love for her best friend in San Francisco in 1924 only for the man to say he was about to propose to someone else. Then he told her about a painter Blake watched who lost his love of art when the woman he loved left him for someone else.

Each story was heartbreaking and different from Mae's dreams, but the undertones felt the same. Loneliness and a sense of loss and despair permeated both Blake's episodes and Mae's dreams.

The dream she'd woken up to that morning was number

nine. The last three had each been three days apart. As much as she hated them, she figured she could live with them if they stayed three days apart, but she knew that was wishful thinking. Less than two and a half months after Blake's birthday, his curse attacked him daily. If Mae's curse followed the same pattern as Blake's, she would soon be having the dreams every day.

Her phone rang, jarring her. Tea sloshed over the rim of her cup onto her hand. Wiping her hand on the blanket, she held her mug in one hand and picked up her phone with the other, answering on the fourth ring. "Hello?"

"Hi. How're you doing?"

Jake's question warmed her. Every night he asked her how she was, like he did care. "I'm good, but I spilled my tea."

"Did you burn yourself? You should put—Where did you spill it?"

She wondered what he was picturing. "Not down my chest," she said, holding in a laugh.

"That would be difficult to rinse under cold water, wouldn't it?"

"Probably, and I like my showers hot."

"I'm not going to touch that one. You're not hurt?"

"No, the tea wasn't too hot." She could hear Jake breathing. It sounded heavier than usual. "What are you doing?"

"Chewie and I are walking and just trudged through a large snowdrift on the side of the road."

She waited for him to elaborate, and when he didn't, she asked, "The sidewalks haven't been cleared?"

Jake chuckled in the way that said *duh-I'm-so-dumb*. "Sorry. Chewie and I are at my family's cabin for a few days. It's fully powered with services from the nearby town, but because the cell phone coverage can be spotty, we walked out to the main road. I usually come out to the cabin one or two weekends a month in the winter, but this weekend is

Emmie's birthday and I don't want to miss it. I drove out here early this afternoon."

"Emmie is Paige's daughter?"

"Yes. But Blake loves her like she's his own."

Envy of the little girl having the love of two people, or more, nipped at Mae. Shoving the feeling aside, she asked, "How old is she going to be?"

"Four. I bought her a deluxe dollhouse that Blake will have to put together. Paige knew giving me directions was pointless. Malcolm, Cade's son, turned one in September and Cade said we could only buy educational toys, so we got creative."

Mae could hear joy in Jake's voice and it made her smile. "Let me guess, you got him a drum set for hand-eye coordination?"

"Blake did. I got him a musical train with lots of sounds and lights for his birthday and for Christmas we bought some loud, boisterous games that everyone had fun with."

"I hope Blake and Paige realize that Cade might reciprocate."

"Nah. He'll buy an educational toy to try and lead by example."

Mae laughed at the same time another pang hit her inside. "You and my cousins are all close."

"Yes. Blake is my closest friend, but we all work together. Except for Gage, he doesn't live in Blue Mountain, but they're all part owners of Akerman Contracting."

After placing her tea on the coffee table, she put her phone on speaker and laid her head back. Solo took that as his signal to move from her feet to lie lengthwise on her, his head resting on her stomach. As usual, her fingers found their way to his dense, brindle-colored coat. "What's that like?"

"Working with my best friend? Or working with a bunch of brothers?"

"Both."

"It's great because we know what to expect from each other. We head different departments and unless our work overlaps, or when we have meetings, we don't see each other very often. Sometimes we butt heads. Like the time we agreed to upgrade some technology." Jake launched into a story that she expected was embellished, but she laughed so hard she didn't care.

Mae heard Jake call for Chewie and remembered Jake was outside. She could listen to him tell stories for hours. "You must be cold. Do you need to head back?"

"Not yet, but we'll start walking that way. Chewie and I spend a lot of time outside, especially training his tracking skills, so we're good. I know where I'll lose the connection, so I'll stop before that."

"Do you have time to tell me more about Blake's curse? I'm ready now." She wasn't, but she couldn't hide from it anymore.

"Did you have another nightmare?"

"Yes."

"That's nine," he said quietly, as if more to himself, so Mae didn't respond. "I'm trying to remember what I haven't told you. I told you about your aunt's letter, how to break the curse, and about some of Blake's episodes. Anything else?"

"The letters in Aunt Alex's closet and the pictures of me and my mom. You said you were going to tell me about a witch you know and about the spirit who cast the original curse. It's all a little hard to believe, so I'm still struggling with accepting that there is a curse."

"I get that. I'd never lie to you, Mae. Although you probably don't know that either. I hope eventually you'll learn that." He called to Chewie again, his voice distant, like he'd pulled the phone away from his ear.

When he picked up the story again, his tone carried the expectation that she believed in curses. That made sense, since he obviously believed. "The spirit might be a witch, but I'm not sure. She's the one who created the curse hundreds of years ago." He went on to explain how she showed up after Blake's curse broke, and Mae got the feeling that Jake wasn't impressed that she refused to break the curse for the rest of the family.

"What about the witch?"

"Akerman Contracting bought the house the witch used to live in and were renovating it. A woman named Carolyn owned the house first and when she died, her ghost stayed. I don't know how long the witch lived there, but she left her grimoire open and ghost-Carolyn memorized some of the magic. She used it against Blake and Paige."

Mae scoffed. "If I wasn't having my dreams and finally believing that there is a curse, I'd think you're crazy talking about spirits, witches, and ghosts."

"A few months ago, I would have thought the same thing. But I've seen what they can do. Anyone who created a curse that tortured Blake and your mom the way it did, isn't someone I want to mess around with. I'm going to lose reception soon, but I'll be back home tomorrow night."

Jake no longer asked if he could call; he just did. Twice he asked if she wanted to meet in person, but she declined. He hasn't asked again. He would probably continue to call her every night until he either met someone and Mae became a footnote in his history, or the curse pulled her so far under she couldn't answer.

She didn't want to dwell on either outcome, so she forced the choice into focus: see him, try to break the curse, and accept that survival might still end with him walking away;

or keep her distance and let the curse consume her. Abandonment or insanity wasn't much of a choice, but thinking about family pressed just as hard. Should she just call Blake instead? But going to Blake without making peace with Jake, Blake's closest friend, felt like choosing against them both, which left her with the reason she kept pretending wasn't part of it at all: she wanted to see Jake.

"Good night, M—"

"Wait."

"What's wrong?"

"Wouldyouliketomeetthisweekend?" She rushed the words out and then remembered he had plans. "Forget I asked. You have Emmie's birthday."

"I'd love to meet you, Mae. Emmie's party is on Sunday, so I could drive down on Saturday. We could meet at the dog park near your place and let Chewie and Solo meet each other too. How's eleven?"

"Eleven works."

"Great. Chewie and I are going to head back to the cabin. I'll call you tomorrow night. Pleasant dreams, Mae."

"Night." After she hung up, she didn't know if she was more happy or nervous at the prospect of meeting Jake in person. Once she mentioned meeting, he'd thrown out a location, date, and time, probably worried she would back out. She wouldn't. At least right that moment she didn't want to. How could she when she loved talking to Jake and he was the most thoughtful person she'd ever known? Only Jake would recommend they meet at a dog park in the middle of winter, so she wouldn't have to invite an almost-stranger to her home or meet him at a coffee shop where she couldn't bring Solo.

Now, she had to hope she'd chosen right.

Saturday, February 1

WHEN A BARISTA CALLED HIS NAME, Jake picked up the coffees and took a table in the back of the shop. He hadn't even taken his first sip when his sister rushed in.

"Sorry I'm late." Chelsea kissed his bearded cheek before stripping off her coat and mitts and wrapping her hands around her coffee cup.

"You're not." Over the years, he'd learned to run on Chelsea time: arrive fifteen minutes late, grab the coffees, and still beat her by five.

She took a sip. "Yum. Exactly the way I like it. Thank you." She beamed. "This is the first hot coffee I've had all week."

"Then I'm glad I could be of service." If he had a family who kept him too busy to finish a hot coffee, he'd gladly drink it cold forever.

"I wanted to treat this time."

"You more than make up for it by cooking me dinner. Now, tell me what my niece was up to this week and how you're doing."

Jake soaked up Chelsea's update on Chloe's new words and how she'd been feeling. She still had *evening sickness*, as she called it, but she claimed it was worth it.

"Enough about me. What's up with you? You didn't say why you had to meet an hour earlier this morning."

"I've got to swing home for Chewie because we're driving down to Green Springs."

"For work?"

"No." They were close, but he was still her big brother, and it was fun leaving her hanging sometimes.

She raised her brows in question. "Come on. Tell me."

"I'm meeting Mae."

"Why?"

"Why?" That wasn't the reaction he'd been expecting. He thought for sure Chelsea would tease him about meeting with a woman.

"Yes, why. You found her and told her about the curse. If she has any other questions she can ask Blake. She's a grown woman and doesn't need you to protect her."

"That's not why I'm meeting her." Jake sipped his coffee and waited for his sister to catch on.

"Then why—oh my god!" She nearly screeched, then leaned toward him and lowered her voice. "You're going to see her because you like her? Like, like-like her?"

"Yes, like, *like-like* her. And now I feel like a teenage girl." He chuffed a laugh.

"You know what I mean. Tell me more."

"We've been talking every night for a couple of weeks, and the curse aside, we have a lot in common." He told her about Solo, Mae's job, her love of Star Wars, and how well they got along.

"Does she believe in the curse?"

"Yes, I think so. The curse gives her nightmares and they're becoming more frequent. If her curse reacts the same as Blake's, soon she'll have them every day."

"Wow. That sucks. But..." Chelsea hesitated and picked up her coffee.

"Chels, tell me."

"What if you meet her and she's not the one, but you still want to protect her? You won't be able to break the curse, and she could end up resenting you. Or worse, you could miss out on meeting the woman who is *the one* because you're spending all your time with Mae."

"I really like Mae, so let me meet her first. Then I can worry about the rest." Chelsea's points were valid, but nothing could make him not meet Mae.

They chatted for a few more minutes and then Jake walked Chelsea to her car. After he bought a gift for Mae, collected Chewie, and hit the highway, he figured that if traffic cooperated, he'd reach the dog park by eleven, right on time.

"Are you ready to meet a mastiff?" he asked, glancing in the rearview mirror. Of course Chewie didn't answer, he didn't lift his head, though his seat belt gave him room to move.

Jake had researched Solo's breed and saw no reason why the two dogs wouldn't get along. His biggest worry was that once he and Mae met in person, their phone chemistry would evaporate. Talking to Mae had become the highlight of his day.

When his phone rang, his first thought was that Mae was phoning to cancel. His shoulders relaxed after a quick glance at the dash and saw Lyra's name. "Hey Lyra, you got some good news for me?"

"I wish I did, but no. I know some pretty powerful witches, but not a single one could help. The consensus is that a spirit wouldn't need to use witch magic and since she was powerful enough to know when Blake's curse broke to visit him from the beyond, she's more powerful than the strongest witch."

"It was worth a try." He thanked her and hung up.

Mae would have to break the curse the same way Blake did—by falling in love. If Jake could be that person for her, he would, but no one could predict love. Still, it wouldn't be a stretch to consider falling for her, as he thought he might be halfway there already. His thoughts kept drifting that way after talking to her for only a few weeks. She was smart, witty, and quick to challenge him, yet heard him out too. Her loving large dogs and Star Wars was a bonus. He hadn't dared bring up children because they weren't there yet, but if the way she asked about Chloe and Emmie most days was any indication, she liked kids.

He was getting ahead of himself, but he couldn't help it. The one thing he couldn't force was making Mae love him back. From the little she'd told him about her past, he wasn't sure she'd even be open to that kind of love.

6

"Your mom is an idiot," Mae told Solo around a yawn as she sank onto the couch. Solo hopped onto the couch after her, blanketing her in his warmth. "We'll take a short nap."

She set an alarm on her phone and set it on the carpet. The night before two things had been on her mind—how to break the curse, and when she'd be sucked into the next depressing nightmare. In an effort to think about the first and avoid the second, she'd drunk far too much coffee. The caffeine had done such a good job, it kept her up all night and now she was exhausted. "Stupid," she muttered around another yawn.

Her all-nighter had at least given her a plan. She'd already chosen possible abandonment over insanity, and decided to go through with meeting Jake to size him up in person. Then she'd ask him to introduce her to her cousins. If she could love them like family, without getting too attached, it might be enough to break the curse. That's not what Jake had said, but then how could he know for sure? She needed to love and be loved in return. Maybe if they loved her back it could make up for not having a romantic love.

In the wee hours of the morning, when exhaustion and sorrow were eating away at her, she admitted she could call Blake and meet him. Instant family without the risk of getting too close to Jake. But she discarded that idea as quickly as it came. Meeting Jake—a dog lover and Star Wars fanatic like herself—couldn't hurt. She didn't have to get so close to him that she'd be crushed when he eventually walked away. Jake needed to get to know Solo anyway, in case something happened to her. Jake would inevitably move on to bigger and better things than her, but he would know Solo so he could look after him like he promised.

Now she could get a couple of hours of sleep before she and Solo met Jake and Chewie. If a nightmare didn't claim her during her short nap, she might have to live on catnaps. Short naps weren't as healthy as a solid eight hours of sleep, but it wouldn't be the first time she'd done something stupid to survive.

Closing her eyes, she knew it wouldn't be long before sleep claimed her.

Mae used her little hands to grip the bar of the carousel and laughed with the girl beside her. They were best friends. Her name was Haley, and they played together at recess every day. Jumping off the carousel, Mae grabbed one of its upright bars and ran as fast as she could, turning it. The carousel spun so fast, she couldn't get back on, but she didn't care. She tumbled to her butt and laughed with Haley.

When the carousel ground to a halt, Haley jumped off, and they ran to the climbing gym. Other kids joined them, and Mae laughed until her sides hurt. The sound of her friends laughing made her happier than she'd ever been.

She held on tight to the ropes as she leaned back, closed her eyes, and tilted her face to the sun's warmth. When the laughter faded, she opened her eyes. They were gone.

Mae scrambled to get down, looking for her friends. Kids were running away from the playground, but as she called to them, they began to disappear one by one. Running toward them, Mae yelled as loud as she could, but no one turned around. She pushed harder but couldn't catch up.

In the distance, she saw Haley and called her name, but her friend didn't look back as she disappeared into the trees.

Her breath heaving, Mae stopped, resting her hands on her knees. Wondering if the kids would come back if she waited. She walked toward the swings. Where there used to be six swings in a row, only one remained. Mae heaved her butt onto it and scraped her toes on the ground for momentum. With her toes barely touching the earth beneath her, the swing wouldn't budge.

Hopping off, she walked back toward the play structures. As she reached the merry-go-round, it turned to dust. Her nose got stuffy and her vision blurred.

Mae turned around and faced a house that looked familiar. As she took her backpack off her shoulder, the silver rings she'd gotten in high school glinted in the sun. Her black nail polish was chipped and as she wondered when she last applied it, laughter caught her attention.

She walked up the three steps to the front door and tried to turn the knob. The lock held. Using her hands to shield her eyes from the bright sun, she peered into the glass pane beside the door. A family stood at the end of the hallway. She yelled, but the glass was too thick for her voice to carry.

Pulling one of her rings down to her knuckle, she used it to tap on the glass as she continued to stare at the family. Just as someone turned Mae's way, the glass panel shattered, spraying her with shards that dug into her skin.

Mae screamed and felt a wetness on her cheek.

Opening her eyes, she blinked at Solo's dark brown eyes staring at her, as drool hung from his jowls. Only a dream.

Mae grabbed a small towel from a stack she kept on the shelf below the coffee table and wiped the slobber off Solo and then herself. "I'm okay, Solo. Thank you for waking me."

The alarm on her phone sounded. As the dream's desperation clung to her, she wondered about texting Jake to cancel. She reached for her phone as a text chimed.

Jake: Almost there. Looking forward to seeing you.

If she canceled now, Jake might show up at her apartment. She could always lie, but she'd didn't want to. "Park," she told Solo and waited until he slid to the floor before getting up.

A few minutes later, she bundled up, clipped on Solo's leash and headed to the park. For the first time since suggesting she and Jake meet, she was eager to meet someone. In a short time, Jake had become the one person she talked to more than anyone else. It was exciting, but risky too. An image of the empty playground from her dream popped into her mind, but she pushed it out for the time being. She'd think of it later.

Today, she'd decide if her phone impressions of Jake held up, enjoy his company, and see about meeting her cousins to break her curse. All while ignoring the little voice in the back of her mind that said she was developing feelings for Jake.

She and Solo turned the corner onto the same street as the park. Her breath hitched—not from the cold. It caught at the sight of a man standing at the entrance to the park, with a St. Bernard at his side. As she closed the distance, she took him in. She'd seen his pictures, but sometimes people looked different in person. Jake didn't. He stood tall and broadshouldered as he had in his photos. Even in a winter coat, he moved with easy strength. His beard was thick, trimmed, and the perfect frame for his grin.

"Hi," she said when she was a couple of feet away. She'd rehearsed a couple of quotes she could use when she first saw him, but a breathless hello was the best her brain could come with as she finally stood close enough to touch him.

"Hi, Mae."

For several seconds they stared at each other like star-struck teenagers. It wasn't until Solo licked her hand that she pulled out of her trance. "This is Solo," she said, petting his head, and nearly smacked her forehead. *Duh. Ms. Obvious much?*

"He's beautiful. As you can guess, this is Chewie." They gave the dogs time to sniff each other before Jake said, "Why don't we talk while we walk through the park?"

"Sure."

Following the dogs as they sniffed along the path, Mae tried to think of something to say. Their silence was comfortable until it became awkward, as if one of them should say something. Neither of them had a problem while they were on the phone, but being together in person felt different.

After a few minutes, Jake broke the silence between them. "This is weird, isn't it?"

Mae looked up—way up. "I was thinking the same thing." He stopped, facing her, and she did the same. The dogs sat at their feet.

The collar of Jake's shirt peeked above his partly-zipped coat and it suited him, matching his beard, to complete his rugged, mountain-man look. Because of a little sleuthing and finding his photos, she'd been able to picture him every time they'd talked, but it wasn't the same as seeing him in the flesh. "We're not awkward on the phone."

"Maybe because we can't do this."

Before Mae could ask Jake what he meant, he tugged off one glove and cupped her cheek with his large hand. It felt calloused and warm against her cold skin, making her want more of his touch. The little voice in her brain that warned of risk drew a breath to speak, and Mae shoved it into a box and turned the lock. She looked into Jake's blue gaze until he leaned forward. She tilted her chin toward him, closing her eyes.

His lips were cold and soft against hers. He smelled like cedar and citrus, a perfect match to his lumberjack look. His hand slid around to the back of her neck, and she rose onto her toes to deepen the kiss.

A bark snapped them apart.

"I've been wanting to do that since you walked up to me." He put his glove back on and took her hand. Still in a lust-infused daze, she didn't protest.

They continued along the path, with the dogs bounding ahead, then coming back. Jake drew her out about her latest project, the earlier awkwardness gone. Perhaps he'd been right. They had both been anticipating a kiss and now that it was over, they were back to friendship. Except with hand-holding.

After circling the entire park, both dogs flopped down in the snow. Mae didn't want her time with Jake to end, but Solo wasn't quite the cold-weather dog that Chewie was.

She turned to Jake, not wanting to leave, but knowing she should. "I guess I should get Solo home and warmed up."

Jake called Chewie and Solo followed. "We can warm them both up in my truck." He walked the few steps to a three-quarter-ton pickup at the curb and opened the back passenger door. He pulled down a set of steps and Chewie climbed up into the truck. "I'm not ready to leave," Jake said, as if he'd read her thoughts. "Will you let me buy you coffee? We can go through a drive-thru."

The little box in her head—the one she's locked that nagging voice inside— rattled. Mae ignored it. "Sure."

JAKE FOLLOWED Mae's directions to the nearest drive-thru and grabbed a coffee for himself and a tea for her, then parked in the farthest corner of the parking lot.

"One second," he said as he got out of the truck. He popped the bed box of his truck and hauled out two large bones he'd stashed there that morning because he anticipated this.

He slid back into the truck and passed each dog a bone; they both hunkered down with their treat.

Turning in his seat, he faced Mae. She glanced into the back seat at Solo.

"Oh shit. Sorry. I should have asked you before I gave him the bone."

"It's okay. They both seem happy."

"Of course, they've got a treat. Speaking of…" He reached across the seat, popped the upper glove box, and drew out a long, narrow, wrapped box and handed it to her. "A treat for you too."

She didn't reach for the present, so Jake set it between them. Mae eased back against the window, as if the box had teeth.

"It won't bite."

She eyed the box, then him. "Why did you buy me a present?"

"Because I wanted to. It's not much, something you mentioned once."

"I can't remember the last time someone gave me a present," she murmured, as if more to herself.

"If I had known you rarely got presents, I'd have picked something better. It's small—I hope you won't be disappointed."

"I won't be." She picked up the box and turned it over.

He let her take her time, but for the first time since he'd decided on the gift, nerves pricked him. When he'd first came up with the idea, he pictured an inside joke that would make her laugh. It never occurred to him that she didn't get a lot of gifts and any present would be a big deal. He should have realized that.

Finally, Mae put her fingernail under the seam of the paper and lifted. "Oh, I ripped it."

"You're supposed to."

She met his gaze. "It's so pretty I was trying to save it."

His chest ached. She'd had so few gifts she wanted to save the paper from a pre-wrapped box. He kept his tone casual as he said, "It's okay. I'll get you more."

She gave him a small smile and ripped the rest of the paper, revealing the box of gourmet chocolates beneath. "Chocolate?" Her eyes gleamed as she grinned at him.

"Better than toilet papering your house, right?"

Mae laughed, a genuine, carefree sound. "You remembered."

"Of course." He remembered everything she told him.

She pulled the lid off the box to reveal twelve brightly colored balls of handcrafted chocolates. "Wow," she breathed. "They're prettier than the wrapping paper."

"Are you going to have one?"

"Do I have to?"

"No." Heat crept up his neck. After her teasing him about giving her chocolate when he talked about making her two promises, he'd just assumed she liked chocolate, but maybe she couldn't eat it. "Are you allergic to chocolate?"

She put the lid back on the box. "No. I love chocolate. I want to savor them."

"Okay." Jake sipped his coffee to give himself a moment to get a grip on his emotions. Mae was the most amazing woman he'd ever met—independent, quick to challenge him, yet somehow untouched by bitterness. She found joy in the little things.

Mae put the box on the seat between them and picked up her tea. Following her cue, Jake took another drink. Like at the dog park, awkwardness edged back in—something that didn't happen on the phone.

Maybe it was because he found her both fascinating and attractive. If he didn't do something, he felt like he'd self-combust. "Maybe we need to break the ice again."

"Maybe." She set her tea in the cupholder and Jake did the same with his coffee. He braced one hand on the dash and one on the back of her seat, then lowered his mouth to hers. He'd meant to keep it light, like in the park, but when she leaned in, that plan went up in smoke. He lifted his hand from the dash and cupped the back of her neck. It could become his favorite place to hold her while he kissed her. She opened to him and he deepened the kiss. She tasted like her tea and something uniquely Mae, sweet and spicy at the same time.

She fisted his hair and he groaned. She lit him up.

A horn blared, and they both sprang apart as if they were teenagers getting caught making out in his dad's car.

They looked at each other and laughed, the tension broken.

Jake checked the back seat and, seeing both dogs still content, he sat back against the driver's side door. Shifting as subtly as possible, he tried his best to ease the tension in his suddenly tight jeans.

"Got a problem over there?" Mae teased.

"Noticed that, did you? I tried not to be conspicuous."

"I'll take it as a compliment."

"So... Did you catch the hockey game last night?" he asked, knowing she didn't watch sports.

Mae laughed. "Was there a hockey game on last night? I mean, one with a team that you follow?"

"Not that I know of." Once more, they'd broken the ice and their conversation flowed. Mae told him about the book she'd just finished and that got them talking about different literary favorites.

They finished talking about a movie they'd both recently seen, and Jake used the lull to ask something he'd been thinking about. "Mae, have you thought about going to see your mom?"

"Yes, but it's been a long time. I don't know if she'd want to see me."

"I bet she'd love it. When Blake and I first went to meet her, she asked about you right away. She remembered your birthday and wanted us to find you."

Mae looked out the window. "I'll think about it."

"I can go with you, if you'd like."

She looked back at him. "Why?"

Jake frowned. "Because we're friends and friends support each other."

Mae pulled her phone out of her pocket and checked the time. "Okay. I should get back."

"Sure. I'll drive you and Solo back to your place." Jake expected her to protest, but she clicked her seat belt instead.

They reached her apartment. Jake let Solo out of the back and Mae met him by the door, the box of chocolates in her hand. Jake opened his arms and she walked right into them. She barely reached his chin; the top of her head brushed it. He wrapped his arms around her and it felt like she melted right into him.

Once more, he didn't want to let go, but eventually they both pulled back. "I had a great time today, Mae." He kissed her lightly on the lips. "I'll call you when Chewie and I get home." He didn't make it a question.

"Okay. Drive safe." Jake waited until Mae and Solo were in the building before he secured Chewie in his seat.

He enjoyed driving and normally the two-hour drive wouldn't bother him, but he wanted to get home so he could call and talk to Mae. He steadied himself and got into the driver's seat.

As he pulled onto the road, he smiled to himself. No one said he had to be home before he could call Mae. He'd called her from his truck before. But first he had a stop to make. "Ready for a bathroom break, Chewie?" He knew a truck stop on the edge of the city that would work for both him and Chewie.

Then he'd drive for a while before calling Mae and asking her how her day was.

7

Friday, February 7

Mae traced along the back of her mom's fingers —the same motion she'd repeated for three hours. She'd never thought much about her hands. Underappreciated, overused, they were simply part of her. She couldn't imagine valuing them more than any other part of her body, but she would never look at her own hands the same again after studying her mom's. They were the same. How could she not have known that? Could she have blocked out that memory?

Over the years, anger tainted so many memories of her mom. Anger for her mom's abandonment. And for believing her mom wasn't handling her mental illness. Mae had blamed her mom for every horrible thing she'd endured growing up.

She'd never stopped to consider what her mom was going through. With adult hindsight, and now that she knew about the curse, Mae could see how she'd been mired in the hubris and arrogance of her self-entitled teenage years. And she'd ladled self-pity over it, convinced her mom had left her. Mae had painted almost all her experiences and memories with the same dark gray brush.

Only one memory held any warmth. She hadn't been able to see it at the time, but now she could. Even as her mom was slipping away, she tried to make Mae feel special.

Mae was about five, getting ready for bed. She remembered it clearly because it was one of the few lucid nights. Those lucid moments dwindled until a social worker took Mae away.

Mae sat like a queen on a stool in her mom's room, facing a large, ornate mirror, with her mom standing behind her, brushing her hair.

"Mom?"

"Yes, honey?"

"A girl at school looks exactly like her mom. Why don't I look like you?"

Coming to her side and crouching down, her mom turned the stool so Mae could look into her eyes. Light blue eyes that were so different from Mae's dark brown.

"You look like your father. I remember when I met him." Her mom smiled, remembering. She put the brush on the dresser and took Mae's hands in her own, giving them a squeeze. "He was the best-looking man I'd ever seen. Would you like to hear the story again?"

Mae wasn't sure she wanted to—hear about her dad who didn't care about her—but she nodded anyway. Since telling the story made her mom smile, Mae listened as her mom told her about going to a party with friends in college and getting introduced to a man who was visiting his younger sister.

"I'm glad you look like him. You have his rich, dark eyes and hair, and olive complexion. That's so much more special than my ordinary light blue eyes, boring brown hair, and pale skin. You're special, like he was."

"No, I'm not." Mae yanked her hand out of her mom's.

"Yes, you are. Why would you think you're not?"

Mae stared at her mom and blinked back the tears she could feel wanting to well up. She refused to cry because she wasn't a baby and a boy at school said only babies cry. "If my dad was special, you wouldn't have left him, and because he's not special, I'm not special. And you'll leave me too."

Her mom's hand twitched, yanking her out of the memory. She jerked her head up, but her mom's eyes remained closed. "Mom, it's Mae—uh, Maeve." When she'd first arrived, she'd taken her mom's hand in the hope she would know someone was there. Jake had explained the first time he and Blake had come to visit, Blake had been holding her mom's hand when they'd been debating whether to leave. When her hand moved, they'd known she was aware of them and had waited to talk to her.

Looking back down, she mapped her mom's hands again. Mae had her dad's features, but it wasn't until today that she realized that her hands were identical to her mom's. Mae brushed her thumb across the back of her mom's hand. It moved again.

Mae looked up into light blue irises that were anything but ordinary. Mae blinked back the telltale burning behind her eyes. Not because she still thought crying was something babies did, but because she wanted to memorize the moment.

"Hi Mom."

"Maeve. Oh, honey. Look how you've grown."

Mae leaned forward and wrapped her arms around her mom. Jake had warned her time would be short, so she didn't bother explaining she'd changed her name. Giving her mom a quick squeeze, she pulled back so she could see her. "I'm sorry for not coming sooner, Mom." Mae cleared her throat.

"For so long, I—" She didn't finish. Her mom didn't need to hear about her anger.

"I love you, Maeve. You don't need to apologize. I'm the one that should. I'm sorry for being so selfish. Your aunt Alex loved you and wanted to raise you, but instead I moved you away from her. I'm so sorry." Her mom's hand trembled as she lifted it like she'd done all those years ago. "Your curse has started, hasn't it?" At Mae's nod, her mom squeezed her fingers and her eyes glossed. "I'm so sorry," she repeated. "Don't be like me. Find love and hold on to it with everything you have. Don't separate yourself from family. Be with your cous—" Her mom's eyes closed and her hand dropped to her side.

Mae let her tears fall. She cried for her mom and the life she hadn't gotten to live. And she cried for herself. For the childhood that was lonely and lacking love. For her marriage that never should have been. For the family she didn't have, and for the future that might be no different from her mom's.

When her tears finally stopped, she blotted her face with some tissue from a box on the window ledge. She stood and looked around the room for a wastebasket. The photo the social worker had taken sat on the nightstand. Tossing the tissue in the bin in the corner of the room, she picked up the photo. Not wanting her photo taken, she'd been her usual angry, sullen teenage self. The social worker had clicked the picture, just after she'd told a joke, catching Mae with a rare smile.

Mae shook her head. The social worker should have been sainted for putting up with her. She hadn't made it easy on anyone. She'd been angry for years, wasting so much time. Her dreams perfectly reflected the despair and loneliness she'd felt for so long. Maybe the dreams were telling her it *was* too late for her.

She put the photo back and peered out the window, the scene in front of her registering for the first time. The trees were bare of leaves, the sky overcast, but she could imagine the beauty of her mom's surroundings in the spring and summer. If she didn't end up in a room down the hall from her mom, fading away, she'd come back to visit during all the seasons.

"I'll be back," she told her mom before giving her hand a light squeeze and walking to her car. She started the engine and blasted the heat before pulling her phone from her pocket. Jake had texted to say good morning, but she must have already been on the road.

She decided on impulse to make the trip. She woke from a nightmare standing on her balcony. Cold wind whipped around her, sucking the heat from her body, as she stood barefoot on the concrete in her sleep shorts and a tank top. She quickly yanked open the sliding glass door—luckily unlocked—and wrapped her arms around a warm and anxious Solo, when she realized she had no memory of going outside. She glanced up at the glow of the clock on the stove. Four in the morning. She had never sleepwalked before. Right then, she decided it was time to visit her mom and meet her cousins.

Now sleepwalking joined the lengthening daily dreams. They felt like they were getting longer since she'd slept through her alarm twice in the last week. She needed to hurry to meet her cousins. If their combined love couldn't break the curse, at least she'd have this time with them. Perhaps they would visit her when they visited her mom.

Either way, it was time for Mae to meet them. Luckily, the kennel she sometimes used could take Solo for the day, and overnight if needed. She didn't expect she would because after seeing her mom for the first time in years, and then meeting her cousins, she'd probably be peopled-out, but the owner of the kennel had told her it was available, if needed.

With one visit down and one to go, she checked the time on her phone. She would stop and pick up something for a late lunch. Her stomach rumbled, as if agreeing with her. She looked in the rearview mirror out of habit, but of course Solo wasn't there. "Lunch, cousins, and then back home to Solo," she told the empty back seat, then laughed at herself. Talking to Solo was one thing, but talking to him when he wasn't there was a step she wasn't ready to take yet.

She checked her phone again, wondering if she should text Jake back. What she really wanted was to call him and hear his voice. Seeing his face would be even better. After his visit, they switched to video for most of their chats and she loved being able to see him. She'd be able to look into his eyes as he told her everything would be okay. It would probably be a lie, but she'd soak it up anyway.

The same way she'd soaked up the memory of their kisses, running them through her mind over and over. His kisses had made her forget about the curse and feel like anything was possible. Her ex-husband had done the same. Not that she'd been cursed back then, but when he kissed her and told her that together they would make all their dreams come true, she'd believed him. She had continued to believe him right until he walked out the door to another woman and left her all alone.

Even though Jake was completely different from her ex, she'd learned that most people had good intentions until those intentions no longer aligned with what was best for them. Running her finger along Jake's text, it slid down, showing the pictures of Emmie he'd sent her after the little girl's birthday party. In one, she sprawled across Chewie, asleep, looking angelic—as only sleeping children could. The other was of Emmie with a grin showing blue teeth from icing, the remains of a large piece of cake in front of her. Whenever Jake talked about Emmie or his niece, Chloe, the love he had for them was obvious. He was the kind of guy who was meant to be a dad. Mae didn't know if she was mom-material, even if she lived long enough. She didn't have great role models growing up. And if she did live and she wasn't cut out to be a mom, would Jake leave her?

Instead of texting, she locked her phone, slid it into the cupholder, and decided to stick with her plan. Checking her mirrors, she pulled out of the parking lot. Some food and then a trip to meet her cousins.

8

From the curb, Mae peered through her car window at the family business she could have been a part of. She wasn't sure, but her mom told her she'd had a chance to be part of this family.

The stately house Akerman Contracting occupied had been easy to find in downtown Blue Mountain. The sun, what little light there was with the cloud cover, hadn't set yet, but the house glowed, as if to say everyone was welcome. Everything about the place, from the company sign mounted between two short stone pillars, to the railings on the stairs, and the massive front porch, invited her in.

Mae locked her car and headed up the shoveled front walk, mentally crossing her fingers that the welcome would extend to her. She'd second-guessed herself half an hour outside of the city, wondering if she should have called first. Plus, it was quitting time on a Friday—her cousins might not even be around.

Is that what she secretly wished for? Had she subconsciously sabotaged her chances of meeting her family? Forcing her shoulders back and lifting her chin, she took a deep breath of the crisp winter air, turned the doorknob and stepped inside.

Warmth and soft music welcomed her, and an older woman glanced up from behind a large desk, surprised. The woman set down the bag she was packing, circled the desk, and smiled at Mae as she extended her hand.

"Welcome to Akerman Contracting. I'm Denise Leach, the office manager."

Mae shook her hand; Denise's was warmer than her mom's. Denise looked like she was about her mom's age, but with a vibrancy her mom would never have. "Mae McFadden."

"Nice to meet you, Mae. I'm guessing you have an appointment that someone forgot to tell me about?"

"Uh, no—"

"Mae?"

She turned at the sound of Jake's voice. Before she had a chance to say anything, Jake and the man next to him, that she recognized from the company website as Blake, came forward.

"Denise, Mae is family. She's my cousin." Without pausing, Blake walked right into her personal space and hugged her. She hesitated for a few seconds before she wrapped her arms around him. "I'm your oldest cousin, Blake. I'm so happy to finally meet you," he whispered into her ear.

Mae felt a tightness in her throat. Two family members in one day after being on her own for years.

When Blake pulled back, he flashed a big smile. "Come back and meet your other cousins."

"I hope to see you again, Mae," Denise said as she shrugged into her coat. Denise wished them a good weekend and left.

Jake stood so close, his cedar and citrus scent enveloping her, Mae fought the urge to lean into him. It was clear she should have thought this impromptu visit through. She didn't know how to act around Jake when others were around, nor what to say to her cousins.

As if he could read her mind, Jake helped her out. Leaning down, he placed a soft kiss on the side of her forehead. "Go with Blake. Your cousins will be thrilled to meet you. I'll lock the door and be there in a minute."

Blake pointed out the different offices as she followed him down the hall and into a boardroom.

She froze in the doorway. Three men sat at a large table, and a fourth filled the screen on the wall. Jake had told her about her cousins, and she'd seen their pictures on the company website, but seeing them in person was more intimidating than she'd been expecting.

Blake put his hand on her upper arm, as if afraid she'd run away. "This is Mae, our cousin."

A man with dark brown hair swept to the side stood first and approached Mae. She knew from the website that he was Cade, the lawyer, and second oldest.

"I'm Cade," he said and pulled her into a hug. She didn't mind the hugs, but wasn't used to it. "It's so good to finally meet you."

Dane introduced himself next, and she was ready for his hug. Then Ford. She didn't explain that she already knew who each of them was and had practically memorized their bios. No need to come off as the crazy cousin on the first meeting.

Gage introduced himself from the screen.

She felt a hand on her lower back and instinctively leaned back into Jake before she caught herself. Her plan was to get to know her cousins and create a familial bond of love to break the curse. Not to fall even harder for Jake.

That was becoming more difficult to avoid every day. Especially, when he did things like pull out a chair for her and grab her a drink from the fridge in the corner of the room. He crossed to the far wall, behind Cade and Dane, and braced against it. If anyone else had moved to a position solely to observe her, she might have freaked out, but she was coming to know Jake. His need to protect made him an observer. She gave him a small smile before turning back to Blake.

He pursed his lips. "I'm so sorry we didn't know about you sooner. We would have been there for you."

"It's okay." She took a drink, needing a moment to tamp down the emotions threatening to drown her.

"It's not, but there isn't anything we can do about it," Cade said. "We learned about you at the end of December, and we all would have reached out earlier, but didn't want to over- whelm you."

She laughed, nervous. "That's probably a good thing. Did Jake tell you I hung up on him?"

The brothers all chuckled. "Yes, but we're not sure that's an uncommon thing when Jake calls a woman," Ford teased.

"Thanks, man." Jake added a small smile to his sarcasm.

"Any time. Tell us about yourself, Mae." Ford held up his hand. "That sounds too much like an interview. We can tell you about us first." Dressed in an expensive-looking suit, he seemed like he could command the room, but charm everyone in it at the same time. "I'm third oldest and the VP of Sales and Marketing. Unlike our buddy Jake here, I'm not obsessed with a space opera movie franchise. I like to run, and I'm an avid hockey fan."

Mae bit the inside of her cheek to stop from smiling. "I'm obsessed with a space opera movie franchise."

Everyone laughed, even Ford. Each brother took a turn telling her similar details about themselves. There was lots of ribbing and laughter in between. She got the feeling that it was a normal thing and could only imagine how long their regular meetings took with all the interruptions and teasing.

Mae had never been part of a group like that. Not even when she lived with foster families. As much as she wanted to have a family, they were a bit overwhelming all together. She wasn't sure if meeting them all at once had been such a good idea.

By the time each brother finished and Cade mentioned introducing Mae to his girlfriend, Jessica, and their son Malcolm, Mae could feel a tension climbing up her spine.

She must have hidden it well because Blake pulled out his phone to text his fiancée, Paige, so she could come and meet her.

"Blake," Jake said, a low warning in his voice. "I think that meeting the five of you may be enough for Mae for one day."

Mae wasn't sure whether to be thankful or annoyed that Jake was so in tune with her. If Jake's comment let her off the hook, would she appear rude? "I'd love to meet everyone, but Jake is right. It's overwhelming. I—" She took a deep breath. "I visited my mom before I came here."

Blake put down his phone and patted her arm. "Jake is right." He looked at his brothers and paused. Then, as if on cue, comments about pigs flying, hell freezing over, and "it happens to everyone once in a lifetime" flew out of his brothers. Jake laughed along with them, and when the teasing and laughter died down, Blake grinned and turned back to Mae. "Meeting all of us can be overwhelming." She heard Jake snort, but Blake ignored him as he asked her, "Did you talk to your mom?"

"Yes." The conversation settled heavy across her shoulders. "Since her facility is halfway between my place and here, I decided to drop in. Sorry. I should have called first."

"No sorry needed. Drop by anytime," Cade said. "I'd like

to plan a time so you can meet the rest of the family, but I'm guessing you've got other things to deal with right now."

Mae doubted he meant her mom, but it felt weird talking about a curse with people she didn't know. It felt weird talking about the curse, period.

"How are you doing with the curse?" Gage asked.

She looked up at the screen. His expression was serious, as if he rarely smiled. "I'm handling it. I get depressing dreams." She waved her hand in dismissal as she did her best to downplay how bad they were getting.

"Every day?"

Mae hesitated for a moment. She wondered if she should lie and avoid burdening her cousins, then decided against it and nodded. If she was going to be part of this family, honesty was the only way to go.

Dane leaned on his forearms, grabbing her attention. "Would you like to tell us about some of them?"

Did she? The dreams felt too personal to divulge to these men she didn't know, but if anyone could understand and help her, it would be them.

As Mae told her cousins about one of her first dreams—her standing inside a massive, hollowed-out tree—Jake noticed subtle differences in her appearance he'd never noticed on video.

A week ago, he'd thought Mae was too thin. Not because he liked to see women a particular size, but because her skin didn't have the glow he associated with health and her clothes hung loosely on her already small frame. If he'd mentioned his concerns to his sister, she would have told him that the health of Mae's skin was none of his business and perhaps Mae liked wearing baggy clothes.

Since he considered himself a smart brother, he hadn't mentioned a thing to Chelsea. He also hadn't had a frame of reference for Mae's health. Until now.

Mae had lost weight in the last week. The bags under her eyes were deeper and her skin was paler than when they'd met. He caught the way she shrugged off Gage's question about how she was handling her curse, but her appearance spoke for her.

If Mae didn't fall in love soon and have her love reciprocated, the effects of the curse would only increase. He couldn't force himself to fall in love with her, but since he'd met her in person, it felt possible. If he believed his sister's words from New Year's Eve, he'd never really been in love—he mistook his need to protect as love. What he felt for Mae was more than that. She drew him in and he was helpless to resist.

He couldn't deny that being around Mae spiked his protective nature. Chelsea could be right about him having never been in love, but he was beginning to care deeply for Mae. He loved talking to her, hearing about her day, joking with her, and being around her. If that wasn't a foundation for a loving relationship, he didn't know what was.

"Then the tree collapsed and turned to dust, leaving me standing under a stormy sky," Mae finished. Blake leaned in with a question.

No matter how strong his protective instinct was, Jake hadn't been able to help his best friend fight the curse, and he felt like he was failing Mae now too. If her curse followed the same pattern as Blake's, she didn't have much time before she would be fully incapacitated, or worse. Nearly three months to the day from Blake's thirtieth birthday, he almost died. That could have had a lot to do with the crazy ghost that trapped him, but it was also because the ghost sensed the curse. She hadn't hurt anyone else who'd been working in the house, only Blake.

Mae's thirtieth birthday had passed over two and a half months earlier. Chances of her running into a ghost who knew witchcraft were slim, although six months ago he would have said that of Blake too. Barely seven months ago, he didn't believe that witches, curses, or ghosts even existed.

Setting ghosts aside, Mae could survive her curse—her mom had—but that wasn't living.

Mae stood. "I should probably be going."

"Mae," Gage said, grabbing everyone's attention. "Don't be a stranger." He nodded, and the screen went black.

All the brothers now stood, and Jake walked up to Mae's side. Dane, Ford, and Cade said their goodbyes and promised they'd see Mae again soon.

"Will you take my number?" Blake asked.

"Sure." Mae pulled out her phone and entered the number Blake told her. His phone pinged with a new text. "You've got mine now too."

"Thanks." His gaze shot to Jake for a second before he looked back at Mae. "I can't help you break the curse, but I'm here if you need me. The curse is going—" He shook his head. "Call anytime." Blake hugged her and headed out.

Mae turned to him. "Do you know what Blake was going to say?"

"No." Jake pulled Mae into his arms and she melted against him. He hadn't lied, because he wasn't a mind reader and couldn't know for sure what Blake was going to say. But he knew his friend. Jake expected that Blake wanted to warn Mae that the curse will keep worsening until it consumes her. Like her mom. He likely wanted to prepare her for the worst, but there wasn't any point. Knowing how bad things would get wouldn't help her find love.

Chewie bumped his head against them and Mae let go. She ruffled Chewie's fur and spoke in the same singsong voice she used with Solo. "It's so good to see you. Have you been good?"

Jake grabbed some tissue from a box on the table and handed them to Mae.

"Thanks." She rid her hand of slobber. During one of their first conversations they'd talked about always having tissues or rags handy to deal with slobber. Something only a large dog owner could appreciate.

She threw the tissue into a wastebasket. "I need to go."

He gestured to the hallway and followed her out. "Where is Solo?"

"At the dog boarding kennel I use. He gets spoiled because it's like a doggy daycare. I dropped him off this morning. Visiting my mom had been a last-minute impulse. Luckily, the kennel was able to take him."

They'd reached the front door and Mae hesitated as if she wasn't ready to leave.

Taking the opening, he said, "I'd like to follow you home."

She gave a quick snort. "You want to follow me all the way to Green Springs? I don't need a protector, Jake."

He heard the irritation in her tone, but he wasn't going to back down. He brushed the back of his knuckles along her cheek. "I know you don't, but I want to spend time with you." When she didn't say anything, he jumped in with both feet. "I'd planned on calling you this afternoon, but a couple of things came up, and then you were here. I packed a bag this morning, hoping Chewie and I could visit."

Her lips curved up in a teasing smile. "Presumptuous of you, don't you think?"

"Yes."

"Sure. Solo and Chewie can spend some more time together. It'll be good for them to socialize."

He didn't argue. If that's how Mae chose to explain it, he didn't care, as long as he could be with her. "Give me a minute? I've got to grab my coat from my office and lock up."

"Can I come?"

"Of course." Jake led her to his office on the other side of the house from Blake's office and the boardroom. "Some weeks I'm here a lot, and others I'm out at job sites."

"Your parents?" Mae walked over to the photos he had on a bookshelf in the corner.

"Yes. It's from a few years ago, and this," he said, picking up a frame decorated with crayons, "is Chloe."

"She's adorable." Mae took the frame from him and he wished he knew what she was thinking.

Before he had a chance to say anything, she put the frame back. "Ready to go?"

He turned off his computer and lifted his coat off a hook. "I am now. Did you park at the curb?"

"I'm right out front."

"I'm parked in the back, so I'll pull around front and follow you. That work?"

Mae nodded, then he walked into her space and wrapped his hand gently around the back of her neck. She looked up at him, then closed her eyes as he lowered his lips to hers. He kept the kiss soft and slow. Passion would come later. At that moment, all he needed was to feel her.

A few minutes later, with Chewie buckled into the back-seat, Jake followed Mae's vehicle through the city and then onto the interstate. His phone rang and he answered on the truck's hands-free. "Hello?"

"Here's a two-fer. What was the first draft of Star Wars called, and in it, what did Lucas want to call Yoda?"

Jake grinned. He loved that Mae was comfortable enough with him, even while in separate vehicles, to blurt out questions. No formalities needed. "Starkiller and Buffy."

"Drat. I thought I'd at least get you on the draft name."

He mocked a villain's cackle. "You'll have to try harder than that."

"Okay, let me think."

"You do that because it's my turn. Who built C-3PO?"

"Anakin Skywalker," Mae said in a not-bad imitation of Yoda.

Trivia questions and answers flew between them for several more minutes until Mae stumped him on a question and she claimed victory for the day. Their conversation drifted to other favorite movies until they stopped at the midway point for some coffee and to let Chewie out for a quick break.

Back on the road, Jake called Mae. "Since I can't see your face, you want to talk about visiting your mom?" Like with the dreams, she'd brushed off the visit with her mom when Blake had asked earlier. If Mae did that with him, he'd let it drop, but he knew her well enough now that he figured seeing her mom for the first time in years had stayed in her mind all afternoon.

"I have her hands."

At Mae's quiet response, Jake turned up the volume and waited.

"She'd always told me I look like my dad, but when I held her hand this morning, I noticed we could be hand-twins." She snorted. "Is hand-twins a thing?"

"If my hands and my dad's are anything to go by, it is."

"In one of the foster homes I was in, the family had two little girls and they were exact mini-mes to their mom, but I never noticed their hands."

She'd never said much about the families she'd lived with, only a stray comment here and there. Coming from a loving and secure home, foster families were an unknown to him.

He'd chosen to let Mae lead the conversations when it came to her past. Each one had been short.

He glanced in his rear-view mirror to see Chewie asleep and let the line go quiet, the silence filling the cab of his truck.

"She remembered me," Mae finally said. "I wasn't sure she would."

"When Blake and I met her, she asked about you right away. I don't think you're ever far from her mind."

"Maybe."

Keeping his voice neutral to avoid sounding like an accusation, he asked, "You don't think so?"

"If she thought about me so much, why didn't she do more so she could keep me?"

"From what I saw with Blake, the curse hit fast. There likely wasn't time for her to fall in love. Let alone ensure that her love was returned."

"I guess not," Mae said quietly, ending their conversation as they entered the city limits.

A few minutes later, Mae broke the silence. "I need to swing by the kennel and pick up Solo. It's not far from my place. You want to follow me or head to my place to wait?"

"Since I'm already behind you, I might as well follow." He tried to make it sound like no big deal, while inside he worried that if he went to her place, she'd disappear on him. Mae hadn't given him any indication that she would, and she hadn't put up much of a fight for him to follow her home, but he had this strange fear that something would happen to her when she was out of his sight.

9

Mae pulled away from Jake's warmth. "Can you pause the movie?" She tossed the blanket off her legs and stood. "I'm going to make some tea. I'm still a bit cold from the walk."

Jake reached for the remote. "Sure."

She set the kettle on and watched it. Not to will it to boil faster, but to buy time to decide what to do about Jake. After they arrived home with the dogs, they'd taken them out for a snowy walk and ordered pizza on the way. Dinner came soon after they got back. They settled in front of the TV with an action flick that had released a couple of months earlier, one neither of them had seen.

They sat together on the couch. At first, only their thighs touched. Then Jake pulled a blanket over them and drew her to his side.

Halfway through the movie, the heat of him pressed against her hijacked her focus. All she could do was breathe in his fabulous scent and keep one hand on his thigh, the other in her lap to stop herself from pouncing on him. She couldn't even say how the movie ended. She was too aware of him.

Mae couldn't ever remember being so pulled to a man. A few problems, though, kept her from having her way with him. He was clearly as drawn to her as she was to him, so that wasn't an issue. The curse was. After seeing her mom, she couldn't deny it anymore, not that she had a solution. She'd told herself she'd choose abandonment over insanity. Now that she knew her mom hadn't gone mad, abandonment was still on the table.

Even if it was melodramatic, too many people had walked out of her life for her to invite it again. But she wanted Jake. She hadn't been with anyone in a long time and the chemistry between them was impossible to ignore. She also wanted to feel intimacy a time or two before the curse took its toll. Maybe he'd agree to sex without strings.

Jake came up beside her and lifted the kettle off the stove. Mae hadn't noticed it was already boiling. "Is something wrong?" he asked, rubbing his hand along her back.

"No." She met his eyes. "I decided I wanted something besides tea."

"What's that?"

"Sex."

His eyes darkened. He lowered, close enough for his breath to tease her lips, but he didn't kiss her. "Have you been thinking about it long?"

"Maybe." She went up on her toes and ran her tongue lightly across his lips. "Have you?"

"It's crossed my mind." He threaded his fingers with hers and headed for the bedroom.

"No." She held her ground, not letting him pull her.

"What's wrong?"

"I only want sex. No strings. I don't want a relationship."

"Mae, we already have a relationship. We're friends. Good friends."

She huffed. "Fine. We're good friends. When it comes to sex, it's just sex."

An expression flickered across Jake's face, then vanished before she could read it.

"It's no secret that I'm attracted to you, Mae. I'd love to be with you, but I want more. I'll take this for now because there's no way I can resist you, and then I'll try my damnedest to show you how good we could be together." He tugged gently on her hand.

She slipped her hand free. "You're not listening, Jake. I don't want to make love. I want to have sex. And not in the bedroom."

He tipped his head toward the living room. "Out here, in front of both dogs?"

"Good point." Mae took his hand and led him to her office. It had a couch lining one wall. She closed the door behind them, clicked on the desk lamp and killed the overhead light. He was giving her the reins, and now nerves fluttered in her stomach.

He sat on the couch and offered his hand. "Are you sure?"

She placed her hand in his. "Yes." The word came out so breathy, she barely recognized her own voice.

"Do you have a condom?"

"Oh." Leave it to Jake to be sensible. "Be right back."

She rushed to her bathroom and found the unopened box under the sink. She'd bought them when she'd dated a guy a couple of years back. He'd turned out to be seeing other women at the same time—didn't believe in exclusivity—so they'd never needed condoms. Mae didn't want anything serious with Jake, but she wasn't into sharing either. She checked the expiration date. "Phew."

She ripped open the box and scooped up a handful, then

stared at the packages in her fist. "Too eager." She put all but two back and hurried back to Jake.

She closed the door behind her and tossed the condoms on the couch beside him. Standing in front of him, she pulled her shirt over her head and reached for the button on her jeans. She shimmied them over her hips, watching him watch her.

"You're beautiful," he whispered, as if saying the words any louder might break the moment.

She'd never been very big, and she'd lost weight recently, but Jake made her feel beautiful. She unclasped her bra and shrugged out of the straps, letting the material fall to the floor, then slid her panties down and stepped free. Completely naked, she knelt in front of him and reached for his jeans. He didn't rush her and try to take over. When she had them open, he lifted his hips so she could ease them, and his briefs, down.

He gripped the collar of his shirt and yanked it over his head, tossing it to the side. Then he reached for her, pulling her up onto his lap. Straddling him, her knees bracketing his hips, she felt the solid line of him against her core. He picked up a condom and shifted just enough to sheath himself. Watching him, heat coiled low within her.

Leaning forward, he cupped her face in his large palms and kissed her. He didn't rush. When he pulled back, she licked her lips, wanting to savor his taste. Desire burned in his eyes and she couldn't look away. One of his thumbs caressed her cheekbone while his other hand trailed down her stomach, his fingers slowly lighting her up until she felt like she was on fire. When his fingers finally reached her core, she was wetter than she remembered being. She melted against him with a soft sound she couldn't hold back and squirmed in his lap. "Please, Jake. I need you."

"Like this?" He stroked her, lazy at first, then deeper,

guiding her higher. His free hand anchored at the nape of her neck, drawing her mouth back to his. The steady rhythm built fast; she rocked into his hand, breath catching. The world narrowed to heat and pulse and him.

Pressure gathered tight, bright, and inevitable. It swept through her, and she came apart against his mouth, the sound of it swallowed by his kiss. Before she'd fully drifted down, he eased his hand away and steadied her by the hips.

"Mae," he said roughly, "take me in."

She looked down, guided him, and sank onto him with a slow, delicious slide that burned just enough to make her gasp. She rocked her hips, deeper, and he filled his palms with her, mouth brushing over her skin, teasing, tasting. She found a rhythm and rode it harder, faster, with heat coiling again, startling at how quickly it returned. "Please, Jake. Again."

"My pleasure." He met her, thrust for thrust, his hand finding that sensitive spot and circling until everything inside her pulled tight.

"Oh, god." She shattered with a cry, stars sparking at the edges of her vision. He surged once more and held her tight as a low groan tore from his chest, his body shuddering beneath hers.

She slumped against him, loose and boneless.

"Hey, you okay?" he asked a few moments later.

"I think you broke me. But in the best possible way."

Laughter rumbled from his chest. "Good to know."

He lifted her carefully and laid her on the couch. A minute later, he was back with a warm washcloth and wiped her gently. She still couldn't make herself move when Jake slid his hands under her and picked her up.

"What're you doing?" she asked, not bothering to lift her head from his shoulder.

"Taking you to bed."

"Okay." He set her down and the mattress dipped beside her, snapping her awake like a bucket of freezing cold water. "What are you doing now?"

"I'm getting into bed."

Holding down her panic, Mae put her hand on his chest. "You can't."

"Can't what?"

"You can't sleep with me. Jake, you need to sleep in my spare room."

"Why?"

Mae could come up with a couple of reasons, such as she wasn't used to sleeping with anyone or she could wake from a nightmare. But the truth was simpler: she couldn't risk becoming too attached. "Because it was just sex."

Jake held her gaze for a long moment before he walked out of the room. Mae lay back on her pillow and wondered if she'd done the right thing. Not about sending Jake to the spare room—about having sex with him.

She reminded herself: she was cursed, and when she attached to someone, they didn't stay.

Saturday, February 8

JAKE LAY AWAKE, staring at the ceiling when Chewie, lying at the end of the bed, lifted his head. "Hey boy, what's up?"

Chewie shifted to get off the bed when a sound came from Mae's room. Jake flung back the covers. Having slept in his boxers, he didn't bother with a shirt as he rushed to Mae's room.

Her door was ajar, so he didn't knock and shouldered it wider. There was enough light from her partially open bathroom door for him to see. Solo crouched over Mae, gently nudging her with his snout. Mae thrashed in the throes of a nightmare, Solo pinning her legs.

"Mae?" He walked to the opposite side of the bed, the space he'd left minutes ago. "Mae, wake up." Lying on the bed, he faced her and brushed his knuckles along her cheek. "Mae, you're having a nightmare. Wake up."

As he repeated his words, Solo stretched forward and licked her chin. Wanting to help, Chewie licked her hand from where he sat beside the bed, his head resting on the comforter.

Watching her struggle, her eyes flickering beneath her lids, he would have sworn eternal love if it would help. He'd nearly said those three words while they made love—as far as he was concerned, that's exactly what they'd done, even if neither had said the words yet. It had been more than just sex. The only thing that had stopped him was the fear she'd feel obligated to say them back and the curse still wouldn't break. He might crush them both.

He pushed her short hair off her face as he kept repeating her name. Finally, after what felt like far too long, Mae opened her eyes. "Jake?" She glanced around the room, and then back at him. "I woke you."

It wasn't a question, and he didn't care that she'd woken him. "You want to tell me about it?"

She stroked Solo's short fur. "It was another nightmare."

Jake sat up against the headboard and pulled Mae against him, needing to hold her. "Tell me. Please."

She sucked in a breath and let it out slowly. "I was walking on a sandy beach. Which is funny because I've never been to the beach. I guess I've seen enough on TV and in movies for my brain to fake it. Someone was beside me, holding my hand. I… I don't know who it was."

At Mae's hesitation, he wondered if it had been him. Or maybe he just wished he could always be the one beside her.

"We were talking and laughing. Then suddenly I was alone. I turned around, looking for the person. That's when I noticed our footprints—two sets of prints in a long line. The other person's prints began disappearing one by one. I knew the footprints weren't mine because mine were so much smaller.

"I started to run toward the prints, trying to catch up to them before they all vanished. As I ran, I called the person's name, but I don't know what it was. In the dream I did. I'm not sure how far I ran, but I eventually became so winded I had to stop. That's when the quiet hit. Well… not truly quiet… no voices or laughter, only waves. The sand stretched endlessly in front of me and the only noise was the crashing of the waves."

Chewie sprang onto the bed, jostling it before he settled against Mae. Jake was on one side of her, Chewie on the other, and Solo still sprawled across her, as if all three of them were trying to keep her safe. He knew it was only an illusion.

Mae stroked Solo with one hand, then threaded the other through Chewie's longer fur.

When she continued, her tone dropped, distant, as if she was reliving the dream instead of explaining it to him.

"The dream morphed, as they all seem to do. I climbed a spiral staircase, already halfway up what felt like a never-ending number of steps. Someone was ahead of me. Not close enough that I could see them clearly, but I knew they were there. I also knew I could trust them, but I don't know if it was the same person who was on the beach with me."

The dream had the same theme as all the others Mae had told him about. Like with Blake, the curse picked a theme and repeated it, though the details of each episode differed. Blake's episodes had all been about failed love. Each time Blake told him about another one, Jake got the feeling the episodes were trying to tell him to hang on to love. Except that they were only showing him the heartache left behind when love didn't last. He hadn't been able to see how witnessing so much heartbreak could convince Blake to risk love.

The same thing was happening with Mae. All her dreams kept leaving her behind. One night on the phone, she'd told him that they left her aching with loss and despair. Like with Blake, Jake didn't see how that would push her toward friendship—let alone love—when anyone could still walk away.

Jake tugged her closer, wanting her to know that he wasn't going to leave. He kept the words to himself because he wasn't sure she'd believe him.

"I think I caught up to the person on the stairs. I kept calling out their name. Again, I don't know what it was but dream me did. At every turn, I called again. Then I yelled as loud as I could. I begged them to wait for me to catch up, but they didn't. I kept climbing and climbing. My lungs and legs burned more the higher I climbed.

"Then, like with so many of the other dreams, the treads crumbled beneath my feet. I gripped the railings on either side of me as I tried to move faster, but my legs felt like hardening cement."

When Mae didn't continue after a few moments, Jake urged her to finish. Regardless of how the dream ended, she was still here and needed to acknowledge that. "What happened next?"

"The staircase collapsed. The only noise was concrete and

metal tearing apart. They dropped silently into a void. Then I fell too. I didn't hit anything as I continued to fall."

Jake eased down onto the bed, lying flat. He pulled Mae down too, not an easy feat with hundreds of pounds of dog sprawled across them, but finally they lay side by side. He wrapped his arm around her shoulders, drawing her into him. "You're safe. I'm here." Inadequate words, but it was all he had.

10

Friday, February 14

Déjà vu settled over Mae as she sat in her SUV and stared out the passenger window at Akerman Contracting. Another Friday afternoon, but this time, she brought Solo with her. Blake and Cade had each called during the week to chat with her—get-to-know-you type of calls—neither one of them mentioning the curse.

Her cousins had invited her to visit again and even offered to come to her. None of them had mentioned any dates, and Mae hadn't expected to be there today. Not until she'd woken up out of a nightmare at three-thirty in the morning to find herself standing in the kitchen with a boiling pot on the stove.

She squinted into the dark, the only light leaking through the gap in the patio-door curtains. Relief hit her. At least she wasn't on the balcony in a tank and shorts. Then she saw it: the pot nearly boiled dry. The pantry handle dug into her spine as Solo pressed against her legs. Panic bubbled up. This had been so much worse than being outside in the cold. She could have set her kitchen on fire. Then her entire apartment building.

Nudging Solo to get him to move, she reached over for the tea towel she always hung on the stove's handle. She turned off the burner, grabbed the pot with the towel, and dropped it in the sink. When she flicked on the tap, the blackened pot sizzled louder than the rush of water. Then a crack, gunshot-sharp, cut through everything as the pan warped from the heat and sudden cold.

She let the water run for a few more minutes, then turned it off and dropped to her knees, wrapping her arms as far around Solo as she could manage. He saved her life. If he hadn't pushed her away from the stove, she likely would have been scalded by the boiling water and who knew what else she could have done in a sleep state. She knew without a doubt that his push finally yanked her out of the nightmare.

Fear rippled down her spine at how close she'd come to dying. She continued to sit on the floor with Solo, not caring about time passing. When she finally peeled herself off the floor, she went to the bathroom with Solo right next to her. He wouldn't even let her close the door.

Still too shaken to go to bed, she pulled on some clothes. They'd gone for a walk in the crisp morning air, then sat on her couch with the blinds open and watched the sun rise.

After breakfast, she worked for a few hours on a project a client was waiting on. Twice while she'd been working, she thought she heard someone call her name, but Solo hadn't reacted either time. She worried that the voices calling out to her in her dreams were now taking over her waking hours. Although there was no way to know for sure, it could mean the curse was progressing faster now.

Right then she decided to visit her cousins and get to know them better. She hadn't thought about how she expected them to form a loving bond if she didn't spend time with them. Deep down she expected that her cousins' love couldn't break the curse, but no one knew for sure.

Once again, she didn't call ahead. She tried to tell herself it was just a last-minute trip, but deep down, she knew the real reason was because she didn't want them to say it wasn't a good time.

The night before, Jake told her he wouldn't be in the office because he'd be out at one of their projects. This time she told herself that it was okay if she didn't see Jake, because getting to know her cousins was her main goal for coming. The same way she'd tried all week to convince herself that Jake staying the whole weekend wasn't a big deal. He'd held her and listened as she relayed her nightmare early Saturday morning, spent a lazy day with her, then soothed her from her nightmare that night. *Yup, no big deal.* She snorted out loud. Lying to herself was a new habit, one she needed to break.

She got out, then helped Solo out and clipped on his leash. As she walked up the front path, she didn't feel as much like an intruder as she had the week before. Knowing Jake wasn't going to be there might not be such a bad thing. When she was being truthful with herself, she could admit she wanted to see him, but she didn't know how he'd react after their phone call the night before. When he told her he'd be on a job site, she said it was fine. The rest of the conversation was fine too, until right before they ended the video call.

His tension was so obvious, it was almost tangible. When she'd questioned him, he admitted he felt helpless where she was concerned. He wanted to do something to help her. If he'd said the same thing a few weeks ago, she would have been pissed; she could take care of herself. Now, after seeing her mom, she had a better understanding of where Jake was coming from. Seeing someone you care about struggle or hurt, even a friend, and knowing you could help them, was harder than going through the pain yourself. She tried to reassure Jake that she'd be okay—even if it was another lie—but he saw right through her. The next time she spoke to him, she would apologize for brushing off his concerns. Now, she had some cousins to see.

Once again, she found the door unlocked and walked in. No one greeted her.

Mae checked her phone for the time. It was later than she thought. Solo sat at her feet in the empty lobby as she debated what to do. Should she call out or maybe text Blake or Cade?

"Whoa. He's bigger than Chewie," Blake said as he stepped out of an office.

"Yeah, Jake's dog is kind of small," Mae joked. "This is Solo. He's very friendly."

"Hi, Solo." Blake lowered his fist for Solo to sniff, then scratched his head before pulling Mae into a hug. He released her and frowned. "I didn't know you were coming. Was Jake supposed to tell me?"

Mae regretted coming on a whim. "Jake didn't know." She shrugged, trying to make it seem like no big deal. She managed to hold in a snort. "It was a last-minute decision. If you're busy, that's okay. Solo and I enjoy driving."

"I've got a few minutes. My brothers are in the board-room. We end most Fridays with a meeting and once the non-family executives leave, my brothers, Jake, and I hang around for a bit longer. Jake went to a job site and isn't back yet."

"That's okay. He told me he'd be at a project site today." She followed Blake with Solo glued to her side into the same boardroom she'd been in the week before.

"Holy shit. He's bigger than Chewie," Dane said as he came around the table.

Blake laughed. "That's exactly what I said."

Dane pulled her in for a hug. "Good to see you, Mae. Is he friendly?"

"Yes, very."

Dane repeated the same ritual with Solo that Blake had, introducing himself, before turning a chair around to sit. It brought Solo and Dane to eye level. "How old is he?"

"Two and a half."

Next, Ford greeted Solo before giving Mae a hug. They were a huggy family—something she wasn't used to but could be.

"Mae, good to see you again," Gage said from the screen. "One day we'll meet in person. Sorry to cut out, but I've got a job to finish before Ford and Greta come up for the night." He nodded, she assumed, at his brothers and the screen went blank.

"Speaking of… I've got to pick up Greta. We're driving down to Green Springs to see Gage. We decided since it's Valentine's Day and none of us are dating, we'd turn it into a singles' night."

Ford grinned and she remembered Jake telling her what a charmer Ford was. Not in a slimy way, but she could definitely see it.

"Next time you're up, I'll introduce you to Greta. She's been my best friend for years. You'll love her." Ford waved at his brothers and left.

Dane gave Solo another pat and stood. "Sorry to rush out too, but I've got to go. I've got a couple of errands to run before I meet some buddies at a sports bar." He gave her a hug and then he was gone too. All the fast hugs and goodbyes were giving her whip lash.

Cade glanced at his watch and regret flickered across his face. "I wish I could stay longer, but I've got to pick up Malcolm, and then the babysitter. Jessica has been out of town a lot, so we've got a reservation at our favorite restaurant. She wanted a kid-free night. Are you going to stay the weekend? The family is coming to my house for Sunday dinner." He grimaced. "My twenty-ninth birthday."

"Early happy birthday and no, sorry, I'm not staying." Mae felt like an idiot dropping in but plastered on a smile for her cousin. "Another time. I'm sure there'll be lots." Another lie. She wasn't lying to herself this time, but she didn't want Cade to feel bad.

"Of course." Cade waved and left.

Mae turned back to Blake, the last one left, to see him looking at his watch. She knew what was coming and didn't want him to feel like he was letting her down. Beating him to the punch, she told him, "I should have called, but I enjoyed the drive with Solo and it was good to see you again, even if only for a few minutes. You and Paige have big plans tonight?"

"Not big. Jake's parents offered to babysit Emmie, because they'll already have Chloe, Jake's niece. Have you met Jake's sister, Chelsea, and her husband, Cam, yet?"

"No, but I'm sure I will soon." She forced another smile and walked into the hallway with Solo so it wouldn't be awkward with Blake trying to hurry her out the door. He followed her into the front lobby.

"Mae?"

Jake, with Chewie trotting beside him, walked up to them from the back of the house. If he made an excuse to leave because he had a date too, she could only hope that the floor would open up and swallow her.

Instead, he closed the distance and kissed her. It was one of those soft, non-lingering kisses he gave her when someone was around. "It's good to see you," he said quietly, then turned to Blake. "Hey, I stopped by my parents at lunch and Mom said they're looking after Emmie tonight. You and Paige have reservations?"

Blake wiggled his eyebrows. "No. We're staying in."

They laughed, then Blake left, leaving her with Jake.

Chewie and Solo circled each other, sniffing, then trailed behind Mae as she followed Jake to his office.

Jake perched on the corner of his desk. "I wasn't expecting you. Is everything alright?"

As he spoke, both dogs flopped onto the large dog bed, side by side, content to relax, like they didn't have a care in the world. Unlike Mae, who stood in front of Jake, millionth-guessing her choice to drop by without calling first. "Everything's fine. Uh, do you have plans?" *Please say no.*

"Actually..." he grinned. "I'd been planning to drive to your place and pretend I *just happened* to be in the area and decided to drop by."

Mae's shoulders unclenched. She took a step forward to stand between his legs, and he placed his hands on her hips. "And what would we have done?" she asked, drawing out her words.

JAKE GAVE HER A SLY SMILE. He loved seeing this teasing side of Mae. All sides of her, really. He hated the deepening shadows under her eyes and that she'd dropped more weight in the last five days, but he loved being with her. She hadn't banished him to the spare room on Saturday night, and he'd held her through yet another nightmare. After that, she'd barely slept. He could only imagine what her nightmares had been like since then. He finally left on Sunday afternoon, but one sign from her and he would've stayed.

"Well..." He tapped his chin in mock contemplation. "I suppose we would have taken the dogs for a walk. Then maybe had dinner..." He let the sentence trail off.

"Sounds good. Then what?"

"Hmmm… We could have played a lively game of Scrabble."

Mae half laughed, half choked. "Scrabble? That's lively?"

"Oh, sure. Or we could do this." He slid his hand to the back of her neck, gentle but possessive, and pulled her closer. His kiss wasn't soft and demure this time. It contained all the passion and pent-up tension he'd been holding in since he'd held her through her dream on Saturday night.

She gripped his biceps and kissed him back. Her tongue explored his mouth as her hands roamed up his arms. He was hooked to the taste that was uniquely Mae.

They broke apart, breathless. "I think I like that better than Scrabble."

He laughed. "I'll admit it was good, but then we've never played Scrabble together." He had a feeling anything they did together would be good. "Come to the cabin with me."

"Now?"

"Now. We've got the dogs, you can follow me in your SUV. The forecast calls for light snow, but you'll be fine."

"I didn't check the weather. Or the date." A red flush rose in her cheeks.

"Why the date?"

"I didn't know it was Valentine's Day. My cousins had plans."

"And now you do too."

She grinned. "Scrabble."

He pulled her back for another kiss. "If that's what you want to call it, I'm game."

In the middle of their kiss, Mae pulled back. "Did you invite me because you pity me?"

"Why would I pity you?"

She took a step back. "Because all my cousins have Valentine's Day plans and I'm all alone."

"I said I had planned to stop by. That's not pity. I wanted to see you. And if I didn't see you, I'd be alone on Valentine's Day too. Would you pity me?"

She tilted her head as if she had to process his words. "No."

"Right. But let's talk about pity for a moment." He lifted from the desk enough to reach out and pull her back between his legs. "I think pity means compassion for someone's suffering. If we're both suffering from loneliness, wouldn't it be alright to feel compassion for that?"

"I suppose."

"What about your curse? I know you're not sleeping well. Can't I feel compassion for you suffering through the nightmares and not getting enough sleep? What's wrong with that? I think we'd be living a pretty sad life if we don't care about other people. You've been alone for so long, I think you need to reframe how you look at pity."

"Maybe."

"And." He purposely didn't finish.

"And what?"

"I like you. I want to hang out with you."

"Okay. Let's hang. And maybe play Scrabble."

He chuckled. "Yes, Scrabble."

Like the week before, it didn't take them long to get on the road, this time with Mae following him. He was about to call her when his phone rang.

"Do we need to stop for food?" she asked.

"When I was there a couple of weeks ago, I stocked up on canned and packaged foods. Even dog food. And replaced the clothes my parents had brought back to wash. The entire family keeps extra clothes at the cabin, so there will be something that will fit you. We'll hit the store before the turnoff and grab perishables."

"I've never been to a cabin before."

Mae was a knot of feelings he wanted to protect and slowly unravel. She didn't want pity, but she hadn't tried to hide the sadness in her tone that she was never taken to a cabin—almost a rite of passage for kids in Colorado. He couldn't change the past, but he would enjoy showing her everything she'd missed out on growing up.

"I've got a feeling you're going to love it." He launched into his family's history with the cabin and then spent the rest of the trip telling her stories about the summers he'd spent there and all the trouble he and Blake had gotten into.

By the time they pulled up in front of the cabin, after a quick stop at the local store, snow was falling steadily. Both dogs bounded through the snow as he grabbed his bag and Chewie's dog bed from the truck's bed.

Mae came up beside him, carrying the grocery bags. "You don't have a bed for Chewie in the cabin?"

"I do, but now Solo will have one too. I tossed a spare in the truck this morning for Chewie, so he'd have it when, you know... I *just happened* to be in your area..." He wiggled his eyebrows suggestively.

11

Mae's lips twitched at Jake's eyebrow wiggle and her heart skipped a beat. After a month of talking with Jake she knew putting others first came naturally to him. She'd mentioned it once and he brushed it off, as if it was something everyone did. And maybe it was with his family and friends. But in her world, it wasn't common.

She followed him up the three steps onto the porch.

Once inside, he dropped everything near the door. "The cabin is heated, but we keep it turned down when we're not here. I'll turn it up and get a fire going before I clear off the solar panels."

The dogs bounded off to explore, but Mae didn't move from her spot inside the door.

Crouched down in front of the fireplace, Jake glanced over his shoulder at her. "You okay?"

"Yes. Taking it all in." And freaking out inside. She'd never been in a cabin before and didn't know the first thing about lighting a fire, and the only solar panels she'd ever seen were on TV.

"Come here." He beckoned with his hand and she walked

over to him. "Let me show you what to do. Unless you know how already."

Jake probably knew she was completely clueless about anything even remotely rustic, but was being polite. She shook her head and knelt beside him.

"When we leave the cabin, we prepare everything, so it's easy to start a fire the next time we come. You can help me when it's time, if you'd like, but it's not difficult. We clean out all the old ashes and bring in more firewood. Kindling too." He nodded toward a wrought-iron rack in the corner stacked full of thick hunks of wood, with a section holding smaller pieces and sticks.

"When we don't have a fire going, we close the damper to keep out the cold air, so we open it first."

Jake pointed it out and made sure Mae could open and close it. Definitely not complicated, but she didn't tell him she'd never heard of a damper before.

He then showed her how to prime the flue by igniting a roll of newspaper and holding it up to the damper to warm it up, preventing smoke from pouring into the room. The paper, kindling, and logs were already in place, but Jake walked her through each step.

"Now you'll be a pro."

Mae snorted. "If you say so. Anything else?"

"The screen to catch any sparks." Jake stood and reached for a three-part metal and mesh folding screen she hadn't noticed and set it in front of the fire.

The process was simple, but more involved than striking a match to some wood, as shown on TV. She felt like the proverbial fish out of water, and not only because she'd never been to a cabin or lit a fire before. Her one and only romance had been with her ex-husband, and ended in disaster.

She didn't know what to expect from Jake—except for the

fantastic sex—and she still didn't want a relationship where she would come to rely on someone. Add in the curse and sleepwalking and she wondered, not for the first time that day, if she'd made a mistake in venturing out that morning.

"I'm going to clear the snow off the solar panels and check the battery levels and the generator to make sure it's full. If we lose power, I want to make sure we've got a backup. I'll clear a path to the shed too. There's extra tools and winter gear, like snowshoes and toboggans in there. The code for the keypad is 2580, just in case." He ran the back of his knuckles over her cheek, a habit she was becoming addicted to. "I have plans for us to cozy up together in front of the fireplace, but working appliances and running water are nice too."

"Sounds good." She mentally rolled her eyes at her lame comment but didn't know what else to say.

"I'll take the dogs and let them play in the snow." Then he called both dogs and a minute later, Mae was alone in the cabin.

She was in the middle of nowhere with Jake, and she felt safe.

MAE JUMPED BACK, laughing, as the dogs shook on the front porch. Snow flew everywhere.

Jake opened the door, telling the dogs to stay. "The cabin is pretty wet-dog-proof, but let's get them dried off." He took some towels from a hook by the door and passed one to Mae.

When they were dry, both dogs trundled off to their beds a few feet from the fireplace. They'd be warm, but not too hot. Unlike Mae, who would be absolutely toasty, because earlier she'd asked Jake if he could move the couch closer to the fire. He had smiled and moved it without saying anything. Then he showed her a dresser full of clothes and told her to help herself. She found a thick pair of wool socks that weren't too big.

"Would you like something to drink? We've got some wine left over from dinner. Or would you like some coffee or hot chocolate?" Jake asked as he headed to the kitchen and Mae crossed to the fireplace.

She put another log on the fire and watched it catch and flare. None of her foster families had camped or even had fires in their backyards. Not that she could remember. Such a small thing, adding a log, but it was one more thing she hadn't done growing up. It gave her a sense of pride to know how to do it now.

Sitting on the couch in the corner closest to the fire, she pulled her legs up underneath her.

"Mae?"

It took her a moment to remember his question. "Hot chocolate, please. Want some help?" she asked to be polite, but hoped he'd say no. She didn't want to move away from the warmth. Her limbs were the right amount of tired from their walk in the snow.

"No, I've got it."

Mae sighed in contentment, her gaze not quite focused as she watched the flames. She was in the zone, not wide awake, but not asleep, when a loud crack from the fire snapped her to attention. It sounded too much like the pot when she'd dumped it into the sink and turned on the water after boiling it dry.

She hadn't thought about the incident since earlier in the day. Hard to believe it was still the same day, but she second-guessed herself again. Had she chosen right when she visited her cousins, which had led her to be here with Jake? Last weekend, she'd felt bad enough when she'd woken him with her nightmares. Tonight, would her sleepwalking wake him? What if she did something to endanger them both?

"You okay?" Jake asked as he handed her a mug and sat beside her.

"Worried about the snow. It's coming down hard." The lie slipped out, not wanting to tell Jake what she'd really been thinking and burden him. Like everyone, her upbringing had shaped her, and being in the cabin with Jake was a constant reminder of how much her experiences differed from his. There were so many things she didn't know. On top of that, she had the worries over her curse. She'd rather enjoy the evening with him.

"We'll be fine. We have everything we need, including a backup generator. The forecast says the snow should taper off late tomorrow morning. If the snow is too deep to get out, I've got a plow to attach to the front of my truck to clear the road to the highway."

She sipped her hot chocolate and looked up at him. "You really are a mountain man, aren't you? It's not just the flannels and beard," she teased.

He grinned, his teeth white against his mustache and beard. "I like being comfy, hate shaving, and being out here is peaceful."

"It is."

They fell into a comfortable silence as they enjoyed their drinks and watched the fire. Every so often one of the dogs snored, making her smile.

She was finishing her hot chocolate when Jake set his mug down and stood. "Stay right there."

She looked up, checking to see if he was talking to her or the dogs. "I'm not going anywhere."

"Good. I've got something for you."

Earlier, she'd forgotten it was Valentine's Day, but she knew Jake hadn't. She sat up, placing her own mug on the table. Should she apologize for forgetting what day it was? For not getting him anything? They were friends. Friends who'd had fantastic sex a few times, but they'd never defined their relationship beyond that. Her ex-husband had proved she wasn't relationship material, and now she was cursed and having nightmares. Both relationship killers.

Jake sat beside her again, a wrapped box in his hand. "I can practically see the wheels turning in your mind. Relax, Mae. Consider it a gift between friends."

He moved both mugs to the floor, then placed the box on the table.

She stared at it. The wrapping paper was white, covered in bright dots, like the kind for any occasion. Not something specific to Valentine's Day, which made her feel better. After social services separated her from her mom, the few presents she'd received had always felt so special. Like the chocolates Jake had given her the first day they met in person. She didn't think it was a big deal to him, but to her, it had been monumental.

Gifts filled her with conflicting feelings—pleasure and guilt. The pleasure came from more than the gift itself. Knowing that someone thought about her enough to think about what to get her, then to buy it and wrap it, made her feel loved. The kind of love didn't matter, it was love all the same. Then came the guilt. Did the person buy the gift because they felt obligated? Mae was happy to reciprocate, but what if the person didn't want her to, or she bought the wrong thing?

"Mae, open it, please."

His tone carried a hint of worry. Not wanting to ruin his joy in giving her a gift, and having learned from the chocolates not to fuss, she reached for the box and pulled it into her lap. The lightness of it surprised her, considering the box stretched more than a foot long.

Sticking her fingers under the seam of the paper, she lifted and ripped the paper wide. At the sight of the image on the box, she laughed as she scrambled to tear off the rest of the wrapping.

"Over one thousand pieces," she murmured. She lifted the box and turned it back to front several times, examining each picture displayed. If she wasn't so excited, she might have cried at Jake's thoughtfulness.

She put the box back on the table and threw her arms around him. "Thank you."

He hugged her and pressed a kiss to her hair. "You're welcome."

Mae turned back to the table, opened the end of the box, and tipped the contents onto the table. She glanced at him over her shoulder. "You remembered." Just like with the chocolates.

"Of course. Now you have a new LEGO kit of your own." He gave her a wink. "I didn't think lingerie would be appropriate."

"This is way better than lingerie."

"I'll remember that for next time."

"My birthday isn't until November." If she continued to sleepwalk, she might not make it until her birthday, but she didn't say anything, not wanting to ruin the moment.

"Memorial Day is in May."

She huffed a laugh. "People don't give presents on Memorial Day."

"There isn't a law against it." He nudged her shoulder with his. "This gift is all yours, but I wouldn't say no to helping you put it together."

"I'd like that." She turned back to the table. "I didn't expect so many bags of pieces."

"Wait until we put together the biggest Millennium Falcon set. It's over 7,500 pieces."

"I don't think I'm ready for that many pieces yet." She glanced over at Jake, his face suddenly flushed. It wasn't from the heat of the fire. "Oh my god! You almost got me that one, didn't you?"

He nudged her shoulder again. "Nah, not for your first set. How about I look for the pieces and you build?"

They worked through about a third of the bags before calling it a night. She never would have guessed how much fun putting a LEGO kit together with someone would be.

They stepped onto the porch and let the dogs out once more before Jake put out the fire. Mae used the bathroom after Jake handed her a spare toothbrush from the extra his mom always stocked, and borrowed one of his T-shirts.

She slipped into bed to wait for him. She shouldn't have been nervous, but she was. It wasn't like they hadn't had sex before, but for some reason, this time seemed different.

When he crawled in with her, she knew that no matter what happened in the future, she wanted this time to be more than just sex. Maybe she could have everything. Could Jake be the one person who sticks? If he did, would she still be around?

12

Jake lay beside Mae on the bed and bent his elbow, propping his head on his hand so he could look down at her. He loved looking at her. He'd hated leaving her on Sunday and it had been a hellish five days without her. "I've said it before, but I'll keep saying it… You're exquisite. Inside and out."

With the light from the moon shining through the window, Jake could see Mae blush. She wasn't used to compliments, touches, presents, and so many other things. He wanted to give them all to her.

Leaning over, he kissed her. Running his tongue along the seam of her lips, he waited for her to invite him in. She stoked a fire in him, and he refused to rush. He intended to savor her.

Seeing her in his T-shirt triggered his protective side, bringing out his inner caveman. He'd been worried about women's safety before, but never had he felt the possessive urges he felt with Mae. He pushed them aside, needing only to pleasure her.

He set his palm on the T-shirt over her sternum. She

sucked in a breath as she watched him. Slowly, he dragged his hand downward, trailing his fingers over her, feeling her warmth through the material. She shivered, and not from the cold. He loved that he could elicit that type of response from her, and he hadn't yet touched her skin.

When he reached the hem, she lifted her arms to help him take it off.

"Nuh uh. Not yet." Jake lifted it up only a few inches. Leaning over, he ran his tongue along her skin, just above the edge of her panties. He kissed a little higher, lifting her shirt as he went. He used his lips, his tongue, and his fingers to drive her wild. By the time he reached the area under her breasts, she was pushing up against him, urging him on.

"Please, Jake. Don't tease. I need more." He didn't want her to ever have to beg for his touch—he'd touch her anytime —but he didn't want to rush.

"I want to cherish you. Unwrap you like a present," he said against her skin. He pushed his shirt up a little higher, still not exposing her breasts as he kissed the bottom of each globe. "You're so stunning, Mae." He lifted his head, looking into her eyes, wanting her to hear and to see he meant what he said. Then he resumed his task of showing her how beautiful he thought she was. How much he cherished her. He lavished attention on her breasts before he kissed her breathless. Then he moved back down her body. He kissed her jaw and neck and moved lower, showing her breasts some more love.

"Please, Jake. Please, please, please."

By the time he'd worked his way back down to her panties, she was squirming under him. Her fingers trailed along his shoulders and neck, her nails blazing a trail all over his skin, making him want to squirm as much as she did.

He slipped his fingers under the edge of her panties and pulled them down her legs, his lips following their path.

Laying his body between her legs, he peppered kisses down the inside of her thighs and back up. She gripped his hair, sending sparks of heat from his scalp right to his groin.

Sliding his hands under her, he cupped her ass and lifted her up, kissing along her seam. She jerked at his first touch and groaned when his tongue split her folds. He continued to torment her until she was pleading, "Please, Jake, please."

He smiled against her skin, not sure what she was asking for, but loved that he was pleasing her. He sucked her clit into his mouth and slipped two fingers into her core, curving them toward him. He'd found the right spot when she bucked against him. Her entire body tensed and her core tightened around his fingers, hot moisture coating them.

He pulled his hands free to kiss his way back up her body. She loosened her grip on his hair and gave him a dazed smile.

"Here," she said passing him the condom he brought to bed with him.

Hovering over her, he peeled off his shirt then kissed her lips, knowing she could taste herself on him. "In a rush?" he teased.

"I want you in me, Jake. I need you."

He took the package from her, ripped it open, and sheathed himself in seconds. "I need you too." More than he ever imagined he could when he made that first phone call to her. Now, she lay beneath him like a work of art.

Kneeling between her legs, he gripped his length and slid the head through her folds. They both moaned at the delicious sensations. He dropped to his elbows and their gazes locked on each other as he slowly slid home.

He went still, killing himself, waiting for her to adjust. When he felt her ease around his girth, he couldn't hold back any longer. He drove his hips, an easy rhythm at first. He lifted one of her legs, bringing her knee up, and adjusted his position, sending himself deeper into her core. She hooked her other leg around his hip, digging her heel into him. Increasing his pace, he thrust harder and deeper. She gripped his shoulders and pulled him down, kissing him with the same uncontrolled passion he felt roaring through him.

Barely holding himself back, he waited for Mae to reach the pinnacle first. As soon as she did, he pumped harder. Once, twice, a third time, before exquisite flares of pleasure ripped through him, lighting up his entire body.

He lowered down, wrapping his arms around her as his breathing returned to normal.

"Wow," Mae whispered below him.

He lifted his head, grinning down at her. "Wow?"

She nodded and stretched up. As she stroked his beard along one side of his jaw with her hand, her tongue lightly stroked his lower lip. "Yes, wow."

Wow worked. When he had enough strength to finally move, he disposed of the condom and got a warm washcloth to clean her up. He helped her redress in panties, his T-shirt, and the wool socks before tucking her into his side and pulling the blankets around them.

Within seconds, Mae was fast asleep in his arms, safe and warm. As he drifted off to sleep, his caveman side wanted to keep her there, always.

Saturday, February 15

JAKE JERKED AWAKE. Chewie was pushing at his side, letting out a low whine. "Hey, boy. What's wrong?" He petted Chewie's head to reassure him while turning to see if they'd woken Mae. She wasn't there.

The moon shone through the window, telling him it was still night, but he picked up his phone from the nightstand anyway. Almost three in the morning.

"Mae?" He got up and pulled on his jeans, telling himself not to panic. She may have wanted to be by the fire.

As soon as he stepped off the rug beside the bed, the cold registered. The floor bit with cold, and a draft swept into the room. "Mae?"

The cabin was deathly quiet. He looked out to see now fell lightly again, having stopped by the time they'd gone to bed. The moon was bright, highlighting the falling flakes.

He walked into the main room hoping to see the fire crackling away and Mae playing with her LEGO kit. Before he could glance that way, a gust of wind hit his bare chest. The front door of the cabin stood wide open, the wind ushering swirls of snow inside.

Fear hit him hard. Unthinkable images of Mae in the snow flitted through his mind. Then he moved. Donning his coat, he saw Mae's still hanging on the next hook, and he ran back into the bedroom and grabbed a pair of wool socks. As much as he wanted to hurry and rush outside, he wouldn't be any good to Mae if he didn't take care of himself. He put on his socks and shoved his feet into his boots, refusing to dwell on the fact that both Mae's borrowed boots, and the dress boots she'd worn for her trip were lined up beside his.

Socks. Boots. Hat. Gloves. He yanked them all on, before shutting the door after Chewie. Outside, the wind knifed his face. "Mae!" He held his breath, listening. Nothing.

Jake bounded off the porch and stopped, not knowing which way to go. More wind hit his face like an arctic blast, reminding him of every statistic he'd ever read of people dying from frostbite and hypothermia. They shook him as violently as the wind, ready to amp up his fear if he let them.

"Focus." Pushing all thoughts but finding Mae out of his

mind, he looked for tracks in the snow. Their prints from earlier in the evening were covered over by the falling and blowing snow. Keeping his gaze on the ground, he turned in a slow circle, searching for any sign of her. Again... nothing.

"Chewie, find Mae." As Chewie angled one direction, Jake took the other, scanning the snow in the moon.

As he rounded the corner of the cabin, Chewie's bark sounded behind him. Trudging back, Jake cursed under his breath as the deep snow slowed his pace while the minutes ticked by.

Finally at Chewie's side, he looked down. A single, small footprint dented the snow. At least that's what he hoped it was, and not an mark left by a chunk of falling ice. Wool-socked feet didn't leave prints like boots.

"Good job. Find Mae."

Chewie didn't bound away, but moved methodically, sniffing the snow as he went. Every few feet, he stopped and let out a single bark. After the third one, a faint bark echoed back, as if carried on the wind. "Good job, Chewie. Find Mae and Solo."

Taking off, Chewie ran toward the lake. Jake sprinted after him. Both dogs continued to bark back and forth, Chewie to track, Solo to guard.

Years ago, Jake's family had cleared a path to the lake. Chewie would know it, but instead of taking it, he led Jake through a copse of dense trees. Branches clawed at his face and arms as he pushed through, trusting Chewie to lead him straight to Mae and Solo.

They broke through the trees near the shoreline.

Still trusting his St. Bernard, Jake turned to the left.

His breath seized.

Clothed in only wool socks and one of Jake's T-shirts, Mae stood on the frozen lake, the shirt billowing around her pale legs. Her arms hung limply at her sides. A thin veil of snow clung to her dark hair.

Mae stood about twenty feet from the shore, facing him. Solo shifted on his paws, on the far side of her, as if blocking her from heading further out onto the lake.

"Mae!" Jake shouted against the wind.

Her eyes were open, but she showed no signs of hearing him. He yelled her name again, and still nothing. Mae hadn't mentioned that she sleepwalked, but it could be new. She'd zoned out a few times in the evening, only saying she was lost in thought when he'd questioned her. He hadn't been sure that's all it was, but he knew better than to push.

Chewie put one paw on the edge of the ice and whined, getting Jake's attention. His dog wanted his permission to head onto the lake—the instinct to rescue lived in his breed's bones. With one person and a dog already out on the ice, Jake wouldn't risk adding any more weight to the possibly fragile surface if it could be avoided. It was cold, but they'd had a few days of warmer weather the week before. He had no way of knowing how thick the ice was.

The wind whipped across Jake's face again, like an icicle stabbing his skin, reminding him time was bleeding away. "Stay," he ordered Chewie before spinning and running back to the cabin, skirting the trees.

When he reached the shed at the back of the cabin, he stopped at the door. Blowing out a breath, he tried to slow his breathing enough to concentrate and force his stiff fingers to enter the code. When his dad had first put the heavy-duty padlock with a code keypad on the shed door, Jake thought it was overkill. A simple lock would have worked. If someone wanted in, they'd find a way. A padlock wasn't going to stop them.

Probably not, his dad had said, but this way no one would need to track water or snow into the cabin to get a key.

"I owe you, Dad," he whispered as he worked to enter the code. It took Jake two tries before he heard it click open. He threw off the lock, wrenched open the door, grabbed the rope hanging on a hook inside the door, and ran back to the lake.

Chewie hadn't moved from the edge of the water. He let out a single bark when he saw Jake. "I know, bud. I'm going as fast as I can." Jake knelt in the snow in front of Chewie and tied one end of the rope to the dog's collar. He wrapped the other around his own waist, pulling it as tight as possible. At only twenty-five feet in length, the rope wasn't long enough to anchor on any nearby trees.

He braced himself in the snow. "Go get Mae."

Chewie took a couple of tentative steps onto the ice, then steadily made his way toward Mae and Solo. The rope stopped Chewie about a yard shy of Mae's feet.

Probably a good thing. The weight of both dogs together could be too much for the ice if they stood close together. Chewie looked as if he was still close enough for Mae to grab onto him without leaning too far forward.

Solo paws slid on the ice as he clamped the hem of Mae's T-shirt in his jaws and tugged. Mae still didn't move.

"Mae!" Jake called her name over and over. The possibility of startling her into a panic crossed his mind for a moment. It was a risk he was willing to take to avoid her freezing to death.

After another minute, and still no response from Mae, Jake knelt down on the ice. Dropping his gloved hands to the ice, he went on all fours, spreading out his body weight. He didn't weigh as much as Solo and so far the dog was fine. When he inched closer to Mae, Jake would go onto stomach, if he had to.

He'd inched out about five feet when a sharp crack echoed through the night.

Jake jerked his head up.

Mae's eyes were as wide as saucers. "J-Jake?"

He didn't know how much she'd taken in, but they were out of time. "Grab onto Chewie. Now!" he yelled at her.

The dogs sensed the danger. Or his barely leashed fear. Chewie inched closer to Mae, using the slack in the rope Jake had created by moving onto the ice. Solo pulled on her T-shirt again.

Mae took a step forward and stumbled. Her arms windmilled at her sides and she fell to her knees. Her hands fumbled and her knees wobbled as hypothermia creeped in, inhibiting her ability to move.

Still on his hands and knees, Jake crawled forward another couple of feet, giving Chewie more slack in the rope.

Keeping his gaze on Mae, Jake saw the exact moment she realized where she was. She looked down at the ice, then at him.

"O-oh g-god. O-oh g-god," she repeated the mantra faster and faster, tripping over the words. Panic caused her voice to rise.

"It's going to be okay," he said, trying to reassure her. Raising his voice while trying not to sound as panicked as he felt, he did his best to get Mae to act. "I know you're cold, but I need you to hold on to Chewie. Grab his fur with both hands. He'll pull you in. Solo will push you."

Chewie crowded in front of Mae, with Solo still at her back. The combined weight of the three of them registered at the exact same time another loud crack split the air.

"Hold Chewie! NOW!" Thin fractures in the ice spread out from their position in all directions.

Mae threw herself on top of Chewie. The dog didn't wait, rushing forward with Solo pushing Mae from behind.

As fast as he could, Jake flung his body into the prone

position on the ice. Spread-eagle, he widened his surface area as large as possible and reached forward.

Freezing water bubbled up between the cracks in the ice. The frigid water cut through Jake's clothes like a thousand little knives pricking his skin, but his gaze never wavered from Mae. He had to be ready.

When the dogs slid the last few feet to reach him, Jake reached up and grabbed Mae, rolling them both toward the shore.

As soon as he felt a solid surface beneath him, he scrambled to his feet, Mae still in his arms. The instant the cold air hit his soaked jeans, they stuck, heavy and frozen to his legs. Cold had already zapped his strength, making his muscles feel like they'd been dipped in concrete. Mae shivered in his arms, reminding him of the danger they were still in, and provided a final burst of adrenaline, urging him to move faster.

"J-J-Jake."

"It's okay. You'll be w-warm s-soon." He started to tremble almost as badly as Mae, but he didn't stop moving forward. Rounding the cabin, he saw the three steps up to the porch and almost stopped. In that moment they looked as insurmountable as Everest would have been.

Then he felt a nudge on the back of his thighs. And another. With the help from the dogs, he made it up the stairs while holding Mae. His wet-gloved fingers fumbled on the doorknob before he made it into the cabin.

As gently as he could, he laid Mae on the couch, whipped his gloves off, and snatched several blankets from the basket by the hearth. His fingers were stiff and painful, and he had to flex them several times to get them working. Ignoring the pins and needles shooting through his limbs as best as he could, he layered the blankets on top of each other. He went back to the basket and grabbed four more blankets, adding them one at a time to the layers.

"I-I'm s-so cold." The clicking of Mae's teeth sounded louder than her words.

"I know. I'll get you warm." She wasn't out of danger yet. Turning away from her shaking form, he faced the fireplace. He couldn't dwell on how scared he was of losing her. Some-time in the last few weeks Mae had come to mean more to him than any other person. It had taken seeing her out in the middle of the lake for him to come to grips with his feelings. He couldn't lose her.

Even as he grabbed some newspaper and balled it up, he thought of the curse. He knew without a doubt that the curse had made Mae sleepwalk into the cold night. He would do everything he could to get her warm and stop the hypothermia from progressing, but that wouldn't stop the curse. Only love could. Even if he could get himself to that point, he wasn't sure Mae could. She believed that everyone eventually left her, and with the curse reinforcing that lie every night, he wasn't sure how she'd be able to let that false belief go.

From long practice, he built the fire to a blazing roar, the crackling of the wood loud in the room.

Still, his thoughts wouldn't stop. Besides all the doubts the dreams reinforced in Mae, next time the curse could hit her with something worse than sleepwalking. He shuddered at the thought of what that could even be.

PEEKING out of the top of the pile of blankets, Mae stared at Jake's back as he started the fire, her mind muddled. She remembered going to sleep in Jake's arms. Then she heard

Jake call her name while she stood freezing in the middle of the lake.

He shoved the couch, with her on it, a foot from the hearth, but it wasn't enough. Her thoughts fogged and fragmented; she couldn't imagine ever feeling warm again.

Jake placed one knee on the couch beside her and reached under the blankets. "Mae, we need to get you out of your wet clothes." He stripped off her socks as he spoke, then removed her panties and shirt.

The entire time, he exposed only the skin necessary to remove each article of clothing, keeping the blankets covering her, but they still weren't enough. "I-I-c-c-an't st-stop-shak-ing." She could see her breath. That couldn't be good.

"I know." Jake stripped off his own shirt and then his jeans and socks. "That's a good sign. Your body is shivering to keep you warm."

Mae would have rolled her eyes at him if she had enough energy. "It's n-not w-working."

"I'll get you warm in a minute." He disappeared and returned with a wool hat. He pulled it down over her head, covering her ears and eyebrows. "I've turned up the thermostat, so with that and the fireplace, it will be warm in here soon."

Jake stepped behind her again. This time he returned with towels and he dried Solo and then Chewie, examining their paws at the same time. He dragged their dog beds closer to the fire, but not right in front, and directed each dog to lie down.

Mae was a terrible dog mom. She hadn't even thought about how cold Solo must have been. "Th-they o-kay?" she asked, forcing the words out.

"Yes, they both look fine. I don't see any signs of frostbite on either of them, but we'll watch them, just in case." Still naked, Jake went back into the kitchen and returned with two bowls of water. "This is warm water, not hot, but it will help them warm up," he told her as he placed a bowl in front of each dog.

Jake lavished each dog with attention, praising them, before he strode back to Mae. He lifted her, blankets and all, and sat on the couch, positioning her sideways onto his lap. Draping the blankets over them both, he snugged her against his bare chest and wrapped his arms tight around her. His skin, even chilled, felt warmer than hers. Holding her arms tight to her chest, she burrowed into him as much as she could.

After a while, she felt sleepy. She jerked herself upright, not wanting to sleep. Going to sleep used to mean warmth and rest. Now it could mean death. A violent shiver ran through her, but this time she wasn't sure if it was purely from the cold.

Jake ran his knuckles along her cheek. "It's okay. You can sleep. I'll keep you safe." She let her eyelids fall closed, and drifted in that dozy, not-quite-asleep state. While she continued to shiver, Jake checked her fingers, then her toes, exposing only what he needed to before tucking the blankets back around her. "I don't see any sign of frostbite. That's a good thing."

"I-I'm st-st-ill c-cold." She shivered so hard, she worried her teeth would crack. It kept getting worse, not better.

"You'll get warm soon. If you're freezing and stop shivering, that's when we worry." Jake gently eased her off his lap, tucking the blankets in around her and called to both dogs. "Chewie, Solo, come." He directed the dogs to jump onto the couch, one on each side of her. "They'll help keep you warm until I get back."

Their weight and warmth beat any weighted, heated blanket, although she missed having Jake's bare skin against hers. She opened her eyes and, for a moment, enjoyed the view as Jake walked naked into the kitchen. He set the kettle on to heat before he disappeared into the bedroom. She'd always considered herself a sucker for broad shoulders, but she might amend that to include a muscled backside. Jake was nice to look at.

Soon, he reappeared covered up in sweatpants, wool socks and a hoodie, but she couldn't blame him. The cabin felt cold, though it was warming. She exhaled, no vapor this time.

Jake added another log to the fire, stoking it. The flames roared up for a moment before settling back down. He pushed the couch back from the hearth a few inches for room to kneel. He chuckled. "Not much room on the couch at the moment." Reaching under the blankets, he took her foot in his hands and put a wool sock on it, then layered another one on top. He did the same with her other foot.

Once both her feet were tucked back under the blankets, he headed into the kitchen and came back with mugs of steaming liquid. He placed them on the coffee table before calling the dogs. "Chewie, Solo, come." He settled them on their beds near the fire again and went back into the kitchen once more, returning with large rubber chew toys.

"I've stuffed them with peanut butter and dog treats. They deserve them." Jake gave each dog a chew toy. "They'll both be okay," he told her, glancing over his shoulder as he went to the fireplace. He added another log, then dropped beside her on the couch, pulling her back onto his lap. He handed her one of the mugs from the coffee table, helping her get her hands free to hold the mug, but not exposing the rest of her. "It's hot chocolate. Not too hot, but it will help warm you up inside. When you're finished, I can make you a hotter one." He picked up his own mug, snugged the blankets in around them again, and relaxed with her.

She couldn't move, but Jake had been everywhere, taking care of everything. All because she nearly killed them all in the middle of the frozen lake. Everything she'd ever wanted had been within reach when she'd fallen asleep. Had she deluded herself because of the fun evening and fantastic sex? Could the curse become too much for Jake before they had a chance to break it—if they even could? Jake hadn't said anything about loving her. No one had ever stuck with her before, so why would Jake be any different? Everything he'd done told her she shouldn't doubt his staying power, but what if dealing with the curse became too much for him?

Pushing the thoughts from her mind for now, she sipped her chocolate and snuggled into Jake. She was sure her curse would remind her of reality before too long.

"HOLD IT UP A BIT HIGHER," Jake said, snapping another photo of Mae with her finished LEGO set. Her smile was one of the biggest he'd ever seen. He wanted to put that smile on her face every day. He took a couple more shots, then lowered his phone. "I think that's good."

Mae gave him a mock scowl. "Really, you think the two hundred pictures you took will be enough?"

"Funny woman." He watched her place her building set inside the box he'd scrounged for her, then hooked an arm around her waist and hauled her onto his lap.

"Thank you for getting that for me," she whispered. He knew her well enough now to know she whispered when she worried she was about to jinx something or her emotions were running high. He'd never believed in jinxes, and still didn't—even after learning that curses were real—and he hoped that one day, between him and her cousins, gifts would become more common.

Jake wrapped his arms around her as they sat in comfortable silence watching the fire. All day, he'd kept the fire high, not letting it die down once. Once Mae was warm, they slept on the couch for several hours, then he'd gone outside to chop more wood and haul it inside to dry.

Overall, it had been a lazy day, one they both needed. They'd let the dogs out several times, but even they hadn't wanted to venture far from the cabin. In the late afternoon, after another nap, he pulled out the family laptop and queued up a comedy. It was the light distraction they both needed.

After they cooked dinner together, she finished her building set and now they were winding down. When she hadn't said anything for several minutes, he looked down to see her eyes were closed. He shifted her easily and stretched out on the couch, keeping her tucked against him. He positioned a pillow under his head and Mae's head on his arm, then pulled several blankets around them.

"Jake?" Mae asked, sounding barely awake.

"Shhhh. Go to sleep. I was just getting us comfortable."

"You don't want to go to the bedroom?"

"No, let's stay by the fire where it's warm."

"Okay."

He was sure she'd fall back asleep, but instead she began telling him about some of her first days with Solo. She'd already told several of the stories, but he didn't say anything. He wanted to hold her and listen to her happy memories. She was telling him about the time Solo started gnawing on her coffee table when she stopped talking.

Figuring she'd fallen asleep, he tucked the blankets higher around her neck and noticed her eyes were open. "Mae? Mae, can you hear me?"

He eased her flat on the couch and hovered over her,

running his hand along her hair. "Mae, wake up, sweetheart." He let out a slow breath, trying not to panic. Seeing her with her eyes open but unresponsive, was scarier than knowing she was in a nightmare.

"Mae!" he raised his voice.

"Jake?" She looked around, then closed her eyes. "I zoned out, didn't I?"

"Yes. Has that happened before?"

"A couple of times, I think, but it's hard to tell if I'm lying on the couch, because it feels like I just fell asleep for a few minutes."

Every protective instinct in Jake kicked into overdrive. "I don't think you should be living on your own anymore, Mae. It's not safe. You need someone to watch out for you. You need to break the curse."

She sat up, forcing him to do the same. "Really? Oh gee, Jake, I didn't know that."

He raked a hand through his hair. "You know what I mean."

"No, maybe I don't. You think I can just fall in love and everything will be hunky dory? Is it that easy? What about you, Jake? Are you going to fall in love with me, or do you just want to fix me?"

"I care about you, Mae."

"I care about you too, Jake, but I can't just break the curse. You know that. And sometimes it feels like that's all you care about."

"What?!" Jake jumped up and fed another log to a fire that didn't need it. He took a moment to calm down and turned to face Mae. "How can you say that? Haven't I shown you how much I care about you? That we have a lot in common? You mean so much more to me than just the curse."

Mae hung her head for a moment, then patted the cushion beside her. "Sorry. You're right. I do know that. But I also know that you're protective and it often feels like you're trying to fix me. Like this morning, you did everything and I just sat here like a lump."

Jake settled on the couch beside her and pulled the blankets up over both of them, not just her, showing he was in this with her. "Anyone would have done the same to keep it from getting worse. If our positions had been reversed, you would have done the same thing. As for you sitting like a lump…" He braced his back against the couch arm so he could see her face and raised his eyebrows. "You were still thawing."

She snorted and swatted his stomach. "Okay, after that."

"Someone doesn't come back from hypothermia in a few minutes, Mae. It takes a toll on your body. You'll be tired for several days."

"I get that, but besides that, it always feels like you're trying to fix me. I never know if you want to be with me just because I'm me. I don't even know if you're the right person for me yet. I care about you, but…"

She let the words hang and Jake tried not to take them personally, but he did. Her words hurt. Neither of them could force love, but he cared about her deeply and loved being with her.

He opened his arms and waited to see what she would do, trying not to hold his breath. She only hesitated for a second before she moved back into his arms, her back to his front. Once more, he maneuvered them, flipping them onto their sides and pulled the blankets up around them.

"I know I can be overprotective, but it's not just with you," he said. He needed her to understand something that had shaped his entire life. "I'm protective with my family and friends too. Just ask Blake. He'll tell you some of the things I've said. Okay… maybe don't ask him." He huffed out a laugh.

She squeezed the forearm he had wrapped around her. "Oh, no. Now you know I have to."

"Well, you'll know I'm not just that way with you."

"Were you so protective before the attack on Chelsea?"

"I think I had to have been—at least a little—but not like I am now. But it wasn't only Chelsea's assault that shaped me." He paused. Earlier that morning, seeing Mae standing in the middle of the ice was the first time he'd been that scared since finding Chelsea's lifeless body in her bed.

"Almost a year after Howell assaulted Chelsea, we all thought she was getting better, back to her normal self. By that time, the other girl Howell assaulted had come forward, and his wife. Chelsea was seeing a counselor and had lots of support. She'd gone back to school too. I had been so protective of her that my parents finally told me to lay off. I'd started university and was working at Akerman's, so I was really busy.

"I usually arrived home about dinner time, but one day I came home early because a professor canceled a class. I had texted Chelsea to see if she wanted to go out for coffee and study together. She hadn't answered, but I was trying not to freak out when that happened. Right after her assault, if she didn't answer within five minutes, I thought I was going to lose my mind." He could still remember walking up to Chelsea's door and knocking. He doubted he'd ever forget the details of that afternoon.

"When I went to her room, the door was closed, but it usually was. I knocked and then called her name. When she didn't answer, I tried the knob. It turned, but the door barely budged. She'd pushed her dresser up against the door. I had to kick in the door, snapping one hinge, then muscling the dresser aside. Chelsea lay on the bed, but she looked dead. Her skin was so pale. She has pale skin to begin with, but I'd never seen her that color. I thought she was dead."

He took in a slow breath, hating every time he relived the event, but he knew Mae needed to know what had shaped him. "I called 911 and before they arrived, I managed to find her pulse. For a while, things were touch and go. Telling my parents was almost harder than seeing Chelsea lying there. They thought they had failed her just as much as I did. Obviously, I made it to Chelsea in time, but it was probably a couple of years after that before I could relax at all if I didn't know where she was or what she was doing."

Mae hugged his arm to her chest. "I'm sorry you all had to go through that."

"Chelsea is doing great now… well, you know that. I've told you all about her life, but I wanted you to know because that's why my inner caveman sometimes gets out of control."

"Sometimes?" Mae teased.

"Yes, only sometimes," he laughed. "I'm not admitting to anything else."

"Okay. Sometimes. But… Jake, you can't fix me. And you have to let me make my own decisions and mistakes, just like Chelsea did."

"I know. You'll have to remind me sometimes."

"Is that *sometimes* like with your inner caveman?" she asked, amused.

"Sure, let's go with that." Jake would try to tone it down, but knowing Mae might sleepwalk into danger or zone out like tonight wouldn't make it easy.

Mae wandered slowly down a dimly lit hallway of an old house. With each step, the hall lengthened. Déjà vu washed over her. She'd been in here before, but when, she couldn't place.

Mae stopped and closed her eyes, remembering what she'd seen before. Framed portraits of her ancestors, one after the other, lined up like soldiers at inspection. Their expressions dour, as if a painter had held them too long, wringing out any joy.

Taking a deep breath, Mae opened her eyes and faced one wall.

Her breath caught in her throat.

Mirrors had replaced the portraits. All different sizes covered the wall, the wood paneling visible only in small slivers between them.

She stepped up to one mirror. Her reflection stared back at her.

Something wasn't right. Mae tilted her head, but her reflection didn't do the same. Looking at the mirror above it, she forced a deep frown, but once more, her reflection didn't change.

Each time she stared into a different mirror, the image staring back stayed fixed, as if time seized her reflection. Stopping at a *large mirror, she studied it, looking for a clue as to what the images of herself were trying to tell her.*

It was her—and not. In the large mirror she looked a year or two younger.

She stepped back and scanned over a dozen different mirrors. She was in each one, but not always alone. When she was, something was different in each. In some of them she looked angry or glassy-eyed, and in another she cried. Not a gentle cry, not soft tears rolling down her cheek. No, red blotches mottled her face and neck, her eyes puffy and swollen, and her mouth open on a sob.

Moving further down the hall, she stopped at a cracked mirror. A spiderweb of cracks branched out from the middle. The next mirror was cracked as well. Several long breaks marred its surface from one side to the other.

The one above splintered only across her right cheek. The cracks didn't seem right. Not that she'd seen many broken mirrors. After several minutes studying the different cracks, she gasped, realizing...

The mirror wasn't cracked.

The skin's reflection was.

She turned to look at the other two cracked mirrors. The glass of the one closest to her quivered, like a pebble disturbing still water.

A loud snap echoed down the hall as the mirror solidified and exploded. Shards of glass detonated out from the wall at lightning speed.

Mae flung her arms up as she spun away from the wall. Small pieces of glass stung her skin as the rest fell to the floor around her.

She risked another glance, desperate to know why her image was reflected back at her, and she faced the wall. A mirror she hadn't noticed at first, caught her eye. In it, she held hands with a man, his face blurred and unrecognizable, as the mirror shimmered in the low light.

Leery it might explode, Mae blocked her face with her arms, peering out between them. As she approached the mirror, the reflection faded until it was nothing but a gray haze. "No," she whispered when a loss settled in her chest.

Mae spun around to look at the wall behind her. More mirrors covered its surface, but none of them contained her image. They held reflections similar to the portraits that had previously hung on the walls.

As she stepped closer to the wall, cracks spidered in some of the mirrors. One man aged rapidly and became a pile of dust, his ashes falling to the bottom of the mirror. In another a woman faded to nothing, like Mae had in the one with the man holding her hand.

Feelings of loneliness, despair, and death became heavy in the air. Mae felt them as if they lived within her, threatening to choke her. One by one, the mirrors continued to crack and the images bled out or crumbled to dust. As much as she tried to look away, something deep in her soul kept her gaze glued on the reflections.

Soft voices threaded through the ache, whispering to her. "Love is an illusion, fragile and fleeting," the voices told her. As the last image disappeared, Mae spun back to the other wall.

She watched her last image dissolve to ash.

"No!" she screamed as she reached for the mirror.

"Mae, wake up! It's a nightmare. Mae, you're safe." She heard the words from a distance and then closer as her mind pulled her from the dream. Warm wetness slicked her hand.

Mae opened her eyes, the lamp on the bedside table casting a dim glow in the room. Jake held her in his arms, his back to the headboard as he rocked her gently. Solo let out a low whine, licking her hand as he crowded against her and Jake. "I'm awake."

"Thank god. I didn't think I was going to be able to wake you."

"I'm okay."

"No, Mae, you're not. You're bleeding." He moved her off his lap, and Solo inched closer when Jake went into the bathroom.

She remembered the mirrors breaking and throwing her arms up to protect her face. Pieces of glass had stung her arms. "It was just a dream."

Jake sat on the bed and unzipped a first aid kit. "I'd call it a nightmare. Whatever is happening while you sleep is now affecting you in the waking world."

She bent her arm to see the backside. Cuts covered her skin like latticework, blood oozing from the small wounds. As if seeing blood flipped a switch, she sucked in her breath as she finally felt the sting from the numerous slices.

Then starting with the slice closest to her wrist, Jake gently cleaned it with a cloth, put a small dab of antibiotic cream on it, then a bandage. He'd finished doctoring three cuts before he spoke, his voice not quite steady. "I didn't think I was ever going to get you to wake up."

"You said that already." Mae sucked a breath as Jake cleaned another wound, this one deeper and longer.

"Twenty minutes."

"What?"

His hand stilled as he met her gaze. "It took me twenty minutes to wake you up. I kept saying your name. Then I pulled you onto my lap and rubbed your arms, trying to get through to you. When the cuts began to appear, I shouted your name and began rocking you, hoping—" He shuddered a breath. "The dogs panicked too. I didn't know how to wake you."

She put her hand on his, not knowing what else to do. "I'm sorry."

"You didn't cause this. I just wish…" He shook his head and wrapped his hand around the back of her neck, pulling her to him. She could feel the desperation in his kiss as if he was trying to give her something neither of them were ready for yet.

He pressed his forehead to hers, such an intimate gesture, she'd never thought about it before. They stayed like that for several minutes, breathing each other in.

"Mae, I'd like to come and stay with you for a while."

Her first instinct was to refuse. She was an independent adult and had been living on her own for a long time, but when she saw the sorrow in Jake's eyes, she didn't want to say no. "You're not trying to fix me, are you?"

"No. You don't need fixing. Breaking really," he said, giving her a small smile. "Well, the curse needs breaking. I care about you a lot and because the curse is manifesting in real life, I just want to make sure you're safe. If my staying at your place bothers you, you can ask one of your cousins to come stay with you."

She didn't need to think about it. As much as she wanted to get to know her cousins, having them wake her from sleepwalking in the middle of the night wasn't the way.

"Okay," she said softly. "For safety. No fixing and no caveman antics."

Jake held up three fingers. "Scout's honor."

She tilted her head, eyeing him. "Were you really a scout?"

"Sure." He moved the first aid supplies to the floor, and lay down, pulling her into his arms, her back to his front.

"Sure? That didn't sound very confident." She felt more than heard him chuckle, against her back.

"Blake and I joined scouts together. We were ten and loved to get into trouble."

"Oh, say it isn't so."

"Hey." He squeezed her tight. "Anyway, we thought we were the bee's knees, as my Grandma used to say. The scout leader didn't agree. We lasted one month before he asked us to find another hobby."

"Tell me," she encouraged. She didn't know what was to come, but for the moment, as long as she forgot about the cuts and sleepwalking on ice, she was having the best time of her life. She fell asleep with Jake's voice in her ear.

14

Wednesday, February 19

With a coffee cup in each hand, Jake elbowed open the door to Chrys's room. Mae hadn't moved from her spot by her mom. They'd spent almost every moment together for the last five days but observing her made it clear the curse was wearing her down, and not just mentally.

Her cheeks looked hollower, her clothes looser than last Friday at the cabin. Her eyes weren't quite as bright and he'd hardly heard her laugh in days.

Every day they worked quietly in her apartment, took the dogs for walks and cooked meals together. And each night he fought to wake her from a nightmare. He likely looked hollow too; he'd slept little, worried she wouldn't wake up and something would happen to her.

One night over dinner, she finally admitted how worried she was and confessed to sleepwalking in her apartment. She told him about waking up on the balcony and about boiling a pot dry. Right then, over a plate of pasta, he almost confessed his love for her. It wouldn't have been much of a stretch because he cared deeply about her. The possibility of confusing his protectiveness for love was the only thing that stopped him. If he confessed his love and she didn't return it he would be devastated, but he would live. If they both confessed their love and the curse didn't break, Mae might give up all hope of ever breaking it.

Her mom had lived with her curse for years, but from what Jake had seen, she wasn't in any physical danger. Mae's curse was hell-bent on killing her. More than her nightmares, that's what truly kept him awake. He had no way to know how the curse would progress or what kind of physical threat it posed.

"Hey," Mae whispered, pulling him back to the present.

Walking over to her, he handed her a coffee and brushed a kiss to her mouth.

"Thanks."

Jake settled into the chair beside her. Since discovering Chrys was alive, Mae and her cousins visited Chrys regularly to make sure she knew she wasn't alone. The week before, Blake ordered six stacking chairs so he wouldn't have to stand when he came with Paige. They never knew how long the wait for Chrys to wake up could be.

Growing up with Blake, Jake had witnessed his friend's impatient but thoughtful streak and hadn't been surprised when Blake told them he'd ordered the chairs. Not so with Mae. She'd looked at the chairs and wondered aloud if the staff had brought them in. When Jake told her it was Blake's idea, her eyes had welled with tears before she turned her back on him.

Jake refused to take kind gestures for granted—always wanting to acknowledge them—but they were still commonplace in his world. Having a family, kind gestures or not, was new to Mae. He was happy that Mae finally had some people who cared about her, but he wanted more for her. He wanted to introduce her to his family, and be a part of her family, not just through his close-knit ties with her cousins.

He took a sip of his coffee to steady himself. Neither of them was ready for that kind of talk without questioning the motives behind it. "Any change?"

"No. I think we were lucky that she came out of a trance right after we arrived. The last time I was here I had to wait three hours for her to open her eyes."

"We can wait. There's no rush. The dogs will be alright at your apartment for a few more hours."

Mae held her coffee cup in one hand and her mom's hand in the other, speaking without looking at him. "I'm sorry for saying you're *just* a friend. It seemed the easiest explanation since we didn't have much time."

"It's alright." When Chrys had come out of her trance, she'd been so pleased to see Mae. Then she'd glanced at him over her daughter's shoulder. Jake didn't think Chrys remembered him from when he'd come with Blake, but seeing him with her daughter clearly impressed her. Chrys asked for an introduction, causing Mae to blush and then stumble over her words. She'd finally told her mom that he was *just* a friend.

Jake couldn't guarantee that he would have said anything different if their positions had been reversed. They hadn't defined their relationship beyond friendship. To him it felt like more, and he hoped it did to Mae too, but knowing it and saying it to a loved one were two different things.

They finished their coffees, both lost in their own thoughts. Silence between them was never uncomfortable. Jake appreciated that Mae was a great conversationalist, but that she also didn't feel compelled to talk for the sake of talking.

When their cups were empty, Jake went in search of a garbage bin and stopped in the bathroom on the way back.

He returned to the room in time to hear Chrys say, "I love you, Maeve."

"I love you too, Mom."

Jake stayed by the door, not wanting to interrupt the precious few minutes the two women would have together.

"What day is it?" Chrys asked.

"February nineteenth."

Jake heard Chrys suck in a small breath. "Oh, no honey. Three months since your birthday. You never said how the curse is affecting you."

"It's okay, mom. I only get dreams."

"Don't try to protect me, honey. There is no *just* with the curse. You need to grab onto your man and love him."

"It's not that easy."

"I know, but you have to try. Don't end up like me."

"We're going to find a way to break the curse for you, Mom. I don't know how but..." Mae's voice trailed off and Jake knew the curse had sucked Chrys under again.

He walked over to Mae and pulled her up into his arms, holding her tight. She didn't make a sound but he felt her tears soak his shirt.

When Mae finally pulled back, she turned and grabbed a tissue from the box nearby. "I'm ready to go." She kissed her mom's forehead. "I'll be back."

Jake stacked the folding chairs against the wall to keep them out of the way and squeezed Chrys's hand. He caught up with Mae in the hallway. Silently, he took her hand as they walked to his truck, letting her process her thoughts.

Mae didn't speak until they'd been on the highway for several minutes. "This morning when we talked about grabbing an early dinner, it had seemed like a good idea, but now I'd rather go home, if that's okay."

Keeping one hand on the steering wheel, Jake reached the other back for the bag he'd stowed in the truck before they left. "I'm sure you're tired. Why don't you curl up and catch a nap," he suggested as he passed her the bag.

She peeked in the bag, then leaned over as far as her seat belt would allow, giving him a one-armed hug. "I wondered why you took the blanket and pillow from the spare room. Figured maybe you'd flake out in the truck while I was with my mom."

"I wouldn't have left you." Keeping his eyes on the road, he masked his expression, not wanting her to see how her words had hurt. Never would he be so selfish to let her sit alone waiting for her mom to wake up while he lazed in his truck. For over a month they'd talked almost every day, getting to know each other. If that hadn't been enough for her to see the kind of the man he was, she should have when they'd made love. Or when he talked about his family.

Taking a quick glance at her, he saw her curled up against the passenger door. With the pillow squashed against her cheek and her body half-buried by the blanket, she looked small and fragile. He knew she wasn't. She'd had no choice but to grow up tough and independent but looks could be deceiving.

Mae let the world see only what she wanted them to see. The strong, resourceful woman she'd grown into, not the child inside of her that had been abandoned too many times to count. When Mae said things that pricked at his ego, he had to remember the abandoned child in her. Remind himself that she wasn't used to people looking out for anyone but themselves.

Her earlier words proved she still didn't fully trust him. He would have to make sure he showed her constantly, in small ways, how much he thought of her. Hopefully, she would eventually believe his actions.

About twenty minutes from Mae's place, lost in thoughts of how to show her he cared, she thrashed against the window. He flicked on the childproof door locks, terrified she could try to sleepwalk and open the truck door.

"Mae! Wake up!" he barked at the same time he checked his mirrors and slowed down to pull off the highway. Waking her, was becoming harder and harder. He didn't want to risk her hurting herself as he drove.

The road's shoulder was wide, providing plenty of space between his truck and the passing traffic. Flicking on his hazard lights, he unbuckled his seat belt, then reached over and undid Mae's to pull her into his arms.

He'd bought the half-ton truck for his job, but now he was thankful for the roomy cab and the large gas tank because he kept it running with the heater on. Judging by Mae's dreams from the last week, they could be there for a while.

MAE BALANCED on an old wooden bridge. A fast-moving river below her flashed in and out of view between the spaces of the weathered planks. Faded and splintered, the boards wobbled as she inched forward.

Reaching out to steady herself, she grasped onto the bridge's iron braces. Pieces flaked off in her hand. Once on firmer footing, she brushed off the iron flakes and took another step forward.

Voices from below called up to her. Without looking, she knew who they belonged to—her ancestors. The same as the portraits she'd seen in the hallway of the old house. And like with the voices in the house, feelings of loneliness, despair, and death hung heavy in the air. Like a blanket of fog blocking her path. Over and over, the voices told her to give up. To join them in the river below. She would never win.

Should she listen to them? Join them? She was so tired of the sorrow that swamped her night after night. The voices swelled. They spoke of failed promises and love.

"Mae!"

Hearing her name, as if from a great distance, Mae spun around, searching for the source. Seeing nothing, she edged forward, peering into the fog. The bridge creaked beneath her feet and the planks swayed. She flung her arm out, and caught the flaking iron brace again, still moving.

She kept a white-knuckled grip as her arm stretched back, then lunged for the next brace.

"Mae!"

When the voice called her name again, she knew with certainty that it wasn't coming from far below her. She pressed on, placing each step carefully as the path became treacherous. Planks sheared away, falling into the rushing water below.

Another step and the fog cleared. In the distance, she could see Jake waiting for her on the other end of the bridge.

He called out again. Warmth engulfed her at the sight of him waiting.

She longed to hurry toward him, but the voices calling to her from below, warning of broken promises and love, felt heavy. The warning weighed on her stops, threatening to drag her down to the rushing river where she'd be swept away.

Mae heard the regret and desperation in the voices below, warning her not to trust Jake. His love would eventually wear and fall apart as surely as the old bridge.

"Stay there. I'll come to you!" Jake yelled.

Mae felt warmth swell in her chest, feeling Jake's love as he took a step onto the bridge. She could trust that he would never abandon her. He took another step.

Then gaped as the bridge gave way beneath him and he fell to the raging river below.

Flinging her arms into the void where the bridge had been, she screamed his name, trying to pull him back.

Mae woke with a start, her eyes wide.

"Oh, thank fuck!" Jake crushed her to his chest. Just as quickly, he gently grasped her upper arms and pulled her away from him. "Are you hurt anywhere?"

"Uh. I don't think so." She wasn't sure. Trying to rid her mind of Jake's death, she slid off his lap onto the passenger seat. She realized they were on the highway shoulder in his truck. "What happened?"

Jake ran a shaky hand through his hair. "You began to thrash in your sleep. I pulled over so I could hold you."

She looked around, pulse racing. "The truck's running. We haven't been here long, right?"

"Let's get you home." Jake reached behind him for his seat belt and snapped it into place. Mae did the same with her own as he turned off the hazard lights and checked his mirrors before pulling out onto the highway. "We were here about forty minutes, sweetheart. I kept the truck on so we wouldn't get cold."

"Oh." Neither of them spoke as he drove to her place. As hard as she tried, she couldn't shake the image of Jake falling to his death. The words from her ancestors stayed with her too. They warned her never to trust. That love wouldn't last. She turned the warnings over and over in her mind. In her dream Jake fell, not her. She reasoned that if the bridge had really collapsed, she would have fallen too. But dreams don't owe logic. Jake had died —maybe she was the problem. If she let herself love him, could the curse kill him? Was she willing to take that risk?

As soon as the question entered her mind, she knew the answer. No, she wouldn't risk him. Mae cared for him so deeply, she might be starting to love him. That wouldn't do. Somehow, she had to find a way to turn it off. To never love Jake.

By the time they reached home, her heart ached. Soon it would disintegrate like the bridge in her dream. She'd have nothing but a pile of rubble.

In a daze, she sat frozen in the truck until Jake opened her door. He lifted her, cradled her to his chest, and shut the door with his hip. His heart beat against her ear and she clung to the steady rhythm, knowing she wouldn't have it much longer.

He handed her the spare key she'd given him when he went grocery shopping the other day; she leaned in and unlocked the door. Inside her apartment, he eased her to her feet, his hands lingering on her for a moment with the same type of desperation she wanted to cling to him with. The moment broke when the dogs trotted over.

She did her best to shake the sense of hopelessness that clung to her like she wanted to cling to Jake and pretend that life was good. When they took the dogs for a walk, they kept to safe topics—tomorrow's work tasks and dinner plans.

Once home, they slipped into the routine they'd adopted so quickly over the last few days. Jake toweled the dogs dry and filled their bowls before setting the table, while Mae whipped up a quick fettuccini Alfredo.

She served it up on two plates and sat at the table while Jake opened a bottle of wine.

He stood beside her and poured. "Will you tell me what your dream was about this afternoon?"

His question took her by surprise. It shouldn't have since she told him about each dream she'd had when they'd been together and even some when they hadn't. He poured his own wine and sat across from her, waiting.

"The same as always. Voices of my ancestors warning me

that love always fails." It wasn't a lie—just not the whole truth. She could never tell him that she saw his death. If he didn't freak out because of his protective nature, worried that she'd blame herself, he would dismiss it because it was only a dream. She did blame herself and it wasn't just a dream; it was a curse. They'd already seen that it could control her. Who was to say the curse wouldn't take Jake too? Maybe not directly, but since things in her dream had manifested in reality, she could hurt him in her sleep without even knowing. Her apartment could have gone up in flames because of her, or Solo could have drowned because he followed her onto the lake. She couldn't rule out that she could hurt Jake, or even get him killed, because of something she did in her sleep.

"You've been quiet. Won't talking it through help?"

Mae took a bite of her pasta, barely tasting it, buying herself a moment. Once she swallowed, she took a drink of her wine, still not knowing what to say. Finally, she met Jake's gaze. "No, they're all the same. I don't want to talk about it."

He nodded, hurt flickering in his eyes that she wouldn't let him help. How could she when letting him help and getting closer to him over the last couple of months could end up killing him?

Later that night when Jake held her in bed, she rolled on her side to face him. She ran her fingers lightly along his beard, soaking in everything about him. Needing his image, his scent, and the feel of him forever in her mind to call upon when the loneliness became too much.

"I feel you pulling away," he said softly.

"I'm tired. Today was a lot." She kissed his lips lightly and rolled over so he would spoon her and she'd feel safe for one more night. At least until another dream smothered her in despair.

15

Friday, February 21

A ball of paper hit Jake in the chest. He tore his gaze from his phone and looked over at Blake. "What?"

"I asked you a question. Twice. You've had your head stuck in— Never mind. We can talk about it next week." Blake wrapped up their weekly Friday afternoon meeting, and even though the other executives were like family, they didn't linger on Fridays, giving the brothers time to catch up.

Blake and his brothers had always treated Jake like one of them. He traded stories and jabs just like they did, and when Blake's curse hit, Jake did his best to be there every step of the way, supporting however he could. Now, it was Jake's turn to lean on them.

"You ready to talk?" Blake asked, as if reading his mind.

"I didn't expect you yesterday," Cade said. At Jake's raised eyebrow, Cade continued. "I thought you were working from Mae's and would call in from there."

"I thought I would too." Thursday morning, he'd had a job-site meeting he couldn't miss, but he planned to drive back to Mae's afterward. That was before she told him not to, that she needed some time alone. He argued with her, saying that she shouldn't be alone because of the sleepwalking. Or she could wake up from a dream injured.

She'd refused to budge, telling him she needed time to process everything that was happening between them, as well as the dreams. She said she'd lock her bedroom door and push the dresser in front of it so she couldn't easily get out if sleepwalking.

That hadn't made sense when he could have just stayed, but she wouldn't relent and had given him no choice but to leave. He'd done his best not to panic until she didn't answer his calls the night before. He'd called Chewie, grabbed his keys and was backing out of his garage when a text came in from Mae saying she was fine. All day, he'd second-guessed himself, wondering if he should have gone anyway.

Chewie lumbered up from his spot on the floor and rested his head in Jake's lap. Jake ran his fingers through the St. Bernard's long coat and blew out a frustrated breath. "Mae's curse isn't only affecting her dreams anymore." He quickly recapped the events from the cabin—the sleepwalking on the ice, and the cut from her dream that appeared in the real world. "I convinced her to let me stay at her place for a few days. The dreams are bad enough, but she's zoning out while she's awake too. On Wednesday, I drove her to visit her mom."

Blake frowned. "You're worried the curse could hit her while she's driving. Like me."

"Yes, and more. Except for the last one with that ghost, your episodes didn't physically harm you. What if she gets hurt worse?"

"Unless she falls in love and someone returns her love, there's nothing you can do," Cade said.

"Speaking of," Blake chimed in, "do you love her?"

"I'm beginning to think so." Jake met Blake's gaze, knowing his best friend would understand. "But what if it's not quite love yet and just my protective instincts on overdrive? What if my worry for her is overshadowing my true feelings?"

"When you truly love someone it's natural to worry. And what if it is love? Mae isn't Chelsea. You've never seen any signs that she might attempt suicide, but I know that's where your thoughts go when someone withdraws."

Jake nudged Chewie back and stood. He needed to move, even just a few steps. "I know. But she's dealing with depressing shit and she is withdrawing." Whether Mae would want to end her life, Jake couldn't say. She was a secure, independent adult, while Chelsea hadn't been. But logic didn't stop him from picturing Mae lying on her bed, looking lifeless, the way he'd found his sister.

"Then you shouldn't have left her alone," Gage spit out.

Jake leveled his stare at Gage on the monitor. "I didn't choose that. She's pulling away from me. If I push too much, she could bolt." If anyone should understand withdrawal, it's Gage.

A moment later, Gage gave a barely perceptible nod. "But…" he leaned forward, his image filling the screen. "The curse isn't a surprise anymore. You don't leave someone cursed alone when things escalate. Full stop. No argument."

This time Jake nodded, then paced a few feet back and forth. "On the way back from visiting her mom, Mae fell asleep and had another nightmare. I pulled over and held her. It took me about forty minutes to wake her up that time. She wouldn't tell me what the dream was about. All she said was that it was the same as always—your ancestors warning her that love always fails. But it wasn't just that. Something else happened in that dream. I know it."

"How?" Cade asked.

"Right after, Mae started pulling away from me. We went back to her place, but she stayed quiet. Then she told me not to come back from the job site because she needed time alone. We'd spent several days together working and she didn't need time alone. Not until she had that dream in the truck."

"Have you talked to her?" Dane asked.

Jake shook his head. "No, and that's the thing. In the last five weeks, we've talked every night but one. Until last night. Last night she wouldn't answer my calls. Finally, she texted to say she was alright. Otherwise, I would have driven to her place."

"Text me her address," Gage said. "Since I'm in the same city, it would make sense I decided to drop by to get to know her better."

Jake picked up his phone and sent off Mae's address and phone number.

"Gage," Blake said, getting his brother's attention. "If Mae asks, tell her I gave them to you, since you live so close."

Gage nodded. "Will do. I've got a few things to finish up, then I'll head to her place. Later." Gage ended the call; the screen blinked to black.

Cade stood. "Let us know if you need any help." Dane and Ford agreed, then all three left.

"You can't force her," Blake said. "Even when I thought I was in love with Paige, and likely had been all the years we were apart, I couldn't ignore the curse. It was relentless. If the curse keeps bombarding her with negative messages about love like I was, she's going to have trouble listening to her own feelings. And you're not helping."

"Me? You think I'm being too protective again?"

"No. You're being an idiot. You don't have voices in your

head and you can't even admit that you love her. How the hell do you expect Mae to admit it?"

Jake felt Chewie nudge his leg in reassurance. "What if I'm wrong?"

"What if you're right and you wait too long?"

"You're right."

Blake grinned. "Of course."

Jake walked by Blake, bumping into his shoulder hard enough to knock him into the wall. They'd always been there for each other to speak the truth, even when they might not have wanted to hear it, but that didn't mean they couldn't be boys having fun. They were like brothers, after all.

"Hey," Blake said with mock indignation.

They left the boardroom together, heading to their offices with Chewie leading the way.

Jake stopped by Blake's office. "You heading home?"

"As soon as I shut everything down. You?"

"I'm going to head to the cabin so I'll only be about an hour from Mae's, in case Gage calls."

"You sure that's a good idea? You could miss his call—reception out there can be spotty."

Jake had already weighed the pros and cons, but being closer to Mae won. "I'll check in with Gage before I pull off the highway, and if he leaves a message, I'll still get a notification."

"Let me know if you need anything."

Jake nodded. He'd loaded his truck with supplies before work, so a few minutes later he and Chewie hit the road. His protective instincts were screaming at him to head to Mae's. He shoved them down and concentrated on driving as light snow drifted down.

THE DAY HAD BEEN brutal and was crashing toward the worst possible ending. Knowing Jake would do anything to save her, even claim he loved her when he might not, she hadn't answered a single one of his calls. The night before, she'd finally given in and texted him to say she was alright. A physical ache knotted her stomach when she shut off her phone to prevent her from reaching out to Jake in a moment of weakness. She refused to put him in danger, no matter how slim the chance.

The morning started off with her rocketing awake and gasping for air. Solo had been frantic, licking her face and whining. She spent time reassuring him that she was alright, but he'd shadowed her all day. He was probably still traumatized from their time at the cabin. The ache in her gut worsened with what she was doing to her dog. One more soul she was endangering.

Her condition was only going to get worse. As much as she didn't want to give up Solo, keeping him with her was selfish. More than a dozen times during the day, she mentally weighed all the pros and cons of giving someone else guardianship of Solo. By late afternoon, mentally and physically exhausted, she fell asleep on the couch. When she woke, Solo lay on top of her, a soft growl rumbling from his chest.

That moment decided it for her. Her dog's stress had been enough to convince her she had to do something. But if it hadn't been, seeing her image in the mirror would have clinched it.

After gently reassuring Solo for several minutes, she'd gone into the bathroom before taking him for a walk. She'd dreaded looking in mirrors since the weekend, but it was difficult to avoid the one in her bathroom unless she wanted to fumble around with her eyes closed. The mirror spanned the counter's length and climbed nearly to the ceiling.

She used the toilet, turned on the taps, and lathered soap in her hands when she finally looked up. She knew why Solo had been growling. Blood dripped down her face from a long cut on her right cheek. It started under the outside corner of her eye and ran down to the side of her lip. For several long seconds she couldn't take her eyes off her cheek. Blood seeped down her cheek, landing in the sink like a macabre crimson Rorschach test.

The slice through her skin represented how the curse was slicing through her life, destroying one piece of happiness at a time. She didn't have a chance for love with Jake and now she was going to lose Solo too. Next would be her freedom.

She examined the cut. It didn't look deep enough to need stitches, but no one would mistake it for a simple scratch. The only saving grace was its clean edge, as if a sharp blade had made it. And like with the cuts on her arm from the cabin, it hadn't hurt until she'd seen it.

Now, a low throb pulsed in her cheek. She picked up one of the navy-blue hand towels she kept on a short stand on the counter and pressed it to her cheek. She hissed but pressed harder to stop the bleeding.

Thinking back on her dream, she remembered a church. *She held a bouquet of blood-red roses. Her heart swelled with joy when she'd looked at herself in the mirror. She wore a plain, sleeveless white wedding gown with a square neck. The way it flowed down her body made her feel beautiful. Her veil was soft tulle, woven with pearls. Short in the front to cover her face but flowing down her back to trail behind her as she walked.*

In the next moment she stood in front of her groom, his face a blur in her mind. She tilted her face up to his when he reached for her veil. As his fingers lifted the edge of the tulle and he whispered, "For better or worse," the lace edge turned to glass and brushed her cheek, his vow slicing her skin.

Mae breathed out slowly as if she could breathe out the dream, but her hand still shook as she lifted the towel to check the cut. The bleeding had stopped. She pulled her first aid kit out of the cupboard below the sink and used a disinfectant wipe to clean away the blood, wincing at the sting. Then she applied antibiotic ointment and several butterfly bandages.

The next few hours had flown by as she locked in her plans and took Solo for a final walk.

Now, there was only one thing left to do. Standing by the reception desk of the boarding kennel and doggy daycare she used for Solo, the owner waited for Mae to say goodbye. The woman thought Mae would be gone for a week. She would learn the truth when Mae didn't show up for Solo as planned.

Mae had used the cut as justification when she handed the owner an envelope. Mae told the woman that she'd walked into the edge of a cupboard door and it reminded her accidents happen. The envelope held a Pet Life Care Agreement since Mae was single and didn't have family. Mae had tried to appear nonchalant, brushing it off as if it were a just-in-case form everyone kept. The owner said that many of her dog parents had supplied them and she'd file it.

Knowing it was now or never, Mae flung her arms around Solo. "You be a good boy," she whispered into his neck, unable to stop her eyes welling with tears. "I love you." She choked on the last word, barely able to get it out, and held on for another moment.

When she straightened, she passed Solo's leash to the owner, turned around, and left. Tears tracked down her cheeks, but she didn't care. There was a wound in her heart far worse than anything she'd ever felt on her skin.

By the time she made it home, she was numb. Without

turning on any lights, she walked into her bedroom, tossed her phone on the bed, stripped off her clothes into a pile on the floor, and pulled on a T-shirt Jake had left. With his cedar and citrus scent clinging to her, she grabbed her phone and crawled into bed.

She'd missed a couple of calls from a local number she didn't recognize, but none from Jake. When she noticed a voicemail, she keyed in her code and played it.

"This is Gage. Your cousin. I stopped by your place tonight, thought we could get to know each other since we live close. Maybe go for a beer. Uh, Blake gave me your number. Give me a call."

For years Mae had wanted a family. Now she could have one, yet she might never know them. No matter how often she had told herself that loving her cousins would be enough to break the curse, she knew it would never work.

Sometime during the day, as she listed off pros and cons, she stopped lying to herself. It was time to face the truth. She couldn't trust her own mind anymore. It was too late for her.

Having a loving family hadn't helped her mom and it wouldn't help her. Only true love would break the curse, and Mae was too afraid to try. If Jake rejected her or said he loved her and the curse didn't break, it would shatter her more completely than the curse itself.

She'd even thought about taking her own life but she couldn't do that to Jake. When she'd listened to him tell her about finding Chelsea's lifeless body, his pain, now years later, felt tangible, like she could hold it in the palm of her hand. She wouldn't give him another burden like that to hold.

Instead, she would let the curse take her. He'd still have to live with her death, but he would know it wasn't by her own hand and that there was nothing he could have done to stop it.

Willingly subjecting herself to the risk of rejection and abandonment was far worse than going to sleep and letting the curse take her.

She would say one last goodbye.

16

Glancing at the speedometer, Jake eased off the gas. The snow hadn't let up in the last several hours, making the road slippery. He cursed himself for not heading to Mae's earlier.

At the cabin, he busied himself, but his thoughts hadn't strayed far from Mae, wondering how she was doing. He debated going to her when Gage had called. The connection had cut out once, but he'd heard enough. If Mae had been home when Gage dropped by, she hadn't answered. Nor had she returned his message.

Screw giving her space. For the last several hours he'd gone over his feelings for Mae and even if he was overprotective, it was still love. "I love her," he told Chewie, glancing in the rearview mirror.

He would prove he loved her, not leave her alone with her thoughts. It certainly hadn't helped his sister. Jake hadn't realized it at the time, but the more he and his parents gave Chelsea space, the more she brooded and felt lost. Loving someone meant being there for them.

Jake had closed up the cabin in record time and hit the

road. Mae would have to put up with him hovering, like it or not. He would try to tone down the over protectiveness if he could while he showed her he loved her.

He was only about twenty minutes from Mae's when his phone rang. He answered through the truck's Bluetooth. "Hello?"

"Hi, it's me."

Mae sounded hesitant, as if she wasn't sure she should have phoned.

"I'm glad you called," he told her, keeping his tone as light as he could manage.

"I…uh…"

Jake glanced at the dash, wondering if she'd hung up. "Mae, you there?"

"Yes."

Her tone shifted to neutral. That worried him even more. "Sweetheart, talk to me."

"I don't think it's going to work."

"What isn't?"

"Breaking the curse. I think it's too late. Don't worry about me, I'm not going to do anything stupid. Bye, Jake."

"Mae!" Jake screamed her name, but she'd already hung up. Checking his speed, he pressed the gas as much as he dared. He didn't need to be a genius to understand what Mae had meant by *I'm not going to do anything stupid*. What she meant was that she wasn't going to take her own life.

That didn't mean she still wasn't doing something stupid. Withdrawing from him was stupid. Not risking love and letting the curse win was stupid. Whether she killed herself by her own hand or willingly let the curse kill her, it was the same thing.

He was making assumptions, thinking the curse would kill her, but he was certain. Her mom's curse hadn't killed her, even after decades, but Mae's curse was different. Alex had said the curse affected each person differently, and there was no doubt in his mind that Mae's curse was different—it physically hurt her.

Blake's had been different too. After it had broken, he and Blake had spent several hours with numerous beers, talking through what happened and what might have. Blake believed the curse would have eventually killed him by locking him into a never-ending trance until he withered away. Or it would have killed him by hitting him at the wrong time. By the time he broke the curse, it was striking him several times a day. Something as simple as walking down the stairs could have been deadly if the curse seized him at that moment.

Jake refused to accept that it was too late for Mae. He wanted to pull her into his arms and confess his love. He'd been so stupid thinking he needed a one hundred percent guarantee that what he felt was love, that he wasn't confusing his desire to protect with love. Life didn't offer guarantees.

After hours of worry, he realized that he and Mae were the same. She pushed everyone away for fear that they would abandon her. She wanted a guarantee too. A guarantee that if she loved someone, they wouldn't leave her.

He had to trust himself that what he felt for her was real and take the risk. That was the scary part—the risk. He was ready. He loved her. But what if Mae wasn't ready? If he told her he loved her now, she wouldn't believe him. She would think he was only doing it to break the curse. But whether they broke the curse soon or not, Jake was still going to be there for her.

He pulled into her apartment building's parking lot, ready to show Mae he loved her. By the time he reached her door with Chewie beside him, adrenaline surged through him. Her place was silent and all the lights were off, but he knocked on the door anyway. After less than a minute, he dug out the key she'd given him.

Jake opened her door and Chewie pushed past him into the apartment. "Mae?" He called her name, not wanting to scare her if she heard him. Chewie headed for the bedrooms, maybe realizing, as Jake had, that Solo hadn't come out to greet them.

"Mae?" He reached her bedroom door but didn't enter.

Her door stood closed like Chelsea's had that day so long ago.

Chelsea had always kept her door closed.

Mae didn't. She'd told him once that she wanted to make sure Solo could come and go as he pleased.

When Chelsea had decided to take her own life, she hadn't called Jake to say goodbye.

Mae had. She said she wouldn't do anything stupid.

Was he overreacting? Had Gage's call made him jump to conclusions? He'd promised he would give Mae space. Then out of the blue, without consulting with her, he decided to ignore her request all because he finally realized he loved her.

When Chelsea had asked for space, he had given it to her.

And he'd regretted it ever since.

Mae wasn't a lost fifteen-year-old girl. Nor was she his sister. Did he have the right to barge in and check on her? Especially after her call?

She'd accused him of being overprotective and trying to fix her. Was he doing that again? Was he now using his love as an excuse to do that?

Jake stepped back from her door and ran his hands through his hair. He'd convinced himself years ago that taking care of someone was always the right thing to do. Now, he didn't know what to do.

He ducked into the bathroom and flicked on the light. An open first-aid kit lay spread on the counter. Torn wrappers from wipes and several unused butterfly bandages lay on top.

Jake didn't need to step any closer to see the dried drips of blood in the sink.

Regardless of how Mae reacted, he couldn't walk away now until he knew she was okay.

He spun around and had to side-step Chewie to avoid colliding with him, as he headed to Mae's bedroom. This time he didn't hesitate as pushed open her door.

"Mae?" He perched on the edge of her bed and reached for the lamp on the nightstand. "Mae? It's Jake, wake up."

Her favorite purple blanket covered her, but he could hear her soft breathing. He'd spent hours listening to it in the last week, trying to decide when he needed to wake her. She didn't look like she was in the throes of a nightmare, but if she was, it wouldn't be easy to wake her.

He placed his hand on her shoulder and gave it a gentle shake. "Mae, it's Jake. Wake up please, sweetheart."

Mae rolled toward him and pushed up onto her elbows. "Jake? What are you doing here?"

"I needed to check—" She turned more toward him, the right side of her face coming into view. "What the hell happened to your face?"

"I cut it." She moved to the side of the bed, forcing him to stand and step back. "You didn't answer my question. Why are you here, Jake?"

"I was worried about you." The urge to pull her into his arms and confess his love was stronger than ever, but he knew it wasn't the right time. He lifted her hand and cradled it between his palms, but not crowding her. "I care about you, Mae. I needed to know you were okay."

"I am. A small cut aside."

"That's not a small cut."

She pulled her hand out of his. "Jake, I need you to leave."

Jake didn't know how to get through to Mae. How could he show her he loved her if she wouldn't even let him stay? If he couldn't show her, he would have to tell her and hope she'd believe him.

"Mae, I want to be here for you. I love you." As soon as the words left his mouth, he saw the saddened look on her face and wished he could take them back.

Mae shook her head. "No, you don't. You're a protector and you want to save me. You only think you love me because you want to break the curse."

"That's not true. I do love you, Mae."

Chewie nudged his leg and Jake heard Mae's indrawn breath. She sat on the bed, as if she hadn't heard him, then patted her leg for Chewie. He didn't hesitate to go to her. Mae wrapped her arms around him and buried her face in his fur.

Jake looked around the room. He'd expected Solo to be with Mae, but he'd been so distracted by worry he'd forgotten about the dog. "Where's Solo?"

She patted Chewie and then stood, forcing him to move back. "At the kennel. You need to leave, Jake."

"Why is he at the kennel?" People took their dogs to the kennel when they weren't going to be around. He'd bet money that's what Mae had been thinking. "You said you weren't going to do anything stupid."

"I'm not. Unlike some people, I keep my word, Jake."

He let out a harsh breath. "I remember what I promised you. Listening to you doesn't mean pretending this is fine. You almost died at the cabin, and tonight you've got a huge gash on your face. And you've sent Solo away so no one will be here if you're hurt again. Tell me how any of that isn't stupid."

"Jake," she said his name quietly and sat down on the bed as if she didn't have the strength to speak any louder or hold herself up any longer. "Do you remember the two promises you made to me the first time I called you?"

"Of course. I promised that if something ever happened to you, I would make sure Solo was well cared for. And I will. The second promise was that I'd always listen to you. I'd never speak over you. I've never broken either of those promises."

"No? Listening involves more than hearing my words. It means understanding them."

Jake's stomach dropped. He swallowed before speaking. "I do understand. You're planning to let this curse take you, and you think pushing everyone away somehow makes it safer for us. Why won't you let me be here for you? If you won't let me stay, at least let someone. I'll call Blake, or Gage—someone needs to be with you when you sleep."

Her eyes shuttered, hurt and determination warring there. "What I need is for you to honor what I'm asking. No reinforcements. No one else worrying over me." She drew in a shaky breath. "It's already too late, Jake."

Jake dropped to his knees in front of her, taking her hands in his again. "It's not too late, Mae."

Mae pulled her hands back and he felt rejected, a bruise deep in his chest.

Slowly, he raised to his feet and called Chewie as he left the room. He used the bathroom, rinsing the blood out of the sink as he washed his hands. When he passed her bedroom, the door was shut. One more sign she was rejecting him.

In her entryway, he slid her key off his ring and set it on the table by the door. He opened the door, thumbed the manual lock, then paused. "No." He snatched up the key, shut her door, and twisted the key back onto his ring as he and Chewie walked to his truck. He might be leaving alone tonight, but he wouldn't let her push him away forever. Somehow he would find a way to show her he loved her.

When he and Chewie were both strapped in, he dropped his head back on the seat as he waited for the truck to warm up. Finding Chelsea looking lifeless had rocked his world, but it had been nothing compared to how he felt now. With Chelsea he'd been able to call 911 and get her the help she needed.

Mae had left him stranded. His brain tried to insist there was no one to call, no way to help her, but that wasn't quite true. His hand drifted toward his phone in the console and Blake's name in his message app. If she wouldn't let him stay, maybe he could at least make sure someone else checked on her. Not tonight. Give her the space she asked for. Tomorrow, if she still brushed him off, he'd pull Blake in whether she liked it or not.

Turning on his wipers, he cleared the window of snow and gave her apartment one last glance as he drove out of the parking lot. He considered calling Gage and crashing at his place since it was close. It was late, but Gage wouldn't mind. The problem was that as emotionally drained as Jake felt, he knew sleep wouldn't come easily. He headed for the highway that would take him back to his cabin.

The snow had lessened by the time he was close to the turnoff. It looked like it hadn't snowed as much in the area as it had closer to Green Springs. His truck would easily be able to make the side road.

He checked his mirrors, slowed down, and signaled to turn left. Headlights set high—an SUV or truck—came out of nowhere, heading straight for him in his lane.

Jake yanked the steering wheel hard to the right to avoid the vehicle.

He exhaled in a huff, thinking he was clear, when the SUV—now clear in his lane—fishtailed and lost control.

Time slowed as the SUV came toward him. Jake felt helpless for the second time that night.

17

Saturday, February 22

Mae hadn't slept much, then woke with the sun rising. Sweaty and disoriented, she struggled to shed the last vestiges of her restless sleep. Her most recent dream fought for real estate in her mind, not letting her forget.

She'd stood in a large, empty room, but she hadn't been there alone. Someone important to her had been with her. Their voice warmed and soothed Mae when they spoke, giving her a sense of comfort. Dream Mae listened to their every word. She didn't comprehend a single one, but that didn't matter. Only that she listened.

So, she did. But over time, the person's words muffled and drifted away as if they'd turned their back and walked away from Mae. Frantic to catch up with the unknown person, Mae quickened her pace to close the distance. No matter how far or how fast she walked, the person remained out of reach, until finally the voice completely faded, leaving Mae all alone.

After remembering the dream, her first thought had been

of Jake. Had the dream tried to tell her that she was right in thinking Jake would eventually abandon her? Or was it saying she was all alone because she'd pushed Jake away the night before?

Mae should have known he would come—he was that type of person. Jake wanted to protect those he cared about. She didn't have any doubt that he cared for her, but life had taught her that caring wasn't always enough.

In the dark of night, she'd been so sure that turning Jake away was right choice. Now, in the light, she second-guessed herself. Something she'd done often these last couple of months. "No. My plan is solid," she told the empty room.

In all the years she'd been on her own, never had she felt the utter isolation that blanketed her that morning, waking up alone. But more than that, she couldn't shake the feeling she'd abandoned Jake as surely as others had done to her all her life. Regardless of whether he truly cared for her or if his feelings were only a misplaced sense of protectiveness, she had turned him away. Whatever his motivation, Jake had treated her better than anyone else.

Everyone has doubts about a plan right before they carry it out. She needed to apologize to Jake. He deserved that and one last goodbye. She considered texting him, then recoiled from the idea, refusing to take the coward's way out. She picked up her phone and called his number. It rang several times before his voicemail picked up. "This is Jake. Please leave a message."

She'd never heard his voicemail before. He always called her. Was that another way he showed he cared? That he was thinking of her because he called first? The phone beeped, startling her. "Uh, hi, Jake. It's Mae. I'm sorry for turning you away last night. I shouldn't have treated you that way. Please call me."

The few times she'd initiated a text, he hadn't kept her

waiting long before he responded. At a loss for what to do while she waited, she cleaned her apartment. An hour later, when he still hadn't called, she walked to the park.

Every step she took was a reminder that she had not only sent Jake away, she'd done the same to Solo. She'd sent them both away because of her plan.

It was a good one, she was just having jitters.

Her plan: lie down and let the dreams take her. Without water, she expected she wouldn't live more than a few days and wouldn't notice the time passing. First, because she was caught up in her dreams, and then because she would eventually be unconscious.

Too bad her plan had one major flaw.

For it to work, her dreams had to be continuous and consuming her. She knew they would, but she couldn't say why she'd assumed it would happen instantly. The curse directed her dreams every night and sometimes during the day, but not twenty-four seven. Zoning out had become common with the episodes happening more and more, but they didn't consume every minute of the day and night. At least not yet.

At one point in Mae's never-ending morning, she opened a calendar on her phone to calculate how long she thought it would be before her dreams took over her life. The first dream had come on the eleventh day after her birthday. As the dreams increased in frequency, the days between them dwindled over the following eleven weeks until the dreams occurred every night. In the three weeks since they'd become a daily routine, the episodes had grown longer and harsher. The dream walking and zoning out had started too.

After staring at the calendar for a minute, she closed it in disgust, powered down her phone, and tossed it on the couch cushion beside her. Using the past week as a rough guide, she figured it would take another week or two before her dreams consumed her all day and night.

Coming out of a dream physically injured was scary. She'd come to terms with the curse but hadn't thought much about the details. Waking up after sleepwalking had scared the crap out of her, but lots of people sleepwalked. But her dreams were more than that—something tangible.

It wasn't until she realized that she could hurt Jake or Solo that the truth of her reality finally sank in. The curse created the dreams that affected her, and when she connected the events that surfaced in reality with Jake dying in the dream, she'd been terrified. If one thing could manifest in real life, others could too. Who was she to say she couldn't hurt Jake or Solo, or anyone else?

She couldn't. It proved to her that her plan to wither away and not put anyone else in danger had merit. If only her timing hadn't been off.

Jake hadn't returned her call. Maybe he finally realized what a burden Mae would be in his life. He could be happy she'd turned him away.

Sinking deep into the couch cushions, she didn't move, except her eyes. Her gaze fixed on Solo's empty dog bed. He had three of them, one in her bedroom, one in the office, and the one in the living room she stared at now. She'd wanted Solo to have a place to chill with her no matter what room she was in.

She snorted at the thought as a burning lump filled her throat. The joke had been on her. The last time Solo used a dog bed had been at Jake's cabin. In her living room, Solo loved spreading out on the couch. She'd bought him a bed for in the office, but he kept wandering into the living room to make himself comfortable on the couch. Being the softy that she was, she bought a couch for her office. They spent a lot of hours curled up on it together. The same with her bed.

When Jake had stayed over, they laughed about both dogs trying to sleep with them at night.

Maybe when she was gone, Jake would train Solo to finally use the dog beds. During one of her many video calls with Jake, he'd walked around his house, giving Mae a tour, which included pointing out Chewie's dog beds. She had to trust that Jake would keep his promise to her and take care of Solo.

She leaned forward as she realized another flaw in her plan. She'd told the owner of the kennel that she'd be gone a week. When Mae didn't show up as planned, the owner would check the agreement to see what to do. Mae left instructions to contact Jake. If he couldn't be reached, then Blake was next in line, followed by Cade. Custody of Solo would go to Jake.

Three days had been Mae's original estimate for the curse to do its thing. She'd told the dog kennel owner she would be gone a week to give the curse a couple of extra days, just in case. What if it wasn't enough? She couldn't have Jake realize something was wrong and check on her when the curse hadn't consumed her yet.

Mae grabbed her phone and turned it back on. She called the kennel owner to explain that her plans had changed and she would be gone another week. The woman sounded concerned and asked how Mae's cheek was healing, before reassuring her that she'd be happy to keep Solo the extra week.

Feeling drained, Mae shut off her phone again and curled up on the couch. For the first time since her curse started in November, Mae welcomed being lost in a dream.

She stood in a house, a stack of letters in her hand. Opening the flap of the first envelope, she withdrew a heavy sheet of handmade paper. The scent of vanilla reached her as she read the letter filled with promises of love. As Mae read the last word of the letter, the bottom of the paper caught fire. She let go as the letter turned to ash. Each time Mae pulled out a letter, it went up in flames as she read the final word. She tried to save some of them but each one disintegrated no matter what she did.

Mae woke with a start and lifted her hands in front of her face. Her fingers stung as if she'd burned them, the tips red. Out of habit more than for concern for healing her fingers, since she wouldn't be around long, she went into the kitchen and ran them under cold water.

After a couple of minutes, she turned off the tap, grabbed a cold bottle of water from the fridge and flopped back on the couch. Picking up her phone, she unlocked it.

She had eight missed calls and five text messages. Expecting them all to be from Jake, she smiled and opened the app. She frowned, noticing four calls were from Blake, two from the number she now knew was Gage's, and the other two were from Cade. The text messages were the same —all from her cousins—not a single one from Jake. Each one asked her to call.

If she didn't call, they might decide to drop by. Her chest tightened as she clicked on Blake's last call.

"Mae?" Blake answered.

"It's me. Uh, sorry I missed your call."

"Jake was in an accident early this morning after leaving your place."

Jake in an accident. For a beat, Blake's words barely registered. All she could see was the dream—Jake on the crumbling bridge, boards splitting under his feet, his body dropping through empty air while she screamed his name and couldn't reach him. She'd taken it as a warning, proof the curse would go after the people she loved, so she'd walked away from Jake, cut him off, and done everything the curse whispered she should do to keep him safe. And it hadn't been enough.

Maybe the dream hadn't been literal. Maybe the curse didn't care which way it took him, as long as it made her watch. And if this wasn't the curse at all—if it was just bad roads and worse timing—that almost felt worse, because then she'd blown up the best thing in her life for nothing.

18

Jake opened his eyes and groaned, then let them fall closed. A jackhammer throbbing in his skull and aches everywhere reminded him of last night. His heart escaped damage in the accident, yet it felt worse than any other part of him. It ached for Mae.

"Oh, the blinds," Chelsea said, her voice a few octaves too high.

A chair scraped along the floor, the sound worse than the light, spiking pain through his head.

"Shhhh, Chels," he murmured.

"Right." A few moments passed. "You can open your eyes now."

He didn't want to but opened them anyway to see his sister. "How long have you been here?"

"About an hour. I passed mom and dad in the hallway. They said you fell asleep while they were here, so I didn't want to wake you."

"Thanks." He sounded like a two-pack-a-day smoker. "Water?"

"Here." She held a cup of water with a straw for him.

The cool water felt like ambrosia to his throat. "Thanks," he said again. "Time?"

"Almost four in the afternoon. So…." Her lips twitched and she looked around the empty room before leaning closer to him and lowering her voice to a conspiratorial whisper. "You look like shit."

"Why do I love you?"

Chelsea laughed. "Sorry. Couldn't resist. Dad said you have a concussion, two broken ribs, several bruised ribs, and a contusion and small laceration on your spleen, so the doctors are keeping you here for observation. Oh… and your face looks like you went a couple of rounds with a heavy-weight boxer and lost. But otherwise, you're lucky, even if you don't look it."

He remembered the SUV sliding toward him when it lost control. In that moment, luck had felt impossible. People say your life flashes before your eyes when they think you might die. His didn't. In the blinding lights of the SUV, he saw only Mae and felt only regret for how things had ended. He cursed softly under his breath.

Chelsea squeezed his hand. "Are you in pain? Want me to get someone?"

"No, I'm good." He forced his lips up into a smile to reassure her. "This morning is foggy. I think Dad told me Blake had Chewie. Is that right?"

"Yes. And Chewie's fine, not a scratch on him. Animal control picked him up and called Blake early this morning. I'd never have thought to add a backup number to his tag. Smart." She grinned. "Although, maybe you should have put my number on the tag. You might have to fight little Emmie to get Chewie back."

"I think I'd win." He shifted, and pain rippled across his chest. "Well, maybe not today. Distract me. How have you been feeling?"

"I'm good. The morning-to-evening sickness is letting up. If this pregnancy is like my first, I should be through it in another week or so when I hit my second trimester. Having a toddler while pregnant has entirely changed the game this time around. I'm tired of being tired all the time, but it's worth it. Enough about me. How is Mae?" Chelsea frowned at him. "And why were you leaving her place so late at night?"

"She kicked me out."

"You went all caveman on her, didn't you?"

Jake pushed up and winced. "Why do you automatically think it's my fault?"

"Because I know you." Chelsea reached for the bed controls and raised the head of the bed. "That better?"

"Yeah, thanks."

She raised her eyebrows. "So? Did you go caveman on Mae?"

"Not really caveman. She asked for some space and—" He held up his hand when Chelsea opened her mouth to object. "Chels, the curse is hurting her. Physically. Some of her dream injuries show up in real life. She's scared and thinks it's too late. I got the feeling she was just going to lie down and let the curse take her."

"Do you love her?"

"Yes."

Chelsea stood and perched on the edge of the mattress to face him. "Then, big brother, here's some tough love."

"Oh, please no," he groaned.

She stuck her tongue out at him. "I know you've always felt responsible for what happened to me. For what I did. I've told you a million times, but I'll tell you again. It wasn't your fault and I wasn't your responsibility. It wasn't mom's and dad's either, even though I was only sixteen. They got me help and checked in constantly. It was on me—I decided to hide what I was going through. That's on me. They couldn't have known how I was feeling, and neither could you, because I didn't want you to. I didn't know how to speak up. I'll always regret that you had to find me like you did, but I'll always be grateful too. I'm not sure that I wanted to die, but I didn't know how to voice what I was feeling. I think taking the pills was my way of getting someone to force me to get better. I'm ashamed I chose that route." She leaned closer to the bed. "Jake, I need you to finally believe me. It's time to let go of your guilt."

Jake's throat tightened, but it had nothing to do with his injuries. His sister's happiness meant the world to him and he hadn't been able to fix it.

She sat back and rubbed her eyes with her fists, then locked her gaze on his. "Now, here's the tough love. I had all the love a sixteen-year-old girl could possibly ask for and I still struggled. Mae hasn't had anyone be there for her and show her the love she deserves. You need to show her that love, Jake. You need to take the risk and love her. Show her that you'll be there for her, like you were there for me, even if you think you weren't. Then it's up to Mae to decide what to do with that love. You can't force her to accept it or act a certain way. You can only be there for her."

"I was doing that."

Chelsea let out a long-suffering sigh. "I doubt it."

"Why the hell would you say that?"

"Because you can be overprotective to the extreme. I bet you could have found a lot of ways to show her you cared without being a jerk. Instead, she asked you for space and you probably barged in and demanded she accept your help and love all at once."

Jake wouldn't have framed it that way, but he knew when it was best to keep his mouth shut. His sister was wrong. Sort of. Maybe.

"Just think about it."

He nodded. After she left, he laid back and shut his eyes, thinking of Mae. Of the slice on her cheek. Of the defeat in her expression when she'd accused him of not understanding what she'd been telling him. She had asked for space but he knew she was going to let the curse take her. What else could he have done?

"Jake?"

Mae stood by the door. Her gaze darted around the room before landing on him. The bandages were gone from the cut on her cheek, but it was still red and stood out against the pallor of her skin. Every time he saw her, she looked frailer than the last time. She was slipping through his fingers and he had no idea what to do.

He offered his hand. She hesitated, then crossed to the bed and took it. "Blake called me, but all he said was that you're here and were okay. You don't look okay."

"A little roughed up, but I'm fine."

"How long do you have to stay?"

"A couple of nights I think. For observation." His injuries were nothing compared to what Mae was dealing with. He lifted his free hand and grazed the uninjured skin beside her cut with his knuckles. "How are you?"

"I'm okay." She glanced toward the door. "I needed to see you, but I should go so you can rest."

She went skittish, ready to bolt. He worried this could be his last chance to convince her how much he cared about her. How much he loved her. "Last night you said I wasn't understanding what you meant when you said you needed space. I do understand. You're scared. I get that—love is risky. I care about you. I love you. I want you to risk love." She opened her mouth to speak, and he held up his hand, knowing she was going to object because he was pushing her again. "But I can't force you."

Mae took a step back. "What do you mean by that?"

"That I want you to love me back, but if you can't, I won't push you anymore."

"You won't push me?"

"No." Jake didn't understand why she repeated his words.

"Thank you. Bye, Jake." She turned and left.

He'd done his best to follow Chelsea's advice, not pushing Mae, so she could make her own decision. The ache in his heart told him that this time Mae was the one who hadn't understood.

When he got out of the hospital, he would prove he loved her, but right now he was sore and exhausted. He shut his eyes and let sleep pull him under.

Sunday, February 23

SLEEP WOULDN'T COME. Mae had given up pretending an hour ago and now she paced from the couch to the bedroom door and back, Solo's absence a hollow echo in every room.

She stopped at the glass doors to the balcony. The last time she'd been out there, she'd woken to knives made from the wind on her skin and no memory of opening the door.

Tonight, she slid the lock back herself. She needed the cold and the reminder of exactly what waited for her.

Mae stepped out onto the balcony and curled her fingers around the top rail. The cold steel bit into her palms and fingers like sharp little daggers. She hoped if she held on long enough a numbness would replace the pain. Her bare feet on the icy cement floor were already that way.

Leaning over, Mae peered down at the street, three stories below. The streetlights illuminated the empty sidewalks. Before the curse, she hadn't made it a habit of being awake at three o'clock in the morning.

She snorted. Not a conscious habit at least. Sleepwalking in the middle of the night likely didn't count for being awake.

By the time she got home from the hospital she was set to head back and shake some sense into Jake. Fighting back wasn't usually her way, but maybe that's where she'd gone wrong for so long. All her life she'd pushed on. Every time someone didn't want her—each time someone left—she got on with life. She didn't know when it happened, but at one point she accepted she was better off on her own. Except for Solo, she learned not to rely on anyone's love.

Damn Jake for barging into her life. If he didn't have that protective streak of his, he could let her be. If he'd never called her on New Year's Eve, she would have gone on with her life until the curse consumed her. But he had called and planted the seed of love and family in her mind. Revealed that her mom's illness was a curse. Instead of thinking she would end up with her mom's illness, Mae hoped she had a curse she could break.

She'd been foolish to think the love of her cousins would be enough to break the curse. If she was honest with herself, she'd known that right from the beginning. To break the curse, she would have to fall in love and have someone love her back. Scary as hell, but then she'd do more than just shed the curse, she'd open herself to the one thing she'd always wanted—family. More than cousins, a true love, and possible children in her future, maybe grandchildren.

While at the cabin, Jake showed her what was possible. Sleepwalking and shattered mirrors had stopped her from grasping onto that reality with both hands, but she'd caught glimpses of it. Seeing Jake's death in her dream had rocked all that.

She was so scared for him, she'd panicked. Like always,

she accepted what fate handed her. Then got on with life and made a plan to keep Jake and Solo safe, accepting it as her only option. Whether being thrust into foster homes, or watching her husband say he didn't love her anymore and walking into the arms of his pregnant lover, Mae had always forged the pragmatic path and got on with life.

The plan to go to sleep and let the curse consume her seemed perfect. The few minor glitches aside—like the timeline—it was still a good plan.

Then Blake called. *Jake was in an accident.* In that moment, those five words sharpened her world to one thing—she didn't know how she would go on without Jake. She'd known for weeks that she cared deeply for him. If what she felt wasn't yet love, it would come. None of that had been the problem. Him eventually leaving her had been. And this time, the curse wouldn't allow her to pick herself back up and get on with life.

That all changed with Blake's call. Like a dip in ice-cold water, she'd emerged with clarity. It was time to stop accepting what was happening to her as fate. She could make her own destiny.

Her nerves had all morphed into live wires, making her a nervous wreck by the time she walked into Jake's hospital room. Seeing him bruised and in pain was far harder than enduring anything the curse had done to her. She had wanted to go to him and tell him she loved him. Not because it would break the curse, but because it was true. His caring, his love of family, his mountain-man good looks, and even his overprotective ways had wormed their way into her heart. Now, she wasn't so sure.

I want you to risk love. Hearing those words, she'd opened her mouth to tell him she was ready. *But I can't force you* had clamped her mouth shut. Not I *won't* force you. Or I love you and I'll wait until you're ready to love me back. No, he hadn't said any of those things. Sure, he said he loved her, but how could she know it was real and not a byproduct of his overbearing caveman nature. He wanted *her* to risk love.

"And then what, Jake?" she shouted into the night. "I take all the risk and if it's not exactly what you want, you walk away? All because you *can't* force me? Is that your out? Your safety net so you don't have to wait too long?" She yanked the railing the way she wanted to shake Jake.

It didn't move. Her hands hurt and her body shivered. She'd probably been shivering for ages. Numbness and anger had temporarily blinded her to her plight. Not anymore.

Mae went into her apartment and shut the sliding glass door behind her, pulling the drapes closed. Pins and needles bombarded her feet, attacking her with little pricks of pain as she walked to her bedroom. Climbing beneath the blankets, she pulled her favorite purple one up to her chin and curled inti a ball to get warm.

Closing her eyes, she willed a dream to come. She decided to stop being a doormat and to stop letting others choose her fate, so she could go back to her original plan. It wasn't because it was a last resort. She was choosing to protect her cousins from having to worry about her. It was her choice to protect Solo and Jake from harm too. She decided—Mae—not anyone else. Jake didn't have to worry about one day realizing he'd made a mistake and Solo would stay loved.

She took a deep breath and let it out slowly. Her body finally warm and relaxed, she surrendered to the curse.

Mae gazed up at a woman's face, smiling with love in her eyes. Mae was a baby held in her mom's arms, deeply loved and secure.

Her mom gently laid her in a cradle and left. Before Mae could cry out for her mom, the dream morphed.

She was now a young girl holding her mom's hand on the way to school. A car honked. Mae turned her head to see and when she looked back, her hand was empty and her mom was gone. Mae opened her mouth to yell for her mom and the dream changed again.

Now a teenager sitting on the steps of a house, the day turned to night as Mae waited for her foster family to come home. Never given a key to the house, she had no choice but to wait—hungry, tired, and cold. A neighbor—an old lady Mae had never spoken to before—called from her front stoop. She said the family had gone on vacation, they'd left that morning. Mae didn't respond. She'd learned there wasn't any point in objecting. Others dictated her life.

When the dream changed again, Mae found herself walking hand-in-hand with Jake. Like with her mom, she felt loved and secure, but the years had taught her it was only an illusion. When Jake's hand began to dissolve in hers, she didn't yell or fight. Opening her fist, she let the ashes fall from her palm and continued to walk. Alone.

19

Monday, February 24

Moving like a ninety-year-old, Jake turned in the passenger seat toward Blake. "Thanks again for picking me up. And for bringing Chewie." His eyes had burned during the reunion when he wrapped his arms around his St. Bernard. Blake had reassured him the morning after the accident that Chewie was fine, but it didn't matter. Animal Control's vet had checked him out and said Chewie's seat belt restraint had done its job. Jake didn't doubt it, but he felt better now that he'd seen his dog for himself.

"No problem. Emmie loved having Chewie stay with us. Paige and I will need to borrow him now and then."

Jake chuckled. "To give Emmie her dog fix so you don't have to get one?"

"Exactly—at least not yet."

"Anytime."

"Sorry I was late," Blake said as he pulled out of the hospital parking lot onto the main road. Snowplows had cleared the main streets, but banks of snow crowded the curbs. "I'd wanted to be here before lunch, but we had to get Paige's parents settled in my mom's house."

"Shit. Your wedding. I could have asked Cade or Dane."

"Nah, it's all good." Blake shot him a quick glance. "Everything is ready for Saturday and I wanted to come. Where am I going? Home or to Mae's?"

"Part of me wants to go to Mae's, but I'm not sure that's smart."

"Why? Didn't she visit you on Saturday?"

"She did." He'd gone over and over the conversation and didn't know what he'd said wrong. Chelsea had been right, he'd barged in on Mae when she'd asked for space, so that's what he tried to give. After she walked out of his hospital room, he lasted six hours before he finally texted her. Texting seemed like the safest way to reach out. She wouldn't be forced to talk to him and she could text back when she wanted to. He was still waiting for that.

Blake eased into a strip-mall lot and threw the truck into park.

Jake scanned the storefronts. "What did you need?"

"For you to tell me what the hell you did?"

"Why do you and Chelsea always think it's something I did? How do you know it wasn't Mae?"

"I don't, but I know you." Blake ran his hands over his face and exhaled hard. "On Friday you went to the cabin to wait for Gage to call, but Gage told me he didn't reach Mae. You were driving back from her place when you were hit."

Blake didn't pose a question, and Jake wouldn't lie to his friend. "Yes. When Gage couldn't reach Mae, I needed to see for myself that she was okay. I wasn't far from her place when she called." He could still remember the feel of panic rising when Mae had said goodbye and severed the call.

"For Christ's sake, Jake. Don't make me pull it out of you."

"Fine. Mae told me she needed some space, but I went to

her place anyway. I still don't know what she dreamed about that made her pull away and I feared she was going to do something stupid." Jake laid it all out—the mental debate, the blood, the first aid kit… right up until she kicked him out.

"I'd have checked on her after seeing the blood too. Maybe you freaked out, but that doesn't explain why Mae wouldn't want to see you now. On Saturday she hadn't acted like someone who would walk away from you."

"My sister lectured me a bit and I was thinking about it when Mae arrived. Chelsea said that after she was attacked, she had all the love and support she could have asked for, but if she wanted to try to kill herself, nothing I could have done would have stopped her. And that as much as I love someone, they're responsible for their actions." He felt like a kid repeating a script he was supposed to memorize, like he knew all the words but they weren't really sinking in. Mae had been right. He listened but hadn't really understood what she needed. "I need to forgive myself for thinking I should've known what she was going to do."

"I've been saying that for years. Do you now?"

"Forgive myself? I'm trying." It wouldn't happen overnight, but he'd work on it. His parents had sent him to a counsellor when they'd first sent Chelsea. It was time for another visit.

"Good. If you knew all that, what happened when you saw Mae?"

"I thought a lot about her saying I wasn't understanding of her need for space and said I get that she's scared. Then I told her I think I love her and I wanted her to risk love. But that I couldn't force her."

Blake raised his eyebrows. "And?"

"What do you mean, *and?* I did exactly what you and Chelsea told me to do. I told her how I felt. I listened and gave her space to make her own decisions. I didn't push her."

"You're such an idiot."

"What the hell, Blake?"

"I don't think that's what Chelsea meant. Remember the episode I had about my ancestor Colm?"

At his nod, Blake asked him, "What did you say to me?"

Jake had to think about that. "Something about you having to stop hiding or you'd end up like Colm, lonely and taking your own life. This is different, I'm not the one cursed."

"No, but you have to look at it from Mae's point of view. I told you that I hadn't said the words yet, but I wasn't hiding. I couldn't force Paige to love me."

Jake threw up his hands, then winced when his ribs protested. "Exactly. That's what I said. You're talking in circles."

"No, you're not listening. You know I was wrong. I already loved Paige, but I was still afraid she'd leave me. I said I couldn't force her as a safety net. That way she'd have to tell me she loved me first. You've admitted you love her, but you're still waiting for her to say it back." Blake emphasized the words. "You love her. Now you need to be there for her. Full stop. Not ask *her* to risk love. Just *love* her."

Shit. He knew love didn't come with a guarantee, but he'd acted like he needed one. Again. He was an idiot.

"If you're not willing to take the risk, she could see you as just one more person with their foot out the door. Not only are you shitty at taking your own advice, you don't listen."

Jake ran his hand through his hair. "Who else didn't I listen to?"

"Chelsea. She told you she felt loved and supported. I bet she recognized that Mae's never had that. But you got so stuck on the part that Mae needs to take a risk you ignored that part. Not only do you need to pull your head out of your ass and just love her… If Mae's not ready, be patient and show her. Be the first person who doesn't leave her. If you can't do that, then walk away."

"Drive to Mae's."

Blake put the truck in gear and headed toward Mae's.

"One more thing," Blake said, on a roll. "Remember when Paige broke up with me all those years ago and I knew she wanted me to fight for her? I didn't because I was a self-absorbed twenty-one-year old and I wanted her to fight for me too. We don't have any regrets because we have Emmie and we can't turn back the clock anyway. Don't do what I did. Don't put your ego and pride ahead of Mae. She needs someone to fight for her even when she's being stubborn or an idiot. If you don't, you'll lose her, curse or no curse."

Blake's advice was sound, but it didn't help Jake shake the feeling that he was already too late.

When they pulled up at Mae's, Blake got out of the truck when Jake did and got Chewie out. "I'm going with you, just to make sure you're not an idiot again."

"Because you've had so much practice, you'll recognize the behavior."

"If you weren't injured, I'd knock you over. Payback for Friday," Blake said as he waited for Jake to enter the building code.

Feeling like he might keel over, Jake took the elevator with Blake.

Jake knocked on Mae's door, out of respect, but didn't wait long for her to answer, using his key. Darkness and silence greeted them when they stepped inside. Nothing looked different from Friday night.

"Mae? Are you home?" When she didn't answer, he called once more. Chewie didn't wait, and passed him, heading straight for Mae's bedroom.

Blake crossed to the couch. "I'll wait here for now."

"Good idea." They didn't both need to barge into Mae's

bedroom. This time, she'd left her door wide open. A good sign, hoping it meant she'd picked up Solo.

"Mae?" After turning on the small light on the nightstand, he settled on the edge of her bed. "Mae, it's Jake. Wake up." He knew from watching her too many times that she was caught in a nightmare. Skewed blankets covered the bed, showing she'd been thrashing about.

Standing up, he peeled off his coat, letting it fall to the floor, before kicking off his shoes. He called to Blake.

"Is she okay?" Blake stood hesitantly in the doorway.

"No." Jake climbed onto the bed and sat against the headboard. He winced when he gathered Mae into his lap, but pain wasn't going to stop him from holding her. "Check the time for me?" He gestured to the large reading chair Mae kept in the corner. "She's covered up. You might as well get comfortable because we could be here for a while."

Chewie jumped onto the bed, laying at Jake's feet as Blake settled into the chair. "Do her dreams last longer each time?"

Jake pulled the covers up to Mae's chin, tucking the purple one close around her, and looked at his friend. He was so caught up in what was happening with Mae, he forgot for a second what Blake had been through. "Yes. The last one I saw was Wednesday. Over forty minutes."

"Since she hasn't woken up, we'll assume she's having an episode now. We've been here five minutes."

Jake rocked Mae and said her name every few minutes. The cuts on her arms were almost healed. The one on her cheek still looked raw and angry, bruising surrounding it.

They talked about Blake's curse, his upcoming wedding, and work, stopping every so often for Jake to try and wake Mae. They spoke in normal tones. If Mae stirred, she would hear them and hopefully wake up.

"It's been forty minutes," Blake said. "Not counting how long she'd already been in the dream when we got here."

Mae bucked in his arms once, then she settled. "Mae? Can you hear me? Come back to me. Open your eyes, sweetheart. Please."

Chewie growled and inched forward on the bed. He nudged Jake's arm cradling Mae. "She's okay."

Chewie nudged his arm again.

Blake walked to the door and flicked on the overhead light. "Chewie knows something."

"What?" Jake shifted and sucked in a breath at the pain his body didn't want him to forget.

"Let me. Like you said, she's covered." Blake put his hands under Mae's upper back to shift her off Jake and froze. "Jake, are you bleeding? Did you pop some stitches?"

"The only ones I have are on my face." Bracing for the pain, he rolled away from Mae giving Blake room to lower her flat to the mattress. Pushing up onto his knees, Jake sucked in air as his ribs and head protested again. "What do you see?"

"She has shallow cuts across her upper back. I felt moisture and thought I was feeling blood, but I think it's water. Her shirt's soaked." Blake pointed at Jake. "You're wet too."

Jake looked down in disbelief. He'd been cradling Mae with one arm, holding her against him. His sleeve and the entire front of his shirt were drenched. "How could I have missed that?" he whispered.

He'd been talking to himself, but Blake answered anyway. "You were concentrating on Chewie. It might have just happened—something in her dream spilling into the real world."

Jake leaned over Mae to get a better look and the room tilted. He grabbed the headboard to steady himself. The pounding in his head increased to jack-hammer strength.

"Whoa." Blake steadied him with a hand to the shoulder, forcing him back against the headboard. "Jake, this is one of those times I was talking about. Swallow your pride and take it easy, or you're going to pass out."

Blake left the room but was back by the time Jake caught his breath and the room righted itself. Chewie sprawled between Jake's outstretched legs and Mae.

"Drink." Blake pressed a cold bottle of water into his hand after loosening the cap.

Jake didn't whine about needing help to open a bottle. He couldn't remember the last time he'd felt so weak. "Thanks." He drank half the bottle, recapped it, and set it within easy reach.

He looked down at Mae and brushed hair off her forehead. The slice on her cheek amplified her pale skin, more than when they'd arrived. He sat looking at her for ages, not able to tear his gaze away. He'd hoped she'd just open her eyes. "How long has it been now?"

Blake sat back in the chair. "Over an hour since we got here. What do you want to do?"

"I don't know. All the other times I waited for her to wake up." Spots swam in front of his eyes and he closed them until the dizziness passed. He didn't know if he was feeling his injuries or having the beginnings of a panic attack. Mae needed to wake up for him to tell her he loved her. It wasn't about the curse or trying to fix her, or even his overwhelming need to keep her safe. He just loved her. Then he'd find a way to prove to her he would be by her side and wait as long as it took for her to be ready too. Only then could they break the curse.

When he thought he might be too late, he'd been thinking about Mae's feelings. That she might not forgive him. It never occurred to him that she wouldn't wake up. He figured he'd have to wait. But what if waiting was no longer enough? He'd have to find a way to help her wake up. Everything else, including love, could wait.

"Blake, can you grab my phone? It's in my coat on the floor. I need to call Lyra. She said she checked around and couldn't find a modern witch who could break the curse, but maybe she knows how to wake Mae."

He took the phone from Blake. "Thanks." Jake pulled up Lyra's contact information, praying she would answer.

*J*ake swallowed down the bile threatening to choke him, not able to take his eyes off Mae.

Lyra had answered Jake's call on the first ring. She wasn't sure she could help, but knew a spell that might send Jake into Mae's dream. She promised to come right away.

When Lyra told him about the spell, he'd become nearly giddy. Knowing nothing about magic, he assumed Lyra could give him the spell over the phone. She soon set him straight —you can't recite a spell until it's ready to use. As soon as you speak the words, the magic releases. If the recipient of the spell wasn't there and accepting of the magic, it could go into another or rebound and backfire. Lyra couldn't risk reciting the spell and harming someone around her.

As desperate as Jake was, Lyra's explanation made sense. And the solution seemed simple. He asked her to email it. Once more she had to set him straight—a spell works best when you read it straight from the book it's written in.

She would bring the grimoire containing the spell, and when they were ready, he would recite it. It would push him into Mae's dream so he could pull her out. He would declare his love and wait for her to do the same to break the spell.

Then the waiting began.

His mind flooded with worst-case scenarios for ninety minutes—ninety way-too-long minutes.

Ninety minutes for Mae to get hurt.

Ninety minutes for him to come apart.

Logically he knew that depending on where a person was driving from in Blue Mountain, the drive to Green Springs took two hours. His logic had dissolved eighty-nine minutes ago.

His brain ran an endless loop of scenarios with Mae suffering. She became too weak to pull herself out of the dream. She got injured to the point she couldn't help herself. The dream trapped her. The possibilities were endless as the minutes ticked on. In each one she felt alone and abandoned, like she had in the dreams she'd described. He pictured her hurt and lost.

He couldn't stop the thoughts any more than he could stop touching Mae, lightly running his fingers over her face and arms, while he waited for Lyra to come and save the day. If Mae could feel him at all, he wanted her to know he was there.

If he hadn't been such an idiot and let Mae walk away—if he'd shown her he would take the risk of loving her—he might have been able to break the curse. She'd be safe with him, instead of alone and suffering. Playing the *if* game served no purpose, but like worst-case scenarios and touching Mae, it was one more obsession he couldn't stop.

He'd told Blake it was time to forgive himself for what happened to Chelsea, but maybe there would never be forgiveness if he continued to make the same mistakes. He hadn't been there for Chelsea, hadn't seen the signs, and now it was happening again with Mae. Was he doomed to fail those he cared—

"Stop."

Jake lifted his eyes to Blake's. "Stop what?"

"Whatever the hell you're thinking about. I see it on your face. What happened with Chelsea wasn't your fault and this isn't either. And it isn't Mae's. Just like my curse wasn't mine. We had a selfish ancestor who got screwed by a petty spirit. That's just fucked up. And even if my mom had told me about the curse before she died, she still didn't tell us about Mae. And if I knew about the curse I probably wouldn't have believed her anyway. And I wouldn't have been able to make myself fall in love."

Jake scoffed. "No shit. Because you were already in love with Paige and too dumb to know it."

"Thanks for the reminder."

"That's what friends are for."

Blake's lips twitched into a smirk as he gave Jake the finger. "Anyway… As I was saying, none of this is your fault because no one can prepare for this kind of shit and you can't wish yourself in love because you need it. You have to be ready. Sure, if you hadn't been such a dumb ass in the hospital, we might not be here, but then again, we might be because Mae has to be ready too."

"I get it, but your pep talk could use some work."

"Nuh. It worked."

Jake's phone pinged with a text and he unlocked it to look. "Lyra said she's ten minutes out."

Blake stood. "I'll go downstairs and wait for her and take Chewie with me. Give him a chance to go outside for a few minutes. Chewie, come."

Chewie gave Mae's hand a lick and slid off the bed to go with Blake.

Leaning over Mae, Jake kissed her forehead. "Hang on for me, sweetheart. I'm coming."

As eager as he was to get into Mae's dream and wake her up, he was nervous too. He didn't know what to expect and worried he'd screw it up. Less than a year ago he didn't know witches, curses, and spells existed. Now, he planned to enter his—friend's? girlfriend's? lover's?—dream.

He didn't know what they were, but now that he'd pulled his head out of his ass, as Blake liked to say, he knew what he wanted Mae to be. His future wife.

One thing at a time: wake Mae. Break the curse. The rest could come later. He ran his knuckles along Mae's cheek again, her dark lashes a stark contrast against her pale cheeks. "I'm coming," he whispered again.

The door opened, Chewie bounded into the room and up onto the bed, shaking the entire frame. "Settle," Jake directed him as Blake and a woman came in.

As far as Jake knew, he'd never met a witch. Lyra wasn't what he expected—though he didn't know what he'd expected. Tall, with long, curly, sandy-brown hair, dressed in green cargo pants and a baggy orange sweatshirt, she looked like a twenty-something college student who'd just come from a class. She held a large, leather-bound book, with a bag slung over one shoulder.

She walked into the room without hesitation, rounded the bed to the far side and offered her hand to Jake. "Hi, I'm Lyra. I'd say it's nice to meet you in person, but not like this."

"Jake." He shook her hand and introduced Chewie so he'd know Lyra was a friend. "And this is Mae. A dream has her trapped."

"Almost three hours," Blake interjected. "We don't know how long she'd been in the dream before we got here."

"Before we start... Tell me, what the hell happened to

you?" Lyra gestured to Jake's face. "Did Mae's dream do that?"

For a while he'd forgotten about his injuries, so concerned about Mae. "Car accident."

She nodded. "You don't know what you'll find in Mae's dream. It might not be a walk in the park. Will you be strong enough to handle it?"

The thought hadn't crossed his mind. It should have, since he knew whatever happened in the dream would hit Mae in real life. He rubbed his thumb along the back of Mae's hand, where he held hers. It didn't matter if he was strong enough. He would have to be. "Yes. Get me into her dream."

"I'll try. Create some room between you and Mae, but make sure to still hold her hand." He did as instructed, and Lyra placed the book between him and Mae, the words facing him. The leather cover of the book squeaked as she opened it, its pages yellowed with age. She turned to a page in the middle. "Don't look at the spell until it's time," she said.

Leaving the book open, she dug into her bag and pulled out large, squat candles, seven in total. "Blake, please turn off the overhead light, and set these around the room." As Lyra held out the first two candles to Blake, the wicks caught fire without a touch.

Blake took the candles from her. "Cool trick."

Lyra gave him a wink. "Comes in handy." The remaining candles ignited as she passed each one to Blake to set around the room, casting a soft golden glow.

Lyra sat on the edge of the bed beside Mae and met Jake's gaze.

"Everyone I spoke to believes a spirit wouldn't need witch magic, and that since this one's more powerful than the strongest witch, this spell might not work."

He looked down at Mae, pale and still. "I'm willing to try anything."

"I figured. But I needed to tell you. This spell isn't built for a case like this, but it's the only one we—I checked with my brothers and sisters—could think of. It's a bridge, not a guide."

"Meaning?"

"It should get you into Mae's dream, but it won't hold you there… This spell is old and temperamental, but it was the only one we could think of that might work, so if it or the curse senses you're a threat…" She shrugged, her unspoken words saying it all. He could be kicked out of Mae's dream before he could reach her.

"I need to try," Jake insisted. He would do more than try, he promised himself. He would wake Mae up—of if he failed, he would stay with her. The first night Mae reached out to him, he'd promised her two things, but he should have promised a third. He'd promised her that if something happened to her, he would make sure someone cared for Solo and that he would always listen to her. What he hadn't promised out loud was that he would always be there for her. He was making that promise now.

Lyra gave him a single nod. "Hold Mae's hand and read the spell out loud. It should pull you into her dream, but whatever happens, make sure you don't let go of her hand."

Jake tightened his grip on Mae's hand and looked down at the book.

"Wait." Lyra slammed her hand onto the open pages. "I forgot to tell you… When you read each word, you must believe it. Don't just say the words. Feel them."

"I will." Jake swallowed to clear the lump in his throat and read the words.

"I seek my love's heart, her soul, and her light.

In her dreams I need to be this night.
Let love be the thread that reaches out and draws me in.
Take me where her consciousness lies,
That I may wake her with my truth.
Through a dream, through the heart, through the truth."

As the last word left his lips, Jake's body jerked. Something yanked him flat onto the bed. His eyes snapped shut, and the room's sounds warped.

MAE HEARD laughter as she approached the end of a long hallway. She reached a doorway, unsure what to do. She longed to rush in and talk to someone—anyone—just to belong. But fear of rejection glued her feet to the floor. For what felt like hours she'd wandered the grounds; every time she neared someone, they vanished, leaving her wordless and alone.

Voices and more laughter spilled from the room. The pull to step inside proved irresistible. Mae inched one foot into the room, then another.

Decorations hung from the ceiling, enormous ribbons looping down the pillars around the ballroom. A string quartet played at the front of the room—a song she knew she'd heard before, but couldn't place, each note hovering just out of reach in her memory. Dim lighting cast an intimate glow over the parquet floor as couples glided across in each other's arms.

She watched the dancers for several minutes. Each one moved in sync, as if choreographed. Mae had never danced, not even on her wedding day. The longer she watched, the more she yearned to join them. To wanted to someone's hand at the small of her back, an arm around her waist, a place to rest her cheek and pretend the world couldn't touch her.

When a man walked in front of Mae, she gathered her courage and tapped him on the shoulder, prepared to ask him to dance. He turned toward her, his eyes sliding right through her like she wasn't there.

"Excuse me, would you—" Before she could finish, he turned away and dissolved, vanished like smoke on the wind. She reached for another man but he too shattered into nothing, disappearing.

She thought about trying again. Maybe the next person would see her. But the music felt sharper now, the laughter brittle. An ache in her chest spread, turning heavy. Dancing no longer held the same appeal it had a few minutes earlier.

She walked to an empty table and sank into a chair, shoulders slumping. One by one the happy couples dissolved, not just the dancers but the entire roomful of people, pairs disappearing together until only hollow echoes of music remained.

Of course they left in pairs. Of course she was the one sitting alone.

Leaning forward, Mae folded her arms on the table and rested her head. She didn't know how long she stayed like that. Time blurred, stretching and bending, until all that existed was the weight in her chest and the familiar thought that she didn't belong anywhere.

She was always alone. It could have been minutes or days.

The table blinked away.

Mae pitched forward with a gasp, flinging out her arms. Her hands caught nothing but air before her feet found uneven ground. She staggered, arms windmilling, and barely managed to steady herself.

Cold wind whipped around her, sharp enough to sting her eyes and steal her breath. She stood at the edge of a cliff, an endless ocean stretching out in front of her. Waves hurled themselves at the rockface below, slamming into stone with bone-rattling force. Spray exploded upward, impossibly high, flinging mist into the air.

The wind shoved at her back, urging her closer to the edge.

Spray misted her shoes and calves, cold droplets soaking into her skin. Despite the chill, the water wrapped around her ankles like a caress, a strange comfort, as if the ocean itself reached for her.

"Come," the hiss of the surf seemed to say. "No more being left behind. No more being the one who stays."

"Mae!"

Someone shouted her name through the howl of wind. Was the ocean calling to her?

She took a step closer to the edge. Pebbles skittered over the side and vanished into the roar below.

"Mae! Mae, stop. Step back!"

That voice. Not the ocean. Jake.

She turned toward the sound. He stood on another cliff, a deep chasm yawning between them. The gap was too wide to jump, the rock on his side jagged and dark. A gust of wind shoved at her again, making her toes curl inside her shoes to stay upright.

She looked from the churning ocean back to Jake. "How did you get over there?"

"You're dreaming." He raised his voice to fight the wind. "Wake up, Mae. Please, sweetheart. Fight your way out of the dream."

His words were too clear, too sharp to be one of her usual dream phantoms. Still, doubt clung to her. "I don't understand. If this is my dream, how are you here?"

"The curse has trapped you. I got help to get—"

He lifted his hand as if to rub his chest and he flinched. Before she could ask what was wrong, he pushed on. "I'll explain later. Right now, I need you to know that I love you. I love you, Mae. You need to wake up so I can hold you and tell you how much I love you."

His voice sounded raw with sincerity and desperation, and carried to her on the wind. "You love me?" The words tore out of her.

Her ex-husband had said he loved her. He'd promised her forever, right up until he walked out the door with his suitcase and someone else's future on his arm. Her mom said she loved her too. Right up until the curse had swallowed her mind and all the love in the house had become fractured and unpredictable. They'd both left her. Everyone left eventually.

The curse had been showing her that on repeat.

"Yes." His gaze locked on hers. "I love you with everything that I am. I finally understand that love is worth any risk. It doesn't matter how long it takes you to love me back. I'll be here for you."

A wave crashed hard enough to shake the ground beneath her feet. Spray leapt up the cliff face and drenched her shins. Cold seeped into her bones, but under it all something warm flickered low in her chest. He loved her.

She turned her head toward the ocean. Mist curled around her legs, tugging at her like fingers and another wave hit, higher this time, a wall of water that almost reached the cliff's lip before plunging back down.

"Stay with me," the water seemed to whisper. "No more risking people who walk away."

She looked back at Jake. He was solid and real on the opposite cliff, his clothes rumpled, his hair wind-tossed, and the bruises stark against his skin. He looked like he'd already fought through something to get here. For her.

Could she risk love too?

Behind her, the wind rose to a shriek. The ground under her foot crumbled, a line of rock shearing away and tumbling into the churning water below. She rocked forward, arms out, a cry ripping from her throat as pebbles rained past her.

"Mae!" Jake's shout cracked with panic. "I'm going to come to you. I see stairs cut into each cliff. Please, sweetheart, step back."

She tore her gaze from the drop and forced herself to take a step backward. Then another. The edge disappeared from her peripheral vision, leaving only rough stone at her heels. Her lungs burned as if she'd been running, but she could finally breathe.

Jake moved, drawing her eyes back to him. He'd found the stone steps carved into the rock. They wound down the side of his cliff, narrow and broken in places, slick with spray. For a heartbeat she thought they'd vanish like the dancers had, like everyone else always did.

They didn't and he started down. Each step looked too small, too sharp, too close to crumbling. The waves struck the rock below with such force that the entire cliff shuddered. She wanted to tell him to stop, that she wasn't worth this, that nothing good lasted, but the words stuck at the back of her tongue.

Instead, she watched him descend, her fingernails digging into her palms. The wind battered him, jerking at his coat. Twice he stumbled, catching himself on the wall. Once he dropped to one knee when a wave struck hard enough to send spray high up the cliffside, drenching him to the skin.

"Jake!" she yelled, throat tight.

He glanced up, found her, and smiled. Even at this distance she felt the warmth of it. "I'm okay. I'm coming."

The ocean didn't like that. The next wave rose higher than any so far, a towering wall of water. It crashed into the rock with a boom that rattled her teeth. The cliff under her trembled causing a jagged crack to split the stone between her feet, racing toward the edge before zigzagging toward the chasm between them.

He kept going.

Her breath sawed in and out as she tracked his progress. He was almost to the bottom. Just a few more steps, then he'd cross the narrow strip of rock and climb up to her side. Then what? He'd hold her. He'd whisper all the things she'd never believed anyone would say and mean.

Another thought crept in—the curse wouldn't let him just walk in and steal her away. That was what this was about, wasn't it? Not just her, but him. Jake, daring to love her in spite of the curse's hold.

He reached the bottom of the stairs and stepped into the narrow passage leading to her cliff. The wind screamed now, so loud it felt like a living thing. Black fractures spidered along the chasm walls, as if the world itself was cracking apart around them.

"Almost there," he called, his voice hoarse. "Stay with me, Mae. Don't listen to it."

She dropped to her hands and knees and crawled toward the edge, needing to see him. The stone scraped her palms, biting into her skin. She ignored it. Peering over, she caught a glimpse of his dark hair as he climbed the stairs on her side.

Up. Up. Each step brought him closer.

Not far from the top, he looked up again. His smile—soft and sure and utterly focused on her—was the most wonderful thing she'd ever seen.

Then the curse hit back.

A blast of cold tore across the chasm, so fierce it stole her breath. The air between them darkened, shadows coiling and lashing up from the chasm like hands. They grabbed at Jake, wrapping around his chest, his throat, his outstretched arm.

She gasped as she watched Jake struggle to suck in a breath. His body jerked as if yanked by an invisible rope.

"No!" Mae screamed, the word ripping her throat raw. "Let him go!"

His fingers stretched toward her, hand shaking with the effort to reach her, to hold on. "Mae..." His voice broke. "I—"

The world convulsed and for a heartbeat, the cliffs, the ocean, the wind—all of it—seemed to compress around them, pulling tight like a fist. Mae felt something whip through the air between them, a force so strong it slammed her back onto the rock. Her head cracked against stone and sparks burst behind her eyes.

When she blinked the blur away, the shadows were gone.

So was Jake.

The steps below her were empty. The opposing cliff stood bare and jagged, no sign of him at all. Not a footprint. Not a torn scrap of clothing. Nothing.

He hadn't turned away. He hadn't walked off like the dancers in the hall or the people in every other dream. He'd been ripped away from her.

"No," she whispered. "No, no, no."

The ocean roared, louder than ever, as if laughing. Spray lashed her face, salty and cold. The crack beneath her widened, the stone shuddering under her palms.

All her life, people had left her. The curse had reached in and stolen Jake, and she hadn't been able to stop it. She hadn't trusted him soon enough and hadn't moved fast enough.

Mae forced herself to her feet, swaying as the wind shoved at her. For one wild second she thought about stepping forward, letting the cliff take her. At least then she'd choose when she fell. At least then she wouldn't have to watch someone else disappear because of her.

Instead, she stepped toward the space where Jake had been. "Jake?" she called, her voice shaking. "Come back. Please."

Silence answered. Mae stood at the cliff's edge, heart splintering, and took one more step.

She met only air.

One moment Jake had his arms out, waiting for Mae to walk into them. The next, Mae disappeared and his world blacked out.

The air shifted and his eyes flew open. Candles flickered on the dresser across the room. "No!" He lifted their joined hands to his chest as he rolled toward her. "Mae? Mae, sweetheart, wake up." She didn't move. He leaned down and kissed her forehead, her skin cold to his lips. "Please, Mae. Wake up."

"Did you see her?" Lyra asked.

Jake lifted his gaze. "Yes. She was inches from me."

Lyra picked up the grimoire and wrapped her arms tight around it. Until then, Jake hadn't noticed it no longer lay between him and Mae. "I'm so sorry, Jake."

"Sorry?" He shook his head. "No, don't say that. It worked. I just have to get back to her. I'll try again." He let go of Mae's hand and reached toward Lyra. "Give me the book."

"It won't work, Jake. I told you that could happen. Mae's curse kicked you out."

Jake held out his hand. "Lyra, give me the book. Please."

She handed him the grimoire. "It won't work. It was always a long shot."

"I have to try." Jake laid the book between himself and Mae. "What page?"

Leaning over Mae, Lyra opened the book to the bridging spell.

Jake took Mae's hand in his and read the spell again.

"I seek my love's heart, her soul, and her light.
In her dreams I need to be this night.
Let love be the thread that reaches out and draws me in.
Take me where her consciousness lies,
That I may wake her with my truth.
Through a dream, through the heart, through the truth."

As he spoke the last three words, he laid back on the bed and closed his eyes. Nothing happened. He pushed up on his forearm and read the words of the spell again.

Jake looked up when Blake said his name. "Jake. Maybe she'll wake up on her own. Her mom does."

"True, but their curses aren't the same. As far as we know, Chrys has never been physically harmed by her curse. How long was I in her dream?"

Blake glanced at his watch. "About an hour."

"She's been trapped for at least four hours. What's the longest you've waited for your aunt to wake up between episodes?"

"Three hours."

"There has to be something else. Lyra?" Jake didn't care if he sounded desperate. He was.

Lyra sat on the bed and looked at Mae. "There might be one more thing we can try, but I can't do it. My sister Aurora is a dreamwalker."

Jake felt his hopes rise. "She can get into people's dreams?"

"Yes. No." Lyra let out a breath. "Yes, she can, but she won't. Something happened once and we can't risk it again. It's dangerous, but she might be able to help you get back in. Don't get your hopes up." Lyra pulled out her phone and walked out of the bedroom.

Chewie crept up the bed and nudged Jake's hand. He threaded his fingers through Chewie's fur. "We're okay," he whispered. If only he believed it.

Blake sat in the chair near the bed. "I tried to take him out for a quick walk, but he wouldn't leave you and Mae. Jake…" Blake said his name like a warning.

Lyra re-entered, saving Jake from the lecture. No matter what Blake said—or how dangerous it would be to go back into Mae's dream—he was going to try.

A woman with straight, shoulder-skimming hair, and Lyra's height and build, followed her in. Like her sister, she looked as if she'd just come from class, dressed in leggings and an over-sized pink sweatshirt. A man who clearly wasn't happy to be there came in behind them.

Lyra gestured toward the woman. "This is my sister Aurora. And that's Atlas, our older brother. They've been waiting in the car because I was out with them when you called. We had to pick up the grimoire, but Atlas wouldn't let me drop them off at home."

"Not likely," Atlas said, following Aurora further into the room. Broad-shouldered and darker coloring than his sisters, a tattoo peeking above his collar, he didn't smile at Jake. "Lyra told us about your girlfriend. I feel for you, but I won't let Aurora enter someone's dream. It's too dangerous for her."

"Hey!" Aurora went on her toes and kissed her brother's cheek. "I can talk for myself," she whispered, but her words carried in the quiet room.

"I'm Jake. Blake and Chewie," he said lifting his chin toward his friend and then his dog. "And this is Mae."

Aurora stood at the end of the bed. "Lyra said you got close enough to Mae in the dream to talk to her. That means there's a strong bond between the two of you. My guess is that the curse kicked you out of the dream because you're a threat to its ability to control Mae."

"My curse definitely controlled me," Blake said. "But it was only ever me; no one else to threaten it."

Jake nodded. It wasn't what he wanted to hear, but that wasn't Aurora's fault. "Can you get me back into her dream?"

"I think so." Aurora shrugged out of her leather backpack and placed it on the end of the bed in front of her. She rummaged around in the bag and pulled out a wooden bowl, a beaded bracelet, and a dagger with an ornate handle. She placed the bracelet in the bowl and set it on the end of the bed, then moved her bag aside and held the dagger over the bowl. She looked up at him through her lashes. "Don't worry, this isn't to draw blood. It channels the energy."

She waved the dagger over the bowl and muttered a few words too low for Jake to hear. When she finished, the bowl emitted a low glow, like soft candlelight. She handed the dagger to her brother and picked up the bowl, cradling it in her palms as she walked to the side of the bed.

"You will need to wear this bracelet," she said, nodding toward the bowl. "It has a repeating pattern of three stones: agate, clear quartz, and selenite. The agate will protect you and give you strength. The clear quartz will cleanse your mind and clear out any negative energy. The selenite will help with that as well, but it also encourages calm sleep and soothing dreams. Together they should help keep you in Mae's dream long enough to reach her. It will still be up to you to talk her into leaving the dream with you." Aurora held the bowl out to him, the wood plain against her pink sweatshirt.

He reached for the bracelet and Aurora held up her hand to stop him. "There's one more thing. Because of the curse, Mae's dream is more than just a dream. It's a realm of sorrow forged from generations of her ancestors' grief. To penetrate that, the magic we're using is old and demands balance. Nothing is given without a price."

"You're talking about a sacrifice." Jake didn't care what it would cost him to get Mae back. He'd give anything.

"Yes. The magic demands a price. To cross into a cursed dream and bring her back, something of yours will stay behind."

"Whoa. Wait a second." Blake stood and walked over beside Lyra, staring across at Aurora. "When you say something has to stay behind, you're not talking about something simple like a shirt. You mean a part of him?"

"Yes. It could be anything. Like a memory, or a skill, or…" Aurora looked Jake in the eyes. "A part of your soul. The dream will decide. But if the curse decides you don't belong, it will eject you and… it could tear you apart. The only thing that might anchor you is your bond with Mae—your love. Is your love for Mae worth the cost?"

Jake didn't hesitate. "Yes." He took the bracelet out of the bowl. "What do I have to do?"

"Lie back, put the bracelet on the wrist you'll hold Mae's hand with, and I'll say the final words."

Jake looked at his best friend. "You know what you were willing to sacrifice for Paige." When Blake nodded, Jake slipped the bracelet on his wrist, took Mae's hand in his, and laid back.

He focused on the warmth of her fingers, the faint pulse

under his thumb. Whatever the dream took from him, it wasn't going to touch her.

Aurora spoke the final words. "Through the night, and across the veil, guide this soul to his beloved's trail."

The air in the room thickened and cold rushed in from nowhere, hitting Jake square in the chest. For one heartbeat he felt the curse notice him—a hungry thing coiling around the edges of his mind, testing him and searching for what to rip away as payment. Darkness slammed into him, heavy and absolute, and the bed, the candles, and Blake's worried face disappeared.

*M*AE COULDN'T GO ON. *Her legs ached, heavy as concrete, and every breath hurt her throat like she'd been running for miles. Wind clawed at her hair, cold enough to sting her cheeks as she stumbled the last few steps and dropped onto a narrow wooden bench.*

For a moment, she just sat there, hunched over, forearms on her thighs, trying to drag air into her lungs. When she lifted her head, the world around her slid into focus. She was on a train platform.

Except, it wasn't like any station she'd ever seen. The platform clung to the side of a cliff, a long strip of cracked concrete and weathered boards suspended high above a furious ocean. Far below, waves smashed against the jagged rocks and sheets of ice floated on the surface like broken glass. Steam rose in places as boiling water sent up ghostly tendrils that made her think of the pot on her stove that she'd boiled dry.

All her dreams—nightmares—had stitched together and brought her here.

She tipped her head back against the bench seat. Over her head, a metal speaker hung crooked, its casing rusted and its wires exposed.

It crackled to life. "Attention passengers…" The voiced boomed so loud she flinched and the rest of the announcement was lost in a wash of static and the distant roar of the sea.

She pressed her palms against the bench to push herself upright. Something crackled under her hand. Mae looked down. A ticket lay on the wood beside her, creased and damp around the edges like it had been dropped in water and left to dry. Her name was printed in neat, black letters, and underneath it, a destination in bold:

Love and Family.

Her throat tightened. "I'm dreaming," she whispered. Her voice sounded small against the echoing crash of waves. "Just another dream."

Except her hands didn't feel like dream hands when she held the ticket. The paper rasped her fingers, and the ink smudged where her thumb brushed the destination, as if it were fresh.

The speaker crackled again. "Final boarding call for the Love and Family line. Passengers report to Platform One."

She stood and turned slowly in a circle. The platform stretched out in both directions, lit by a scattered line of flickering lamps. Faded signs hung from iron posts, but most were blank. The only one with words was bolted to the wall behind her, an arrow pointing ahead to Platform One.

Her heart sped up. She'd spent so many nights stuck in hall-ways that never ended, doors that opened on empty rooms, parties that dissolved the second she stepped close. People vanished from her grasp without apology.

The dreams always left her alone in the end. But not this time.

Clutching the ticket in her fist, Mae pushed to her feet and followed the arrow.

The platform narrowed as she went, the concrete making way for more of the old wooden boards, some warped and some splin-tered. There wasn't a railing between her and the drop, and when she forced herself to glance down, her stomach lurched. Wind tore at her hair, carrying the tang of salt something metallic—like blood —on her tongue.

Shards of glass glittered on the surface of the water far below, catching what little light filtered through the clouds. One wave hit with such force that droplets sprayed up, scalding hot against her skin.

She jerked back with a gasp. "Okay, point made."

The curse didn't need to whisper to her this time—the message pulsed right through her. You can fall, you can drown, you can boil, you can bleed it said. She kept walking anyway.

Voices drifted toward her, but not the tinny rasp of the speaker this time. They were the low murmur of conversation with laughter, accompanied by the hiss of doors sliding open.

Mae rounded a curve in the platform and almost sobbed with relief. A train waited ahead, sleek silver cars humming with restrained power. Warm light spilled from the windows, gold and inviting—a sharp contrast to the gray sky and jagged cliff.

Bodies jostled her as she rushed for the train. Pushing through a group of travelers, she emerged to see a familiar figure stepped forward, a bag slung over one shoulder and a little girl propped on his hip. A woman walked at his side, dark hair falling around her shoulders, her hand resting on his back.

"Blake," Mae breathed.

Her cousin turned, laughed at something the woman said. The child clapped and pointed at the train.

"Blake!" Mae called, her voice snatching away on the wind. "Blake, wait!"

He didn't look up. No one did.

A knot formed in her chest, tight and hot. She shoved through the small crowd, shoulder to shoulder with people whose faces blurred whenever she tried to focus on them. Each time she reached for an elbow or sleeve, the person she touched simply...wasn't there anymore. They vanished between one heartbeat and the next.

"Please," she said, half to them, half to the uncaring sky. "Don't leave me."

"Final boarding call," the speaker boomed. "Love and Family departing. Doors closing."

The doors slid shut behind Blake and his family. Mae pushed harder, lungs burning, eyes stinging. She reached the nearest car just as the train hissed and lurched forward.

"Blake!" She slapped both hands against the glass. "Blake, look at me!"

His profile passed inches from her fingers. His daughter's face pressed to the glass on the opposite side, mouth open in a delighted squeal as the scenery began to move. None of them reacted to her pounding fists.

They can't see you.

They never do.

The train picked up speed, wheels clacking rhythmically against the tracks that ran along the edge of the cliff. Mae ran with it, boards bouncing under her feet, the ticket clenched in her palm. Every time she thought she was gaining ground, the end car inched farther away.

"Stop," she begged, breath tearing at her throat. "Please, stop. Don't leave me again."

A familiar voice cut through the roar of the train and the crash of waves.

"Mae!"

She stumbled, the voice wasn't the echo she'd heard in hundreds of dreams. Not that fuzzy, half-there presence she could never quite reach. This was clear and solid—Jake.

Mae twisted, searching for him.

"Mae!" He called again, from inside the moving train. "Sweetheart, where are you?"

She spotted him halfway down the length of the train, pressed against the window of one of the middle cars. His palm was flat on the glass, his hair ruffled like he'd run a hand through it one too *many times. There were shadows under his eyes and a cut on his face, but he was real.*

Her chest ached at the sight of him. "I'm here!" she shouted. "Jake, I'm here!"

He turned his head, scanning the platform and panic flared across his features.

Of course he can't see you, the curse murmured. You're always left behind.

"Here!" Mae screamed, forcing her legs to move, shoving past people who flickered and disappeared like smoke. "Jake!"

He jerked, his gaze snapping to her.

Mae's feet faltered. In so many dreams, she'd yelled for him and gotten nothing back. At best, a shadow or the echo of his voice fading before it reached her.

This time his eyes locked with hers, relief and fierce determination blazed there.

"I see you," Jake shouted, and she could hear him over everything—the train, the sea, the wind. "I'm coming to you. Hold on."

The floor under her vibrated harder, the boards rattling. A crack zigzagged across the planks in front of her, splitting them like a fault line. Beyond the edge of the platform, the ocean surged higher, steam and spray swirling together, carrying specks of broken glass on each crest.

If she fell, there'd be nowhere to land. No waking up in her bed with Solo whining and her heart hammering. This is it, she realized. The last dream.

Jake shoved away from the window. She lost sight of him for a moment as he fought through the press of passengers. The train was still moving, inching faster along the cliff, the last car creeping past her.

Realizing what he was going to do, she yelled. "Jake, don't! Stay on the train! You're safe there!" Safe from her. Safe from the curse.

The speaker crackled again, but this time the words weren't the impersonal bark of an announcer. They slid into her ears like oil, familiar and hateful.

"Stay back, Mae," the voice crooned. "Let him go. Let them all go. Love leaves. That's what it does. Stay on the platform. Stay alone, and I'll keep him alive. Reach for him, and I'll drag him down with you."

She'd spent years building her life around that belief. That distance kept people safe and that choosing love meant choosing loss. If she stood still and let the trains leave without her, at least she wouldn't be the one walking away.

Jake burst out of the last car.

The doors weren't supposed to open while the train was moving, but this was a dream and he was stubborn enough to make impossible things happen. He landed on the edge of the platform in a rough crouch, one hand slamming down to steady himself.

The planks under him splintered. A chunk of the platform tore free and dropped away, crashing into the churning sea below. Dark water and boiling steam surged up in a column, reaching for him like grasping hands. For a heartbeat his heel hung over empty air.

"Jake!" Mae lurched toward him.

Another crack raced between them, boards popping, nails shrieking as they were wrenched from wood. The platform split, leaving a gap like a mouth opening down to the rocks.

Jake swayed and a bracelet on his wrist glowed faintly, threads of light running from it down his forearm and into the boards beneath his hand. The light tangled with something darker that seeped up from below, like ink bleeding through paper.

"It doesn't like me being here," he yelled, grimacing. "Mae, listen. We're running out of time."

A gush of hot air blasted up from the fissure, smelling of smoke and salt water. The curse's voice slithered up with it. "Let go of him, little dreamer. Step back, and I'll let him wake up. Reach for him, and I'll have you both. You'll drown together, and he'll wish he never loved you."

Her whole life had been like a series of trains leaving without her: her mother, her father, foster families, her husband. And each time Mae watched from the platform, heart in her throat, pretending it didn't hurt as much as it did.

Jake's gaze locked to hers, steady despite the cracking wood and the boiling sea and the dark magic clawing at his ankles.

"I'm not leaving you," he shouted. "Not again. Not ever. I love you, Mae. I choose you even knowing the curse would come for me. I knew it might take something from me, and I did it anyway." His voice shook on the last word, but he didn't look away.

"You were supposed to pick someone safe," she choked out. Tears blurred her vision, streaking hot down her cheeks only for the wind to dry them. "I was supposed to stay away... I tried."

"I don't want safe," he said, fierce and sure and so achingly Jake that it stole her breath. "I want you. But I can't fight this alone. You have to choose me back. You have to choose love, even if it scares the hell out of you."

The platform shuddered again. A section behind her gave way with a groan, plunging into the ocean. The ground under her feet tilted toward the gap between them, toward the dark.

The speaker hissed. "Stay. Stay. Stay."

If she stepped forward and reached for him, she might fall. He might fall with her. The curse might wrap its hands around both their ankles and drag them under.

If she stayed where she was, he might be able to scramble to safety, back to the train and back to life without her. Then, he'd wake up, heal, and move on.

She'd done that before. Watched a man walk away from her and told herself it was better this way. The ache in her chest cracked wide. She saw Jake at her kitchen table with Solo's heavy head in his lap. Saw him standing in her doorway when he said he didn't want to leave. And she saw him lying in that hospital bed, bruised and broken because he'd left her condo worrying about her.

Then she saw herself, curled up on the couch, convincing herself that dying quietly alone was a favor to everyone. She was so tired of being left behind.

"I don't want safe either," Mae whispered.

She took a step toward the gap. The boards groaned. The fissure widened, splinters flying.

"Mae!" Jake's hand shot out, fingers stretching toward her. "Be careful."

"I'm tired of being careful." Her heart pounded so hard it hurt. "I'm thinking about every time I watched a train leave and told myself I didn't want to be on it. I'm thinking about you driving away from my building and getting hit anyway. I'm thinking about how the curse doesn't care if I stay alone. It'll just keep taking."

The darkness below surged higher, licking at the edges of the platform.

"I am done letting fear choose for me," she said, louder now, so the curse could hear her. "I am done standing on platforms and watching love leave. I love you, Jake Young."

She ran. The distance between them was only a few feet, but it felt like crossing years. The boards slipped under her feet. The gap yawned wider, and for one dizzying second she saw herself plunging into the sea, saw Jake dragged with her, both of them lost in cold and heat and shards of glass.

She jumped anyway.

For an instant, there was nothing but air and falling and the roar of the ocean in her ears. Then Jake's arms closed around her.

Momentum rocked them backward. The cracked boards under his feet gave a protesting shriek, then held. Light exploded outward from the bracelet on his wrist, racing up his arm and over her, searing through the dark threads that had been creeping toward him.

The curse screamed. Not in words this time, but in a sound that vibrated the air and rattled her bones. The platform beneath them convulsed.

Mae buried her face in Jake's chest, breathing in his scent—soap and sweat and the faint smell of dog. His heart thundered against her cheek.

"I've got you," he murmured into her hair, his voice hoarse but steady. "I'm not letting go."

She clutched his shoulders. "I love you," she said again. "I love you, and I'm not letting go either. Not this time."

The world around them began to dissolve.

The boiling ocean smoothed, turning glassy and still. The sharp shards hanging in the air dropped, dissolving into harmless sparkles before they touched the ground. The train faded, its golden windows blinking out one by one until there was only darkness where it had been.

The fissure under their feet sealed, the split boards knitting together. Color bled back into her surroundings—soft greens, deep blues, the warm brown of Jake's eyes.

He pulled back just enough to cup her face in his hands.

"You did it," he whispered. "You chose love."

"I chose you," she corrected, a wobbly smile tugging at her lips. "And love. Both."

He laughed, the sound rough with relief. "Both works for me."

The darkness pressed at the edges of her vision again, different this time. Less like something hunting her and more like a curtain about to be pulled back.

Jake's expression sobered. "We're not finished yet. We broke its hold, but we're still in the dream. You need to wake up, Mae. I need you to come back to me."

Panic flared. "What if I wake up and you're gone?"

"I'm not going anywhere." His thumb brushed a tear from her cheek. "I promised you that. But you have to meet me halfway, remember?"

He held up the hand that wearing a bracelet, the wood warm and solid against his skin. Light glowed faintly along the braided cord.

"In the real world, I'm holding your hand," he said. "This"—he *laced their fingers together—"is our way back. Concentrate on my hand. On how it feels. On us. Follow it home."*

Home. Love and Family. The words from the ticket echoed in her mind. The destination she'd never believed she was allowed to reach.

Mae swallowed hard and tightened her grip on him. "Okay."

She closed her eyes. At first, all she felt was the phantom sway of the platform, the memory of wind and the distant rush of waves. Then those sounds faded, replaced by a slower rhythm—the steady thump of Jake's heartbeat, the slide of his thumb over her knuckles.

Warmth spread from their joined hands, up her arm, across her chest. The dream loosened its fingers, darkness folding in.

Jake squeezed once more. "Come back to me, sweetheart."

Mae held on and pushed.

Wanting to see Jake, she forced her eyes open.

He hovered over her, granting her wish. Bruises and all, he was the best sight in the world. "I love you, Jake."

"I love you, too. I will risk anything for you, Mae." He caught her mouth in a kiss. She didn't hesitate to open her mouth to let him in.

Someone cleared their throat, startling Mae. "Oh my god," she whispered, burying her face in Jake's neck.

She heard Jake's quiet chuckle before he wrapped his arms around her and rolled onto his back, taking her with him. He pushed upright, leaned against the headboard, and drew her between his legs, her back to his chest.

"Welcome back," Blake said.

"Uh, thank you." She smiled at him before looking at the three other people in her bedroom. "It's not usually so crowded in here."

"Didn't think so." A woman with curly, sandy-brown hair stepped to the foot of the bed. "I'm Lyra. That's my sister, Aurora, and my brother, Atlas," she said, pointing to the others in the room. "We gave Jake a hand getting into your dream." She felt Jake's entire body stiffen against her back.

"Thank you." Mae smiled at the woman, and half-turned to see Jake's face. "Are you in pain?"

He shook his head but pain pinched his eyes. Jake's gaze flicked from her to Blake to Lyra and back to her. He frowned and shifted his gaze between them again.

She opened her mouth to question him, but room blazed bright like the sun, temporarily blinding her.

*J*ake blinked several times until the bright light disappeared and his vision returned to normal.

A spirit hovered near the doorway, the same woman he'd glimpsed once before, although he didn't know her name. She cut a striking figure with long, silky black hair and petite features. She floated several inches above the floor, light pouring from her skin and robes billowing as if a gentle wind lifted the fabric. Angelic to the eye, but Jake knew better. Not an angel. A selfish witch.

"Mae, this is the spirit who cursed you," Jake said, unable to keep the bitterness from his voice. The spirit was responsible for more suffering than Jake could quantify. All because five hundred years ago she wanted to teach an arrogant man a lesson.

Irony at its best, the spirit's arrogance made her think she alone was worthy enough to teach the man a lesson. Her lack of humility and empathy toward others hadn't hurt the man at all, only his innocent descendants. Jake felt not an ounce of warmth toward her and saw her only in shades of gray—literally.

Jake kept his gaze on the spirit, not trusting her. Out of the corner of his eye, he saw Blake step in front of Lyra and Aurora as he faced the spirit. Focusing on Blake for the first time in hours—maybe even days—Jake could see the toll his accident and Mae's curse had taken on his friend. There were circles under his eyes and blond stubble covered his usually shaven cheeks. His blue henley hung on him like he'd slept in it for days.

"If you're popping in again to tell us the curse has lifted, save your breath. We can tell," Blake told her.

An expression flickered across the spirit's face—one that, if Jake didn't know better, might have passed for empathy.

"I always come," she whispered. "Each time in the past five hundred years." She looked at Mae, who still leaned against him. "Thank you for risking and embracing love." She faded away, once more leaving her legacy unchanged.

"Well now," Lyra said, her voice too loud in the small room. "That was a new one. I've seen a lot of things, but never a spirit like that." She looked at her brother. "You?"

"No, and let's hope we don't need to see her again." Atlas turned to Jake. "I'm glad you're both alright. Since we've got a couple hours' drive ahead of us, we'll pack up and get out of your hair."

Aurora picked up the wooden bowl and tossed it in her bag. "Jake, I charmed the bracelet for you, so please keep it. Consider it a wacky souvenir." She smiled at him, then her eyes went wide. "Wait. The sacrifice. Do you know what it is?"

Jake looked at Blake and then the three Statera siblings, before easing Mae from his lap to see her face. Pain knifed through his ribs, but he did his best to ignore the pain.

Mae looked sharply at Jake. "What sacrifice?"

Jake didn't regret his decision. He looked into Mae's stunning brown eyes, so full of life, and knew she was worth any sacrifice. He took both of her hands in his, needing to hold her. "You stayed trapped in your dream for hours and wouldn't wake up, so I called Lyra. She had a spell that pulled me into your dream, but the curse felt me there."

"I remember," Mae whispered. "You were on a cliff."

"Yes, I—"

"You disappeared."

Jake paused, waiting for Mae. A part of him needed to confess his sacrifice, but he never wanted to talk over her. She gave him a sheepish smile and nodded for him to continue. "Yes, I finally found you on the cliff, but the curse ripped me out before I could reach you. After that Aurora used her dreamwalking to force a stronger connection and anchor me to you. She warned me the spell would demand payment if it let me stay in there with you. It did."

Mae's eyes filled with tears. "You sacrificed for me."

Cognizant of the others in the room, he squeezed her hands. "You are worth any sacrifice. I love you, Mae." His gaze drifted to Blake in his rumpled blue henley, then over the Stateras to confirm one last time before turning back to Mae.

Her eyes searched his face. "What did you sacrifice for me?"

"Only some color." He shrugged, as if it wasn't a big deal. If he had to do it again, this time knowing what he'd lose, he wouldn't hesitate, no matter how different life would be going forward.

"I don't understand."

He swallowed against the tightness in his throat and met her gaze head on. "I look at you and I see your beautiful brown eyes and the pink that's finally coming back into your skin. I can see Blake's rumpled blue shirt. He glanced at his friend. "And I can see the white and orange of Chewie's fur."

Hearing his name, Chewie nudged Jake's knee with his

snout. Jake took one hand off Mae's and ran his fingers through Chewie's thick fur but kept his eyes on hers. "But that's all the color I see. When I look around your room, I see everything in shades of gray."

Mae's eyes darted around the room as if confirming it still held color. "What about Lyra's orange sweatshirt and Aurora's pink one?"

Her voice held so much hope that he would see what she did. He wanted to give that to her, but he expected the sacrifice was permanent. Loving her meant giving her his honesty. "No. I remember the bright pink and orange, and I remember Lyra's pants are green, but I don't see the colors now. Only shades of gray."

"I'm so sorry," Aurora said softly.

Jake looked at her. "Don't be sorry. I'll always be thankful to you for helping me bring Mae back."

"Why do you see Mae and Blake in color? And Chewie, but not—" Lyra cut herself off, then smiled. "You see the people—and animals—you love in color. You don't know me, Aurora, and Atlas, and obviously don't love us, so you see us in gray scale. How did the spirit appear to you?"

Jake didn't want to think about the spirit but wouldn't be rude to Lyra. "The same as you—grays."

"Mae, were you in the car accident with Jake?" Atlas asked.

"No. Why?"

"The cut on your cheek looks new. Since it wasn't from the accident, it happened in a dream, didn't it? Like the cuts on your arms?"

Jake already knew where Atlas was going with his questions, but didn't interrupt. He couldn't change anything, nor would he, if he could. As long as he had Mae, he'd be okay.

"Yes, but what does that have to do with Jake's vision?"

"I'm guessing anything that happens in the dream, or

through a spell, and shows up in the real world, stays. Although the cuts will heal. Or at least the scars will fade."

"I don't care about scars," Mae told Atlas before meeting Jake's gaze again. "If I hadn't pulled away... If I'd taken a chance, I could have—" She choked on her words as her eyes filled again, this time spilling down her cheeks.

He wrapped his hand around the back of her neck and pulled her close. "I have you," he said quietly. "You are my world and I see you in full color. That's all I need."

Mae snorted a laugh through her tears. "My eyes are brown and my hair is so dark, it's nearly black. I'm not a lot of color."

He brushed his lips to hers. "You're perfect."

Jake looked up when Blake called his name. With his adrenaline waning, seeing his friend in color—his familiar blue henley—vivid against the dull grayscale of the room, sent Jake's head reeling. The clash was too sharp, too unnatural. The contrast of Blake's silhouette was too jarring against the lifeless hues behind him.

Dizziness washed over him. The room swam in front of his vision and he swayed to the side.

Mae pressed a hand to his chest. "Lean back."

With no energy to resist, he yielded, letting her guide him. "I'm okay." He hadn't felt the effects earlier when he looked between the colors and shades of gray. Now, everything caught up to him at once. Between the concussion and aches from the accident, worrying about Mae, and crossing the veil into her dreams—twice—his body and mind wanted to shut down.

Exhaling slowly to steady himself, he looked at Mae, then dragged his gaze to Blake, taking in the dull shades behind him.

The gray suddenly felt loud.

Blake stood at the end of the bed, worry etched in the lines of his face. "I'm going to head out too. You'll be alright?"

Too? Only then did Jake realize the Stateras had left. He needed sleep. "We'll be fine."

"I'll take Chewie out one more time, then let him back in and lock the apartment door behind me." Blake paused in the bedroom doorway. "Since you don't have your truck, Gage offered to pick you both up tomorrow, take you to get Solo, and drive you to Blue Mountain. He was coming for the wedding anyway. He'll be here at noon."

Jake nodded, too tired and choked up to say anything.

"Chewie, come." Blake lifted his hand in a semblance of a wave and left, leaving behind a colorless backdrop.

"Are you really okay?" Mae asked softly.

"Yes." He shifted and groaned. "Maybe my body isn't yet, but I will be." He eased down onto the bed, not able to hold in a wince as he rolled onto his side. He couldn't remember ever being so sore and tired.

She propped her head on one arm and laid her other on his chest. "Even now, you don't see color?"

Experience had taught him that she would have a harder time accepting his fate than he would. Like he had with Chelsea. Guilt could be a real bitch. It would take time, but he'd help her see that everything played out the way it was supposed to and he had no regrets.

He placed his hand over hers, where it lay on his heart. "Your favorite blanket looks gray, even though I know it's purple. Everything else is gray too, until I look at you. I see your gorgeous brown eyes and my navy T-shirt you're wearing. But you know what else I see?"

She licked her lips with cautious hope, her eyes glistening with new tears. "What?"

"You. Not just the colors. You're the brightest thing in my whole world. I love you."

"I know." She wiped at her tears, laughing as she cried.

He leaned in and kissed her. "You can quote Han Solo anytime you want, as long as you love me."

"You may see most things in gray now," she whispered against his lips, "but when I look at you, Jake, you're *every* shade I've ever needed."

EPILOGUE

Saturday, March 1

$\mathcal{M}$ae smoothed her hands down the front of her dress as she looked at herself in Jake's bedroom mirror. Long-sleeved and modest, the deep purple dress with fabric buttons down one side made her feel beautiful. Elegant.

She'd bought the dress on a whim during an end-of-season sale the year before. Black had always been her preference, but something about the purple with the tone-on-tone pattern woven into the material had called to her. She didn't have any place to wear it, so it got pushed further and further to the back in her closet...until five days ago.

She'd been packing to come to Jake's for a few days. Searching through her closet to find something to wear to Blake's and Paige's wedding, she'd come across the dress. She had known right away it would be perfect for the semi-formal winter affair. The style fit the bill, but once again, the color drew her to the dress.

From now on, she'd reach for color first. The day the

"

curse broke she vowed to turn over a new leaf and dress in color. There were moments in the past five days where everything that happened felt like a figment of her imagination. Then something would remind her the nightmare of her life had been all too real. That Jake's sacrifice was real. She might catch a glimpse of her healing scars or see Jake hesitate when he reached for a shirt in his closet, not knowing which one would match.

The weight of Jake's sacrifice sat heavily on her, and maybe it always would. On a recent trip to the grocery store, Jake had hesitated at a traffic light because it was horizontal instead of vertical and he didn't know which light was green. She'd had to tell him. He hesitated in the store too, when he couldn't discern the red bell peppers from the green.

It was all because she hadn't embraced love soon enough. She couldn't turn back the clock, but she could embrace color. As one of only a small group of people who could bring color into his life, she would take every opportunity she could to take away the gray. It might take her a while to work up to the bright pinks and oranges the Statera sisters wore, but she could start with dark, rich colors.

Turning in a slow circle, she checked her dress for slobber stains. Not seeing any—a small miracle with two adorable, drooly dogs around—she smiled at her reflection. Years ago, she'd opted for a short, textured hairstyle that framed her face and today she'd blow-dried the pieces forward. They softened the still-healing slice on her cheek.

"You look breathtaking," Jake said from behind her.

She turned around to face him. "Thank you." He leaned against the doorframe, as if content to admire her. "You clean up pretty good yourself." He wore a short double-breasted, navy pea coat with a white dress shirt underneath and dark trousers.

He took a few steps into the room and she took a few to

meet him. Lifting up on her toes, she kissed the underside of his neatly trimmed beard. "I love your lumberjack look, but this is like lumberjack-meets-fine-dining. It suits you."

He grasped her hips and moved backward until he was sitting on the bed and she stood between his legs. "You suit me."

She huffed an inelegant snort. "You're so cheesy. But I love you."

"I love you too. So much," he rasped.

She tipped her head. "You missed the perfect opportunity. You didn't say, 'I know.'"

"And I never will. That's your line now. I'll even let you practice." He paused for a beat. "I love you."

She grinned. "I know." Lowering to sit on his knee, she gripped his shoulders and leaned into him. Her lips met his, warm and soft. What she'd intended as a simple kiss turned hot in a flash. She felt it all the way to her core. If it hadn't been for the alarm on Jake's phone going off, instead of only telling him how much she loved him, she would have pushed him back onto the bed and shown him.

"Later," he said, giving her another quick kiss and helping her off his lap. Taking her hand in his, he led her over to a small sitting area and coaxed her into the large, comfy, reading chair that could easily fit two. She scooted over to make room for him.

Instead of sitting, Jake knelt in front of her and produced a box from his pocket. Her breath hitched and dizziness washed over her.

Jake smiled. "It's not a ring."

"Good. No. I didn't mean that, I—"

He pressed a finger to her lips, halting her. "I know. I plan to ask you to marry me some day, but right now, let's find our new normal."

"I'd like that."

He lifted the box and flipped the lid open. Inside lay a key and a tag.

She met his gaze. "I get the key. You already have one to my place, but what's the tag for?"

Jake lifted her keyring she hadn't noticed sitting on the small side table. Setting the box down beside his knee, he slid the key onto the ring as he spoke. "This isn't so you can visit, Mae. I want you to move in with me. Nearly losing you made me realize how much I love you and I never want to be without you. I want to fall asleep beside you every night and wake up next to you every morning. I want to be your forever family, but we can start with this."

"Yes." She held out her hand and he placed the keys in her palm, curling her fingers around them. He offered her his hand to help her stand. As she took it, she noticed the opened box still lying on the floor, the tag still inside. "What's the tag for?"

"For Solo." Jake picked it up, handing it to her. Solo's name, registration number, and her phone number were etched on one side, the same as he had on his current dog tag. She turned it over and felt her eyes tear up again. Instead of Mae's address printed on it, it held Jake's. His number was listed as a backup. She'd never had someone else she could list before. No family member, or even a close friend, who could pick up Solo in an emergency. Not until Jake had come into her life and brought her cousins with him.

Jake took the tag from her and held out his hand. "Let's go find the dogs. We have to hurry too. I don't think it would be a good idea for the best man to be late for the wedding."

Hours later, Mae sat at a table off to the side of a room someone had turned into an enchanting winter wonderland, nursing a glass of wine. Some guests still danced as others mingled or prepared to leave. The bride and groom had departed less than ten minutes earlier.

Jake had gone to help Dane and Cade put wedding presents in his SUV. Mae suspected Cade was happy to escape the teasing. He and his girlfriend, Jessica, caught the garter and bouquet, and if tradition held, they'd be next to marry.

During the brief times Mae had spoken to Jessica, she'd seemed standoffish. And when Mae asked about Malcolm, Jessica changed the subject, but Mae understood. Family could be overwhelming and Mae was sure she'd come across as prickly herself when meeting new people. Cade was the exact opposite. Like he'd done before, he'd given Mae a hug as soon as he'd seen her. As did her other cousins. She chatted with all of them during the evening, getting to know them a bit better.

Cade asked the most questions about her curse. It could have been the lawyer in him, or the fact that his thirtieth birthday was next, just over a year away. Lucky for him, he was already in love and didn't have to worry about the curse. When Cade talked about Jessica and his son, his love for them shone through every word.

Since the curse wouldn't be an issue for Cade, Dane would be next. He'd told Mae he wasn't worried as he had more than two years to fall in love. Mae only smiled. If only falling in love was that easy. All she could do was hope that her cousins found love because she wouldn't wish the curse on anyone.

She didn't regret the curse. Not anymore. Without it, she may never have found Jake. As much as she wished she'd recognized love earlier, she hadn't. No one could change the past. But she wouldn't live in it anymore, either. She would walk into the future with her heart wide open. But before she embarked on that journey, a little sleep would be good.

As much as she had loved the wedding and getting to know her cousins and Jake's family, she felt drained. The past several months had taken a toll on her and she was still recovering. She put her empty wine glass down and picked up her purse. Out of the corner of her eye, she caught Jake walking back in. He stopped, scanning the room until he found her.

She might be the brightest thing in his world, but he was her everything—everything she'd never dared dream of.

**The Following Year
Friday, March 13**

CADE LOOKED in the bathroom mirror and the truth stared back at him. He couldn't avoid it any longer. He had enjoyed his thirtieth birthday celebration, one month and two days earlier, believing his love for Jessica had kept him safe from the family curse. Now he knew how wrong he'd been.

Twelve days after his birthday, he noticed gray sprinkled throughout his dark brown hair. More than a few gray hairs seemed to have appeared overnight. The coloring had been unexpected since his older brother and dad hadn't gone prematurely gray.

Thinking logically, it shouldn't have surprised him because he was a busy man. He juggled fatherhood, a relationship, a law career, and the family business, and with that came stress. Stress could gray a man early. Despite his responsibilities, he took good care of himself, but he wasn't vain, so he'd shrugged off the early sign of aging.

The following week the hair at his temples had silvered. The week after that, he noticed the outer corner of his eyelids had begun to droop. None of that was normal for someone who had only just turned thirty.

Each morning when he stared at himself in the mirror, he feared what he would see. Today, his wrinkles appeared deeper. He looked at least ten years older.

"Daddy!" Malcolm let out a happy screech as he burst into the bathroom.

Cade scooped up his son in his arms. His biggest joy. "Morning, buddy. Did you have a good sleep?"

Malcolm nodded, then squirmed to get down. "Hungry."

After one last glance in the mirror, Cade took his son's hand and let him lead them downstairs. At two and a half, Malcolm navigated the stairs well, but they took their time.

"Mommy!" Malcolm pulled his hand out of Cade's and ran to his mom, wrapping his arms around her legs.

Jessica patted her son on the head. "Good morning, Malcolm. Daddy will get you breakfast."

Cade leaned in to Jessica and gave her a kiss on the cheek. "Morning."

She leaned against the counter, watching the news on the TV she'd insisted he mount in the kitchen, and took a sip of her coffee. Jessica had never been an extremely affectionate person, but in the last year, she had pulled back even more. "Do you have a few minutes to talk before you head to the office?" he asked, keeping his voice low so Malcolm didn't hear.

"Sure." She took another sip of her coffee.

Cade slid a piece of bread into the toaster and grabbed a couple of yogurts out of the fridge. He helped Malcolm into his booster seat on the high-backed stool and peeled the top off one yogurt, handing it to him with a spoon. "A banana or an orange this morning?" he asked his son.

"Banana," Malcolm said absently, already digging into his yogurt. Cade grabbed a banana out of the bowl on the counter, peeled it and handed it to his son. When the toast popped, he spread some peanut butter on it and passed that over as well.

"Thank you," Malcolm said, giving him a yogurt-smeared smile.

"You're welcome, buddy." Cade raised his eyebrows in question at Jessica as he picked up the remote to change the channel. She nodded and took her coffee into the living room. He found the kids' channel and turned up the volume. "Mommy and I are going to talk so you can watch some TV while you eat breakfast."

"Yay."

Cade put a coffee pod in the coffee maker, a mug underneath it, but didn't wait for it to brew. He worried that if he waited for it, Jessica might get impatient and leave for work. She liked to get to work early, so he'd get his coffee after they talked.

When he entered the living room Jessica was putting on heels that matched her high-powered suit. She was a beautiful woman and looked every bit the poised attorney that she was.

"I don't have a lot of time, Cade. What did you want to talk about?"

He usually addressed things head-on, but he wasn't quite sure how to put his question into words. "Have you noticed—"

"You're concerned about how you've aged?" Jessica asked, interrupting him. She shrugged into her coat and picked up her briefcase.

"You noticed?"

"It was hard not to. In the last month you looked like you've aged ten years. Your curse must have taken effect. I can't think of another explanation for your rapid aging, and since the curse affects each person in your family differently..." She shrugged.

Cade perched on the arm of the couch. "I don't understand how this is happening. Don't you love me? I love you."

Jessica put her briefcase on the coffee table and gave him the look that had people on the witness stand shrinking back. "No, you don't. I don't think you've ever loved me, Cade. You're a romantic. You're in love with the idea of being in love. You wanted a wife and family, but have you ever asked yourself why we never married?"

He felt like he'd walked into the living room and entered someone else's life. "You didn't want to get married."

"No, you never asked me. I didn't want a baby, but when I got pregnant you begged me not to abort. Then to move in with you. I thought I'd come to love you with time, but you acted like you already had everything you wanted. A big house, your play wife, and a child. You didn't have to do any more work."

Cade shot up. "Do any work?" He glanced over his shoulder to make sure Malcolm was still watching TV. Keeping his voice low, he faced Jessica. "I do everything when it comes to taking care of Malcolm and looking after the house."

"But nothing when it comes to being a loving partner."

He opened his mouth to object, but she held up her hand. "Let me rephrase that," she said like she was in court. "You're a loving man, but you're not in love with me. When Malcolm was about a year old, I knew we would never work, but then your family found out about the curse. After seeing what your brother went through, and then your cousin, I thought if I stayed that maybe I could spare you that."

He wanted to yell at her for not loving him, but some of what she said was the truth. At one time, he thought he would ask her to marry him, but it never seemed the right time. He loved her, but he couldn't say for sure that he was *in love* with her, yet she had stayed to try and prevent the curse. "Thank you," he said softly.

She picked up her briefcase again. "I'll draw up the divorce paperwork, including child support, and I'll grant you full custody of Malcolm."

He couldn't wrap his brain around how Jessica didn't want her own son. Malcolm was a fantastic kid and Cade's whole world. But maybe that was his problem. Malcolm was his whole world, not Malcolm and Jessica.

"I'm sorry it's come to this." He never thought he would be thirty, about to be divorced and become a single father while facing a family curse. *The curse.* His true reality just sank in. "Blake and Mae only had about three months after their thirtieth birthdays before the curse nearly killed both of them."

"Then you have about two months to find love and have it reciprocated, Cade. If you don't, you'll have to name one of your brothers as Malcolm's guardian." She glanced toward the door as if she was anxious to leave. "Speaking of your brothers. Can you take Malcolm to one of their places after work so I can pack? I'll take what I can fit into a couple of suitcases and we can make arrangements for the rest. I'm going to move in with my business partner so I don't need any of the furniture."

"Your business partner—Steven? You already had this planned?"

"Yes. I love him, but I didn't want to leave you in case we could have stopped the curse." She opened the front door and looked back at him. "I'm not the bad guy here, Cade. We both lied to ourselves. I really did care about you and thought I could love you, but I needed real love back. I'll be here after five tonight to pack."

Cade nodded and Jessica walked out the door, closing it behind her.

"Daddy! I'm finished," Malcolm called.

He glanced back at his son and managed a smile. "You watch TV for another minute. Daddy will be right there."

Cade drew a long breath and released it slowly, forcing himself not to panic. He took a minute to steady himself, then he would figure out how to spend every minute of the time he had left with his son. He knew from Blake and Mae that the longer the curse tightened its grip, the faster it sped up. Since he'd already aged a decade in a month, depending on how fast his curse progressed, he figured he had two, maybe three months before the curse aged him to death.

He was an optimistic guy by nature, but even with that outlook, the odds of him falling in love and having it reciprocated in two months weren't great. And if he suddenly looked sixty or seventy by then, his chances were even less likely. He wouldn't give up, but he wouldn't hold his breath either.

Thanks so much for reading *Cursed to Dream,* and you don't have to say goodbye just yet.
Go to:
https://kjwarawa.com/cursed-to-dream-bonus-scene/
to download a **Free Bonus Scene** with more of Mae's & Jake's HEA.

Then find out what happens as Cade ages rapidly and if he find love in
CURSED TO WITHER
https://books2read.com/cursed-to-wither-kj

IN MAGIC SERIES

Hidden in Magic

Truth in Magic

Found in Magic

Courage in Magic

Love in Magic

Forged in Magic

Forever in Magic

CURSED TO LOVE SERIES

Cursed to Love

Cursed to Dream

Cursed to Wither

Cursed to Suffer

ABOUT KJ WARAWA

Paranormal romance writer KJ Warawa had worked every job under the sun, including swimwear seller, switchboard operator, legal secretary, sign language interpreter, soldier, massage therapist, and process improvement advisor, before settling into the career she'd always dreamed about: Author.

She still loves processes and spreadsheets, doesn't love massaging feet, and is currently living out her own love story in Alberta, Canada.

STAY IN TOUCH WITH KJ:
Join KJ's Newsletter at
https://kjwarawa.com/free-book/
to receive a **FREE** book, exclusive deals, special offers, behind-the-scenes info, and learn about new releases, plus more!
www.kjwarawa.com